THE ROOMMATE SITUATION

ONLY IN ATLANTA #1

KATIE BAILEY

Cover Design by
CANVAPRO

Conor & Jess art by
KRISTINACHISTIAKOVA, SIMPLY WHYTE DESIGN
FROM JOANNEWHYTE VIA CANVAPRO

ELEVENTH AVENUE
PUBLISHING

1

JESS

I forgot about the heat.

Big shot destination marketers will try to convince you they call it "Hotlanta" for its sexy nightlife scene. But I'm not fooled for a minute. Oh no. I am one hundred percent sure that the cloying, sticky, wet blanket of heat that suffocates worse than a too-tight sports bra is the actual source of my hometown's nickname (which, by the way, Atlantans tend to loathe).

As I drive south on I-85, the temperature gauge on my dash reads ninety seven. Throw in the fact that the AC in my crappy old car broke months ago, and that I'm still wearing the extra-fleecy sweatpants I put on before leaving New York yesterday morning, and you'll get a pretty good snapshot of how things are going.

T-shirt? Sweat-soaked.

Hair? Damp. Plastered to my skull while simultaneously managing to frizz out in every direction.

Mood? Let's not even go there.

I lift another Twizzler from my lap—conveniently doubling as a plate—and hang it between my lips, cigarette-style. I'll be forever indebted to the delicious chemical-and-sugar-based foods that have kept me company along this journey. Bonus points for the snacks that haven't melted in the blistering sun. Somewhere in North Carolina, I even mastered the art of eating Twizzlers with no hands. Like a turtle.

I consider that to be a win. Which says a lot about the current state of my life.

Pleased that I'm able to finally focus on some (albeit questionable) positive thoughts, I crank the volume on my aptly named "Heartbreak" playlist. The one that's been playing on repeat for the last two days of driving.

It's mostly songs from Adele's 25 album. And I've listened to it so many times, I now have my own lyrics for every song.

"Helloooo, Johnny," I sing off-key. "I drove over 800 miles to flee your smelly feet."

It's pathetic. 850 miles later and the best insult I can come up with for my lying, cheating ex is that his feet smell?

I mean, they don't even smell *that* bad.

Undeterred by the fact that James Corden won't be inviting me to be on Carpool Karaoke anytime soon, I launch into the chorus, waving my Twizzler in the air. My voice cracks on the high notes.

"Hello from I-85

It's been a truly awful drive

And I hope you're sorry for pushing me out that door

But you're prob-*ah*-bly busy with that wh—"

I choke on the last word. Though the rhyme works, I've never been one for swearing, especially not with words that are derogatory to women. Usually, I prefer creative cursing alternatives. Like *snickerdoodle*. Or... *hobknocker*. Plus, Sarah doesn't really deserve to be called any names. Not even hobknocker. She's nice.

Well, she seems nice.

She has nice hair.

So there's that.

But, what she really has going for her is that *she* wasn't the one with a serious girlfriend when she and Johnny got together.

And, by serious, I'm talking six years.

Yup. Six years of my roaring twenties, wasted on someone who would eventually leave me for a tall, slim, attractive go-getter with a dazzling career in the finance world.

And, in the interest of full disclosure, by "roaring twenties," I am referring to being broke, unable to sell a single one of my paintings, and not even being able to enjoy wearing skimpy tank tops due to my freakishly outsized chest. (Maybe I mean "boring twenties?" After all, my idea of a good night is more *Friends* marathon and a cup of cocoa than stilettos and tequila shots.)

Under an array of billboards telling me to "Eat Mor' Chikin," I change lanes. I ignore the terrified glance from the man in the car next to mine as he takes in my Twizzler-wielding, Adele-belting, bedraggled appearance. It'd be just my luck if someone calls in a report of a crazy person in a silver Honda making their way into the Atlanta city limits on the interstate.

The funny thing is, I'm not even that mad at Johnny. I'm more... disappointed. In him, yes. But, more so, in myself. I'm disappointed that I followed him to New York in the first place. That I settled for a mediocre relationship with a man who did the bare minimum. Gave up my hopes and dreams in order to help him fulfill his.

And now, after four years of waitressing sixty hours a week to make ends meet—not to mention appearing at countless uber-boring finance events as Johnny's arm candy

—the man has upgraded from a dumpy malt ball to a hot tamale. Which is why I'm rolling back home with my tail between my legs.

Still broke. Still unsuccessful. Still unable to find a store that sells pretty bras in my size.

Ugh, speaking of slinking home, I need to inform my brother that I'll be crashing with him for the foreseeable future. Because my parents selfishly sold their home and took off on a round-the-world retirement tour.

We don't speak a lot, but last I heard, they were milking yaks in Nepal.

Long story.

I blow a sweaty lock of hair off my face, turn off Adele, and dial Aiden handsfree. The phone rings and rings until I get an eventual, breathless, "Hello?"

"It's me," I reply, and suppress a giggle when I realize what I've done.

"What's up, Jess?" Aiden's voice, tinged with sleep, warms over the syllable of my name.

"You sound tired."

"I am."

"Did I wake you?"

A pause. Then a sigh. "Yeah. But no worries."

I can picture my older brother running his hands through his dark hair as he sits up in bed, face marked with pillow creases. As a successful professional photographer and branding consultant, Aiden works long, hard hours and keeps an unusual sleep schedule.

"Soooooooo..." I segue. Not very delicately.

Aiden laughs. "Okay, J. Why don't you tell me what's going on?"

My brother is always the person I call when I need a pep talk or some tough love. Goodness knows why. Though I love Aiden to death, we are opposites in almost every area that counts. He's tall, I'm short. He's rich and successful, I'm not. Women flock around him, and he takes delight in serial dating all of them—whereas my relationship history consists mainly of Kevin Morrison in Grade Eleven (I dug his blue rubber-banded braces in a major way), and, after that, Johnny.

I take a deep breath. "Johnny and I broke up."

There's a very pregnant pause and the phone line crackles as Aiden passes his cell from one ear to the other. He has a strange habit of doing this every two minutes while he's on the phone. Or maybe he's just afraid of radiation waves melting his brain, or whatever.

I know what Aiden really wants to say right now: that he's pleased. That we should have broken up a long time ago. That Johnny didn't deserve me.

Aiden always hated Johnny.

But, Aiden is a good human, and an even better big brother. So, he bites his tongue on any *I-told-you-so's*. "I'm sorry... Are you okay?"

"I'm in Atlanta."

Aiden chokes. Which is to be expected. I haven't been home in two years.

"What?" He manages to splutter.

"Yeah, I'm about—" I glance at the road sign ahead. "Ten minutes away from your place."

"A heads up would have been helpful, J."

"Uhh... can you consider this a heads up for your favorite sister coming to stay with you for a while?"

"Only sister," Aiden corrects. Unnecessarily. "But J, you see, the thing is—"

"I don't care if the house isn't clean. I'll clean it," I wheedle. What could I offer to make him say yes? "And... Chinese takeout tonight is on me."

"No, Jess—"

5

"Fine, pizza then," I persevere.

"It's not that," Aiden says. "It's just that I'm in LA right now for work."

Frick.

Frick, frick, double frick.

The last thing I need is to have to call someone else. Every relationship I have left in Atlanta is linked in some way to Johnny. I have no close friends left here, and the only family member I'm close with is Aiden. Who I need right now.

I dig around in my brain frantically before retrieving a winning idea. "You still got that spare key hiding under that hideous garden gnome?"

Aiden clicks his tongue, thinking. "Well yeah, but—"

"Perfect," I cut him off swiftly, taking advantage of his slow, sleepy state. "I'll let myself in. When are you back?"

"In about three weeks. But Jess, there's something you—"

"I promise I won't break anything."

"No, I—"

"Loveyoubyeeee," I sing, hanging up before Aiden can protest further.

Harsh? Yup.

But, desperate times call for desperate measures. And, what are big brothers for? I need to retreat to Aiden's place so I can get my feet back on the ground. It's time to start thinking about myself, for a change. Time to get my career on track and chase my own dreams.

I am a strong, independent woman... who just needs a free place to stay. You know, because of that whole broke and jobless thing.

I put on my blinker, and exit the highway.

I'd been pumped to see my brother, and I feel a little

gutted that I won't see him for a few weeks. But, there is one perk to being alone tonight — I can wallow in a sea of wine and popcorn while watching chick flicks on Aiden's big-screen TV without anyone judging me or telling me not to.

I am a grown up, after all.

2

JESS

A sweet sense of familiarity washes over me as I pull up outside Aiden's neat heritage bungalow in Peachtree Hills. He paid way too much for it a few years back and, though the interior is closed-off and dated, my brother loves his house like any normal thirty-one-year-old man would love their human partner.

But not Aiden. Aiden doesn't *do* love. In fact, I'm pretty sure that I'm the only girl he's ever said "I love you" to.

I wipe the sweat off my brow, then open my trunk and retrieve my shabby suitcase and the one household item I snagged from Johnny's apartment—a weepy lemon button fern in a slightly chipped pink pot. It was a sad, straggly brown thing when I bought it for fifty-percent off at Green Fingers Market in Greenwich Village. But, seeing as my own shack of an apartment had zero natural light, I gave it a home in Johnny's sunny living room window on the Upper West Side. I pruned and watered that little plant to full, voluptuous health.

Johnny can take my life, but he can never take my favorite houseplant! I channel my inner *Braveheart* and cackle to myself while hugging Fernie close to my chest.

Soil spills on my t-shirt, but I don't care. It can keep the ketchup and sweat stains company.

I can't wait to shower. The terrifying murder motel I pulled into last night just outside of Richmond promised free parking and cable TV for fifty-nine dollars a night. What it actually delivered was a mattress made of broken springs, and absolutely no hot water.

I'm just grateful I got out of there alive. And without stumbling upon any dead bodies.

"HEY!" A booming voice cuts through my thoughts, and my precious Fernie almost slips out of my hands.

I wheel around, and I'm startled to see a tall, slim lady and two drooling golden retrievers jogging towards me. The woman wears designer athletic-wear, and carries a large, black backpack that bounces as she runs. Her blond hair is pulled into a neat ponytail under a baseball cap. Below the cap, her mouth is screwed up in a grimace. Her blue eyes glitter like morning frost, and her skin is pink and splotchy.

"Sit, Butch. Sit, Cassidy." She tugs on her leashes and both dogs drop their butts to the ground obediently. My first instinct is to compliment her on the cool names and ask if I can pet these golden beauties, but the look on the woman's face makes me take a step backwards instead.

I glance around, but there's nobody else on the street. Which means she must be talking to me.

"Hi?"

In response, she points at me. *Points.*

I take another step backwards, getting ready to run. I lived in New York for long enough to know a crazy person when I see one. And to know the importance of removing yourself from all possible street altercations. I look over my shoulder. Aiden's house is only about ten steps away... I can easily make a run for it. I'll even sacrifice Fernie, if I have to.

"Are you Aiden's?" she asks, her accusing index finger still jabbed in my direction.

The bizarre question catches me so off guard, I forget my plan to flee. "Excuse me?"

"Ai-d-en," she says slowly. Like she's speaking to someone very, very dim. "The guy who owns this house? Are you his latest girlfriend?"

I wrinkle my face in disgust, and she adds, "Gal pal? Partner? Conquest? Flavor of the week? Whatever people are calling it these days."

She waves a cool, dismissive hand—a difficult look to pull off when said hand is attached to two, bright pink dog leashes.

Okay, so she knows my brother's name. And, apparently, doesn't like him very much. She looks about my age... is she a jilted ex? Oh, please no. I can't be dealing with that right now. My Heartbreak Hotel quota is full for the month.

"Why do you want to know?" I ask cautiously.

"Because I need a message relayed to him." She says this like it's the most obvious thing in the world.

"And what would that be?"

"Can you tell your boyfriend to get back to me already? I put a letter through the door a week ago about fence pricing."

At this point, I'm not sure if she's some deranged ex-girlfriend of Aiden's or a terrifyingly persistent fencing saleswoman.

"He's not my boyfriend, he's my brother," I say.

For some reason, she visibly relaxes when I say this. Like, her anger literally drains from her face. *Weird.*

"Oh!" She adjusts her inexplicably large backpack on her shoulder, then sticks out a hand, suddenly all sweetness and light. "I'm Courtney. Aiden's next door neighbor. We share a fence."

"Jess. Aiden's sister," I reiterate, peering at the strange woman as I shake her hand. "If you left something for him, he didn't get it. He's out in LA right now."

"Of course he has," Courtney mutters cryptically. She opens her mouth to say something else, but my overheated, sweaty, exhausted self is in no mood to keep this conversation going.

"Well, nice to meet you." I step away from her, walking backwards up the driveway. I want to get as far away from Aiden's rude neighbor as I can.

"If you can let Aiden know I dropped off the fencing information, that would be great," Courtney says. She tugs her leashes and the golden brother duo climb lazily to their feet. One of the dogs yawns, and I can't help but smile at how sweet he is.

"Sure will." I nod.

"I'll drop by sometime soon."

Please don't.

"Okay," I say with a forced smile. I keep my smile fixed in place as she bounces away, and I watch her carefully to see that she actually lives next door.

When I visually verify that Courtney does, indeed, live next door (or she has a key, at the very least), I retrieve Aiden's spare set of keys. As expected, they're hidden under the ugly, googly-eyed garden gnome on the porch.

But, the scene when I walk through the front door is completely unexpected. My mouth falls open in shock, and I almost drop Fernie again.

Aiden's bungalow has been renovated to the point of being unrecognizable. The previously boxy, closed layout has been transformed to a fully open-concept main floor, with crisp white walls and white oak floors. The ceilings are vaulted, drawing attention to gorgeous, exposed roof beams that are stained a rich espresso brown. The kitchen blends old and new seamlessly, and features shaker-style cabinets and crown molding coupled with stainless steel appliances and subway tile. The granite island with waterfall edging is to die for.

Not to mention it's sparkling clean—like, eat your dinner off the floor clean. There's not a thing out of place.

I am beyond impressed. Aiden must've brought in someone who knew exactly what they were doing. The house's historical elements are perfectly preserved and merged with the modern features for a look that is pure interior magic. This is HGTV-worthy. I glance around, half-expecting Chip and Joanna to pop out and yell "surprise!"

When did Aiden do all of this? I've clearly been away far too long.

Eager to see the rest of the house, I dump my suitcase and trot down the hallway towards the bedrooms.

And that's when I hear it.

A creak.

I freeze, statue-like. Brandish Fernie in front of me like a weapon.

There it is again.

Not just creaking—footsteps.

Definitely footsteps.

My heart jumps erratically, banging around in my ribcage like the spin cycle on an old washing machine.

Is it possible that Aiden's here, pranking me?

I don't think so.

I swallow painfully, all traces of that strong, independent woman vanishing into thin air. Then, another creak right behind me.

A door opens.

I remain perfectly, painfully frozen. Not by choice, but because I'm utterly incapacitated. Adrenaline courses through my body, rushing like icy hot liquid in every vein. This is it. My penance for escaping the murder motel unscathed. The killer tracked me here—a game of cat and mouse fit for any slasher movie. And I'm that idiot girl in every one of those movies. You know—the one you scream and hurl popcorn at because she's doing absolutely everything wrong.

But, I still can't move. Where's my fight or flight instinct? Clearly, it's broken, because my body is doing neither. My brain also isn't helping much. It's turned to a lumpy, useless pile of mashed potatoes.

All I need is a plan. Seriously, any plan would do.

The footsteps get closer.

Within moments, I'll be lying in a pool of my own blood.

In my mind's eye, I see my funeral. Friends and family weeping softly. What would my obituary say? Jessica Shaw was a... what, exactly?

Loving sister?

Decent friend?

Mediocre cook?

Proud plant owner?

The footsteps stop behind me.

Great. I'm going to die without achieving anything noteworthy in my life.

I screw up my eyes and prepare for the blow.

Something touches my arm. "Jessica?"

I can't tell if it's the sensation of fingers on my bare skin, or the fact that my killer knows my name, but some sort of preservation instinct finally—*finally*—kicks in. I unfreeze from my trance and whirl around.

"AGGHHHH!!!!" I scream.

After that, everything happens in slow motion.

Fernie flies out of my hands, sending a shower of dirt into the air before the pot smashes on the floor. I charge forward blindly, and my upper body collides with something hard, warm, and wet.

What the—?

I put my hands out to steady myself, and they immediately make contact with what feels like a strong, muscular chest. But, as firm as my killer's very fit, bare chest is, my palms slip against his damp skin, and I go tumbling to the floor in a heap. I land unceremoniously on top of what's left of poor Fernie.

I lie still for a moment, eyes closed as I curl into the fetal position to wait for my fate.

But, instead of a blow to the head, someone swears.

I blink my eyes open in surprise.

And find myself staring at a man who looks more like a Greek god than a man.

He's kneeling next to me, his dark green eyes crinkled with concern. I can't help myself—my eyes roam over an angular jaw, full lips, tousled golden brown hair and—*oh my gosh*—that chest. This guy isn't just fit. He has muscles on his muscles. And then some.

My eyes travel further south, taking in a tanned, chiselled torso and a glimpse of an inhumanly perfect deep V, just visible above white athletic shorts. Have I died and gone to hottie heaven?

I don't remember dying.

Clearly, that Ted Bundy movie starring Zac Efron has taught me nothing, because my first coherent thought is that this guy doesn't *look* like a murderer. Not one bit. He looks more like the love child of Chris Hemsworth and Bradley Cooper.

Not that that's possible. But, maybe—*hopefully?*—in heaven, it is.

Hottie gently lifts one of my hands. "You're bleeding."

"Am I dead?" I croak, glancing at the soil-splattered hallway.

He laughs. It's a warm, rich sound that I want to bathe in.

"No, not dead." He presses his thumb into my palm and his beautiful lips quirk upward. "It's just a flesh wound. A small one, at that."

I yank my hand away and sit up with a start, head spinning.

"Who are you and why haven't you killed me yet?" I demand.

Hottie's lips tug at the corners again, like he's trying not to laugh.

"I'm Conor Brady." He looks at me quizzically, as if searching for a flash of recognition. When I don't answer, he keeps talking. "I haven't killed you yet because I don't tend to murder people as a pastime. Especially not houseguests who happen to be my roommate's sister."

"Roommate?" I manage. My vocal chords feel like they've been rubbed with sandpaper.

"Yeah. I'm staying with Aiden for a couple of months. I take it you're Jess?" Conor's shoulders shudder a touch.

He's still trying not to laugh. Only now, he's failing.

I peek at him through lowered lashes, mortification pitting in my belly. A furious blush spreads over my skin like a blazing red wildfire.

"Yeah, I'm Jess." I take ownership of my name like I'm admitting I have a highly infectious skin condition. Conor keeps watching me, eyes dancing with amusement. He clearly thinks Aiden's little sister is a nutcase.

Not that I blame him.

Well, this is just my luck. The hottest guy I've ever seen in my life happens to be my brother's roommate. And I happen to be lying in a sweaty, dirty heap on the floor, accusing him of wanting to ax murder me.

Why couldn't Conor have just been a psycho killer?

That would have been way less embarrassing.

3

CONOR

Dark chocolate truffle gelato.

That's what Aiden's little sister's eyes look like. Huge pools of melted gelato in my all-time favorite flavor. Beckoning me to dive right in.

Aiden called me ten minutes ago to warn me of his sister's surprise arrival. I was out for a run, and I wasn't particularly bothered at the thought of a new roommate.

Until I saw her.

Wild-eyed, panicked and brandishing a houseplant, within a split second of laying eyes on her, Jess became the most interesting woman I've met in years. Most women bat their eyelashes; Jess looked like she would have swung a baseball bat at my head, if she'd had one.

Aiden talks about Jess a lot. But, when he told me that Jess lives in New York and dates a Wall St. whiz kid, I'd pictured... oh, I don't know, a bland, paper thin model with a personality to match? Or—if she loves shoes anywhere near as much as her brother does—perhaps a pampered Paris Hilton type with a chihuahua and a major attitude problem?

What I had NOT prepared myself for was a fresh-faced, girl-next-door type. A girl-next-door who's not actually a girl at all, but 100% all curvy, beautiful *woman*. With a death stare and an arm Tom Brady would be impressed with.

I can't drag my eyes away.

So, I just stand here—still shirtless and sweaty from my run—and stare at her. Like a total creep.

I'm *that* guy.

No, I'm not proud of it. And yes, I'm painfully aware that this is not a good look. Especially because I *just* terrified her into thinking I'm Freddie Kruger, here to slash her to pieces.

I'm usually pretty good with women. I'm charming and funny, or so people tell me. But this is not exactly the time to drop in a quick, Joey-esque "How you doin'?" is it?

From her sprawled position on the floor, Jess blinks slowly. And the momentary severing of our eye contact gives me a split second to think.

This is *Aiden's little sister*.

Who's going to be *living here with us*.

And speaking of living, let's not forget that Aiden would kill me if he knew I thought his sister was... well, hot.

"Band-aids," I say, like I've just discovered the solution to global warming. I take a step backwards. "I'll get you a Band-aid."

And then, like the hero I am, I flee. Leaving her in a crumpled, soily heap on the floor.

Proper knight in shining armor stuff. One for the books.

In my room, I run a towel over my torso. I saw her looking at my bare chest, those big eyes like saucers—why had I not thought to put a shirt on and make myself somewhat presentable before introducing myself?

My phone rings, and I slide it to my ear as I open my

closet. I want to get back to Jess with a Band-aid ASAP, but when work calls, I always answer. I'll make it quick.

"Hello?"

"Conor, babe, great news," a smooth voice purrs. It's Karla, my realtor.

"What's up?" I grab a shirt, then put the call on speaker-phone so I can change. I'm only half listening, anyway. Karla is a born salesperson, and she's using her realtor voice... so I take the term "great news" with a pinch of salt.

"You got the house in Edgewood."

"Oh." I'm suddenly paying attention. "That is... news."

I wasn't expecting to get this one. And I don't know how I feel that I did. Since I started my house flipping business a few years ago—Brady Homes, yup, I know I get zero creativity points with that one—I've been careful not to take too many risks.

And having three—four, if you include the one I just bought for myself—houses on the go? Feels risky to me.

I'm already so busy as it stands. My house flipping business has grown alarmingly fast, and Brady Homes has become a sought-after name in the Atlanta market. The money has been a happy side effect of being successful. And my business, along with my bank account, will keep on growing if I take on multiple projects at once. That is, if this pace doesn't kill me first.

"Like I said, *great* news," Karla amends my statement. Everything about Karla, from her pressed two-piece suits to her bottle red hair, screams SHOW ME THE MONEY. She's a nice lady, but I know that, deep down, what she cares about more than anything is success. And that, to her, success means making as much money as possible. She'll stop at nothing to get her commissions, and she gets a lot of them from working with me. She's even got some bigwigs lined up who might be interested in investing in Brady Homes, so I can expand faster.

Unlike Karla, I tend to focus less on the money side of things, and more on giving each renovation the time and attention it deserves. The way I see it, every house has a story, a unique history. I love modernizing houses and making them work for today's buyers, while still retaining the build's original charm and heritage.

"Shall we check it out later?" Karla's voice is low and flirty. "We can go for a drink after."

I wince. Karla does this a lot. And I always try to let her down gently, because while I never want to lead her on or give her the wrong idea, I also don't want to hurt her feelings. It's a tricky balance, like walking a tightrope. But I do know the last thing I want to do tonight is go for a drink with Karla. What I want to do is spend some time getting to know Jess.

Who's currently lying on the floor. Bleeding. Where I left her.

Conor, you idiot.

"Band-aids!" I exclaim.

"Excuse me?"

"Karla, I gotta go," I say. "I'm sorry, I can't do tonight. Maybe we can check out the house tomorrow?"

"Hot date?" Karla laughs, but I hear a sharpness in her voice.

I laugh awkwardly. "No. No date. But I really do have to go—talk later, okay?"

Karla finally hangs up and I spring into action. A quick breath mint and swipe of deodorant later—nothing like locking the stable door after the horse has bolted—I head back to the hallway. I have my first aid kit in hand, and I'm ready to be of service.

But, Jess is gone. A trail of blood droplets and soil tell me she's in Aiden's bedroom.

She probably scarpered the second I left. I don't blame her for wanting to get away from her brother's weird friend.

Or, maybe she still doesn't believe that I'm not a serial killer.

With a sigh, I retrieve the vacuum cleaner.

⚔

Cleaning always relaxes me.

Call me Type A, OCD—whatever. I'm a clean freak and proud of it.

And, once I've vacuumed the floor, scrubbed the walls, and deposited what's left of Jess's plant into a plastic mixing bowl in the kitchen, I decide to take a shower.

A cold shower.

And not just because it is hotter than the fiery infernos of the underworld outside.

Since ending a short-lived relationship a few years back, I've more or less been married to my career. Brady Homes has been my life, and I've been striving for success for two reasons— One, to make enough money to support my mom, and two, to prove to myself that I can.

I always had that kind of drive to succeed. And, as I never had any interest in meeting someone and settling down, I was content with working 70 hour weeks and dating around casually. At least, I was content for a while.

Lately, I've been feeling different. Like I might want something more.

It's probably just because I bought myself a house. A house that I'll be moving into when the renovations are complete... alone. The space is way too big for one person, and for some reason, it's got me thinking about finding someone. Over the past few years, I've been on a lot of first dates. But not so many second dates. Practically no third dates. Work has taken precedence for me, and I never went on a date with anybody who made me feel like I wanted otherwise.

But Jess immediately piqued my curiosity in a way most women don't.

Which is a bummer. As she is obviously off-limits. And thinks I have a staring problem.

Despite my better instincts, I replay every little fact I've heard about Jess from Aiden. I know that she's three years younger than us. That she's lived in New York for the past four years. That she hasn't been home to visit in two.

And I know that Aiden hates her boyfriend. With all the burning passion that only an older brother can summon when it comes to his baby sister.

I decide I hate Jess's boyfriend, too. Although my reasons for hating him are definitely a little bit different than Aiden's.

Which is exactly why I can't be thinking the way I am right now.

I turn off the shower and stand on the bathroom rug, peering into the mirror above the vanity.

"What are you going to do about this?" I ask my reflection.

I should stay away from her. But staying away from your roommate is like trying to cut a steak with a butter knife—tough and unsatisfying. Plus, I need to apologize, anyway. You know, for leaving her on the floor, bleeding and covered in soil.

It doesn't take me long to decide that the best way to do this is with pasta.

It's the hospitable thing to do. I mean, it *is* dinner time. And she needs to eat.

So, I might as well make my new guest dinner. It can't hurt to get to know her a little. Welcome her home to Atlanta.

I'm just being friendly. Like anyone would.

Pleased with my decision, I make a simple, five-step plan:

One: I'm going to make pasta.

Two: I'm going to knock on Jess's door and offer her pasta.

Three: We are going to eat pasta together.

Four: We will have a normal, mundane, get-to-know-each-other conversation.

And finally, by the time dinner is over, I will never think about Jessica Shaw ever again as anything other than Aiden's little sister and a temporary roommate.

A situation that will resolve itself in no time.

Simple, right?

4

JESS

Breathe, Jess. Breathe.

I repeat the mantra to myself at least a dozen times.

After hottie god—sorry, *Conor Brady*—disappeared to get me a Band-aid, I did what any person in my situation would've done: Legged it.

No time to cry over Fernie's death. I swiped my suitcase from its place by the front door and ran.

I then locked myself in Aiden's bedroom. Which, I can't help but notice, has also been beautifully renovated with a gorgeous white and navy color palette. Deep mahogany wood accents give the room just the right touch of masculinity.

Seriously, whoever did these renovations was a certified genius.

I spend a few minutes pressed against Aiden's door, listening. I can hear Conor's voice carrying from the bedroom down the hall. He's on the phone. To a woman, by the sounds of it. Kayla or Marla, or something. She's on speakerphone, and I catch the words "hot date."

She's probably his girlfriend. Of course a guy like that has a girlfriend to go on hot dates with.

I dial my brother and huff out a few breaths while I wait for him to pick up.

"Hello?" Aiden's greeting is tinged with amusement.

"Since when do you have a *roommate*?" I hiss by way of a reply.

Aiden chuckles, clearly getting a kick out of this. "You met Conor?"

"Uh, yeah, I met Conor!" My whisper-yell is a whole lot more yell than whisper. "Why didn't you warn me? I thought he was a serial killer. I... I threw a plant at him!"

Aiden laughs. Long and hard. I hold the phone away from my ear, bristling with annoyance.

Brothers.

The little cut on my palm is bleeding again, and I dab it with a tissue. Poor Fernie. Her little pot exploded into a million pieces after I threw it at Conor. And, instead of murdering me, he'd actually wrapped his hand around mine to check the injury. My cheeks flare at the memory of his touch, but I shake myself off. When I'm done on this call, I have some serious cleaning up to do.

And apologizing.

When Aiden finally finishes cracking up over my apparently hilarious near-brush with death, he proceeds to annoy me further by pointing out the obvious. "You hung up on me. I didn't have a chance to warn you."

I mean, he's right.

But still.

"And why, exactly, do you suddenly have a roommate?" I demand. "One that I have never heard of before?"

I wait while Aiden shifts the phone to his other ear. "We met about a year ago, when Conor did the renos on my house. He does that for a living—flips houses. We hit it off right away, went out for drinks and..."

I stop listening. Why? Because I am no longer capable

of listening. Or thinking clearly. Or doing anything at all, really.

My brain short-circuited after hearing the words "Conor" and "flips houses" so close together. My body heats as my imagination runs wild with mental images of Conor all sweaty and shirtless, wearing work boots and a hard hat and doing manly things that manly contractors do.

Easy, Jess.

"Conor did this to your house?" I squeak, fanning myself with my free hand. Is it very, very hot in here? I need to sit down.

Not wanting to mess up the clean bedsheets with my soil-covered self, I plop down on the floor.

"Yeah," Aiden replies. "Is he okay, by the way?"

"Hmmm?" I say dreamily, my brain far, far away in Conorland. Population: 2.

"You said you threw a plant at him?" Aiden cracks up again.

"Not funny," I snap, jolting back to the harsh reality that Conor would never want me to come live with him in Conorland because he thinks I'm insane. "Most people don't take kindly to being assaulted."

"Good," Aiden says, his tone suddenly serious. Too serious. He shifts his phone again, and sighs. "Look, if I'd known you were coming I never would have gone to LA."

"I'm sorry," I say. I mean it, too. "I didn't intend to barge in like this. I had no idea anyone else lived here."

"It's fine, Jess. You know you're always welcome at my place, and to be honest, I'm glad you've got some space from Johnny."

"I knew you'd be." As much as I hate having to talk about Johnny—especially while it's all so fresh—I can't help but allow myself a smile. Aiden might be annoying, but he always has my back. As far as big brothers go, he's pretty great.

"It's just..."

"What, Aiden?"

"Conor." He pauses, and takes a huge gulp of a drink. "I should tell you something. He's a great guy. The best. But he's a bit of a—" Aiden stops again, grappling for a word. I hold my breath. "Ladies' man."

I exhale in an unladylike snort. "And you're not?"

"Uh, well. Um..." Aiden flounders. I smirk, and he sighs like he can see my smirk through the phone. "That's not the point. You're my little sister. He's a single guy. You're both at my house, and I'm across the country."

I try to ignore the idiotic joy that jumps in my stomach at the news that Conor is single. *Take that, Marla!*

"What are you trying to say, Aiden?"

Silence. I hear footsteps as he swaps over his phone to his other ear. I imagine him pacing around his hotel room. "I'm just saying, Conor goes on a lot of dates. Maybe don't add to that number while I'm away, okay?

"What is this, the 1850s?"

A sigh. "No, this is just your big brother looking out for you. You know that, right?"

This probably isn't a good time to tell Aiden that trying to find a man like Conor unattractive would be about as easy as putting toothpaste back in the tube. My only hope is that he has a terrible personality.

Lucky for Aiden, the truth and my fantasies are at polar opposite ends of the universe, anyway. Conor is a hottie god, and I'm just your run-of-the-mill mortal. I'll bet Conor has women hanging all over him. Women who look like Victoria's Secret models. Which I do not.

Plus, even if there *was* a smidgeon of a chance that a guy like that would look twice at a girl like me, there's the

27

teeny tiny issue that I accused him of trying to kill me. And I attempted to assault him with a fern. So, instead of dreaming about getting cozy with him, I'll have to avoid Conor just to survive my mortification.

Which, you know, should be really easy given that we're living together.

"Thanks, Aiden," I say. "I know you're always looking out for me. But, you have nothing to worry about. I made the worst first impression on the planet."

"I'll be back in a few weeks. I'll see if I can work longer days to get the project wrapped up faster."

"No need, Aiden. I'm a big girl. I can take care of myself."

"Can you?" he teases, and I'm glad to hear the lightness return to his voice.

I laugh, but my heart speeds up a little. I know he's teasing, but to be honest, it's a valid question at this point in my life. "We'll see, I guess."

Aiden sighs again. "Conor will be nothing but a gentleman, I know that. He really is a good guy. And you're right, you're an adult who can make your own decisions. I guess I just worry sometimes."

"Aiden?" I clamber to my feet, and walk to the ensuite bathroom. I take out a towel, eager to get in the shower.

"Yeah, Jess?"

"Thank you," I say sincerely.

"For what?"

I reach into the fancy steam shower and turn it on. "For caring enough to worry about me."

"Anytime, little sis. Is there water running?"

"Yeah, I'm about to shower... Oh, that reminds me," I say, sweet and casual as can be. "Can I stay in your room while you're gone?"

"Absolutely not."

"Would you be really mad if I told you it was too late?"
"HEY, GET OUT OF MY BATHROOM!"

After a very long shower—complete with a double shampoo and condition, and approximately half a bottle of shower gel —I finally feel somewhat clean. Two days' worth of dirt, grime and sweat takes time to wash off, right? Or, maybe I'm just making excuses to stay in the shower so I can put off having to face Conor again.

What am I going to say—sorry I thought you were going to make a human pincushion out of me? So much so, that I tried to smash you over the head with a ceramic pot? Leaving a mess that I still haven't cleaned up?

By the time I hung up with Aiden, I'd completely forgotten that I fled the scene of the incident without tidying up. Meaning that Conor has probably added "extremely selfish and unthoughtful" to his mental list of his new roommate's qualities. Right under "certifiably insane."

I step out of the shower and wrap myself in a big, fluffy towel. The room is full of steam and I breathe it in, hold the heat in my lungs for a few seconds.

I need to look on the bright side. And the one bright spot in the universe of crap that is my life right now is that it can't possibly get any worse. I've hit rock bottom, and the only way to go is up. So, I will get dressed, put on my big girl panties, go out there and talk to him. Apologize. Behave like a regular human being who can live with a hot man in the next bedroom and not collapse in a heap on the floor.

A rap on the door jolts me from my thoughts.

"Jess?" Conor calls.

Ohhhhhh, Lord have mercy. That voice could make me melt into a human puddle.

I glance down at my towel-clad self. "Uhh, just a second."

I dash to my suitcase across the room and change into the first thing my hand lands on—a pair of pink pajama shorts. Then, in a minor panic, I dig through Aiden's drawers for a t-shirt. No time to find a bra. I'll have to opt for the old, oh-so-casually-cross-your-arms-over-your-chest trick.

Breathless from the scramble, I fling open the bedroom door. And promptly freeze.

Somehow, Conor looks even better the second time around. He's freshly showered, and his damp hair hangs across his forehead. He's wearing different athletic shorts— blue, this time—and a white t-shirt that hugs his body in such a way that it forces me to remember what that exact body looks like *sans* shirt.

A blush blooms beneath my skin, and I cross my arms over my chest in the most awkward, least casual way imaginable. I lean dizzily against the doorframe.

"You're wet," I say, and regret my words instantly.

Apparently, my brain has disconnected from my mouth.

He laughs. "Right back atcha."

My hand automatically rises to touch my sodden, drowned-rat hair. Then, way too late, I remember the boobage situation, and snap my hand back down to cover my chest—resulting in an action that looks like I'm giving him some kind of bizarre, half-salute.

Frick.

"Oh, ah, yeah. It was from the, uh... shower," I say wittily.

Double frick.

A slow, sexy smile spreads across Conor's face, and my blush turns into a full-body, third degree burn.

"Are you hungry, Jess?" he asks. When I don't reply, he adds, "I'm making pasta."

He can cook, too?

COME ON.

Conor looks at me, clearly waiting for an answer, and by some miracle, I manage to plug my brain back in long enough to say, "I like pasta."

"Perfect." Conor's green eyes travel over me in the most disconcerting of ways. "In that case, dinner's ready."

Not trusting what might come out of my mouth if I try to speak again, I simply nod.

He pauses for a moment. Our eyes connect.

Is he... waiting for me?

Double frick with hobknockers on.

"I, um, uh...." Helpless as a fly in a Venus flytrap, I flap my hands and gesture over my chest area.

"OH!" Those gorgeous emerald eyes widen in understanding. "I'm so sorry, I'll... see you in the kitchen when you're dressed. Uh, ready. I mean ready. No rush."

And with that, he high-tails it down the hallway like a bat out of hell.

Mere minutes ago, I actually believed that this couldn't get any worse. How had I been so naive?

I close the bedroom door, and begin my quest to find a clean bra. After a few moments of rustling in my suitcase, I locate one poking out of a sneaker.

Once my assets are safely enclosed in a nice, sensible bra, I dress in a blue, floral sundress with a positively Edwardian neckline. In Aiden's bathroom mirror, I peer at myself from all angles to ensure no cleavage will be making a guest appearance over dinner.

To be extra safe, I add a baby blue sweatshirt. Despite the blazing hot weather.

Apparently, I'm a sucker for punishment.

31

I pull my wet hair into a side braid, put on a slick of mascara and lipgloss (for confidence), and an extra layer of deodorant (for necessity). Then, I step outside the safety of Aiden's bedroom.

I'm shocked to discover that the hallway is pristine. All traces of blood and dirt are long gone, like they never even existed in the first place. Did Conor do this? My previous experience living with men (which is, albeit, limited to growing up with Aiden and visiting Johnny's apartment) didn't give me high hopes for having a male roommate. I'm talking old mac and cheese stuck to the inside of the sink, socks EVERYWHERE, and walls covered with scuff marks whose origin I didn't care to hear about. But if Conor did this—well, he's way neater than I am.

The guy seems to be full of surprises...

And they just keep coming. The smooth sounds of chill jazz and the soft clanging of plates carry from the kitchen. The rich scents of garlic and basil make my mouth water in anticipation. I follow my nose and pad barefoot down the hall.

Conor is at the stove, stirring a pot of something that smells positively heavenly.

"Hey," I say, feeling slightly awkward and more than a little out of place. "Thanks for cleaning up. You really didn't have to do that."

He glances over his shoulder to shoot me a smile that could dazzle the brightest of stars. "I wanted to."

And then, I see what's left of Fernie. On the counter. In a mixing bowl.

Conor follows my gaze. "I tried my best to rescue your plant."

Be still, my beating heart.

5

CONOR

Nope.

This is the opposite of simple. In fact, this is messier than a state championship baby back rib-eating contest. The extra-saucy kind.

Because being "just friends" with Jess looks like it's going to be even harder than I thought.

"Mmm." Jess takes another bite of tortellini, closes her eyes and sighs. "This is the best pasta I've ever eaten."

We're out on Aiden's newly-renovated patio, sitting across from each other at the butcher block dining table I built. The sizzling scorch of the day has given way to a balmy late evening, and the sky is streaked with a blaze of pinks and purples. Notes of citronella carry through the thick, warm air. On the table in front of us lies a mouth-watering spread of Italian food. But I barely notice, because under the table, my knees are mere inches away from Jess's.

She has a fleck of tomato sauce on her lower lip. I have the most indescribable urge to reach out and brush it away with my thumb. Apparently, I'm eager to rack up a bunch more creep points.

In order to keep my wayward thumb from executing

regrettable actions of its own accord, I pick up my wine glass and take a massive swig of Merlot. A swig so massive, I almost choke. Classy.

"Glad you like it." I set my glass down with more force than intended, resulting in an unceremonious *clank* that makes Jess jump.

She's Aiden's sister, dude.

I repeat: Aiden's sister.

I'm trying to put all of my confusing feelings aside and treat Jess as a regular, normal human... person. Look at her like she's Aiden in a dress, or something.

But Jess is making it very difficult for my brain to cooperate. Because the more I learn about Jess, the more I want to know.

Over our heaping plates of four cheese tortellini, she tells me about majoring in Art History at Emory and working at a gallery in Cabbagetown after graduation. She moved to New York a year later.

But, what I really learn are the things that lie beneath Jess's words. I learn that her face lights up when we talk about art, and that she purses her lips when she doesn't like a question. I learn that she collects postcards, thinks talk shows are lame, and that she never swears. I learn that she moves her food around on her plate between bites, and drinks her wine in tiny little sips, like she's not quite sure she loves it.

But most of all, I learn that Jess isn't just pretty.

Oh no. Jess is smart, funny, witty, sarcastic and— perhaps most endearingly of all—she has absolutely zero idea.

Like, zilch.

When Aiden called earlier to let me know that Jess was ten minutes away, he'd mentioned she was here due to some kind of trouble with her boyfriend. Maybe they broke up?

"So... how long are you visiting for?" I dig deeper, mental shovel at the ready.

Jess's smile slips off her face.

"Indefinitely." She addresses her plate.

I wait in silence, not wanting to push her.

"I just got out of a relationship," she says, splaying her hands across the table. Her fingers are small, her shell-pink nail polish chipped. "When we broke up, I had no reason to stay in New York. So I gave up my apartment and came home."

The devil on one shoulder tap-dances with joy, while the angel on my other tells me to lay down my shovel and stop digging. I can't get over how sad her tone is, how hopeless she sounds.

I'm sure there's more to the story, but not wanting to upset her, I decide to stop digging for now.

"I'm sorry."

Her eyes flicker to meet mine for a split second and she nods. "It's okay."

She sees the skeptical look on my face, and continues. "Honestly, it is. Johnny and I, we weren't a great match anymore. We were too... comfortable. Worn out. Like old shoes, you know?"

"I do," I say, thinking of my favorite hole-filled Nikes at the back of my closet. Even though I never wear them anymore, I can't bear to part with them.

Jess sighs. "The shoes no longer fit, but I was too scared to throw them away. In case I... never found another pair of shoes."

"Nobody wants to be barefoot forever," I agree, then mentally dropkick myself for saying something so stupid.

But Jess smiles softly. "Exactly."

There is nothing on this earth as attractive as a woman who's beautiful inside and out. From the moment I laid eyes on her, I knew Jess was physically attractive—with her wavy dark hair, gelato eyes, sprinkling of freckles on her nose, and her full, pink lips. But, as we sit here and talk, she becomes more captivating with every word she says.

And all of that without even touching on those killer curves she has. The ones I keep trying to avoid staring at.

You know, because of those creep points.

"So, Conor Brady." Jess's voice makes me jump again. She swirls her wine glass in small circles on the tabletop, creating a whirlpool in her glass. Her eyes dart in all directions, looking anywhere but at me.

She's trying to change the subject in the cutest way possible.

"So, what?" I give her a slow, flirty smile. I swear, I can't help myself.

Jess continues to avoid eye contact. "Tell me about yourself."

I wipe my hands on a napkin and lean towards her. She touches her hair and blinks. I give her another smile. "What do you want to know?"

She frowns slightly and runs her tongue across her teeth. A seemingly innocent action that she needs to stop. Immediately.

"Aiden told me you're a house flipper."

"When I get time off from my ax murdering job," I joke, averting my eyes from her mouth.

Jess winces.

"Too soon?"

"I'll be locking my bedroom door tonight, just in case."

"Wise choice." I grin. "So, what else can I tell you to soothe your nerves about this unexpected roommate situation?"

"Let me see..." Jess taps a finger against her chin. "The

36

first thing that makes me suspicious is that you're a house flipper who doesn't have his own house."

I frown. "I currently have three houses I'm working on."

"But you live with Aiden?"

Ahhh. That's what she's getting at.

"Temporarily," I explain, scooping more pasta onto her empty plate. "Aiden offered me a place to crash for a couple of months while I renovate a house I bought for myself. It's actually the fourth project I have on the go right now. But it's a bit of a gut job, including the kitchen and bathrooms. So Aiden pretty much saved me from having to pitch a tent in my backyard."

Jess reddens, and my less than ideal word choice falls on me like acid rain. Really, Conor? I'm about as smooth as a gravel road right now.

A gravel road full of massive potholes.

I press my lips together and try to blow past the awkwardness. "If you're uncomfortable with me being here, Jess, I can find another place to crash tomorrow. Even sleep in a tent outside tonight. I'd totally understand."

"Stay as long as you like." Jess holds up her hands and I breathe a sigh of relief. Maybe my Freudian slip went over her head, after all. "I'm in no position to judge, after all. You're looking at a twenty-eight-year-old jobless, homeless lady who's had to move in with her brother."

"Quite the catch," I tease, glad she didn't accept my offer and effectively eject me from my cozy bed.

"Says the man shacking up with my brother so he doesn't have to spend the summer camping." Jess shoots me a grin.

I hold up three fingers and tilt my chin. "I was a Boy Scout. I would have managed."

"Did you know how to pitch a tent back then, too?"

My jaw hits the floor and my eyebrows shoot up. She didn't... Did she just go there?

I scan her face, looking for a tell, and she stares right back at me, all big eyes and innocent expression. Like butter won't melt. Does she want a literal answer? Like, whether I know how to actually lay a groundsheet and assemble tent poles and peg down a fly?

I look at that innocent face again and see the ghost of a smile flicker over the edge of her lips.

That SO didn't *go over her head... She's totally playing with me.*

But, I need to behave. I've already crossed so many lines, I could weave myself a blanket. Hopefully one I can hide under. Because I'm supposed to be focusing on being her friend right now.

I shouldn't be flirting with her.

And certainly not cracking inappropriate jokes.

Even if she started it.

I drag my eyes away and force myself to think about something—anything—other than her pink cheeks. And that ridiculously weather-inappropriate baby blue sweater that I'm totally *not* dying to take off of her. Nope, not even in the least.

Awkward silence stretches between my new friend and I.

I finally say, "well..."

Just as Jess says, "so..."

Our eyes meet again, and in a single look, the tension snaps. We both laugh and I breathe a sigh of relief.

"I'd better start clearing up." I veer the conversation to safer pastures.

Because, you know, AIDEN'S SISTER.

I begin stacking empty dishes on the table between us.

Jess jumps to her feet. "I'll help." She reaches out and

her hand touches mine, stopping me mid-stack. "And Conor?"

"Yeah?" I say, looking pointedly at where her fingers brush my skin.

"Because you made dinner and rescued my fern, I won't force you to set up camp in the backyard tonight. Just don't murder me, k?"

And with that, she grins and winks before sashaying to the kitchen, the bottom of her blue dress swinging from side to side.

Leaving me alone on the patio, staring after her, and feeling anything but *friendly* towards my new roommate.

When I learned that Aiden was out of town, I anticipated a night alone in front of the TV. I was going to put on my comfiest sweatpants and watch endless reruns of *Friends* while eating Betty Crocker frosting right out of the carton. And then I would cry, because I was sad, lonely, and I'd just eaten frosting out of the carton.

And so on and so forth, until I ended up in a spiral of failure and regret.

But then, in some miraculous twist of fate, my plans were derailed and I ended up on the best dinner date I'd been on in years.

And yes, I know it wasn't a date.

But it was still the best *not-a-date* I'd been on in forever. Which, quite frankly, says a lot about the state of my ex-relationship.

Conor wined and dined me, and, unlike most men, he actually looked at my face during our conversation instead of leering at my chest. I felt like a very sweaty, slightly fluffy Cinderella. And somewhere between the caesar salad and the second helping of tortellini, my brain even began to function again.

At least, function long enough to discover that Conor's genuinely nice. Which, on top of being clean and not being a murderer, was another unexpected plus. Nobody that good-looking should also be allowed to be so nice. It's like getting dealt a twenty-one hand in Blackjack while us mere mortals clutch threes and fours and wonder why we even bothered playing in the first place.

We talked. Laughed. Even flirted a little... I think. As a genuinely awkward, foot-in-mouth type being, flirting has never been my forte.

So, yeah. Dinner went above and beyond all expectations I might've had of my brother's surprise roommate.

But, while we stood side by side washing and drying the pasta pots, the doorbell rang. And now, just an hour later, I'm not so much starring in Cinderella as I am in Snow White. Only, instead of being the princess surrounded by the seven dwarves, I *am* the dwarf, sticking out like a sore thumb in the midst of a group of Aiden and Conor's glamorous, good looking friends. They're sprawled effortlessly, casually, confidently across the gorgeous, rattan wicker outdoor couches.

Music throbs from built-in, state-of-the-art speakers, and the patio is illuminated by the sparkle of the fairy lights overhead. The yard looks like something out of a movie. Conor is clearly very talented at what he does.

"Want a beer, Jess?" a guy named Luke asks. He's been telling me all about his job as a marketing guru at a tech company downtown. With his designer watch, shades and stubble combo, I don't doubt that he's as big a deal as he claims to be.

He's gorgeous, sure. But I prefer Conor's rugged, smirking, hammering-nails-into-things-for-a-living aura.

Not that I should be thinking about Conor hammering anything at all.

I shake my head. "No, thanks."

I'm exhausted at this point, and the glass of wine I had with dinner is still buzzing through my veins. Last thing I need is to drink too much and get sloppy in front of Aiden's friends. I've already embarrassed myself enough today for one lifetime, thank you very much.

"I'll take one." A woman named Mindy leans right over Conor to accept a beer from Luke. She presses closer than is necessary, brushing her arm against Conor's chest.

A tiny, little green-eyed monster rears its ugly head in me. And yes, I know this is insane. I've known Conor for a matter of hours. Aiden told me himself that the guy's a total ladies' man.

But, still.

Ugh.

"So what brings you to Atlanta, Jess?" Mindy pops the top of her beer and takes a swig. She's dressed in a low-cut tank top and curve-hugging shorts, and her fair hair is scooped in a high ponytail. She's pretty... in that "super chill girl who claims to be one of the guys but is actually trying to steal your boyfriend" kinda way.

Okay, okay. I know I'm being a little unfair to Mindy, especially considering I met her less than an hour ago. She's probably lovely. But then again, I thought Sarah was lovely, too. That she was just my boyfriend's *lovely* colleague.

Oh, gosh. How could I have been so blind? So stupid? Sarah and Johnny worked together for ages. Had it been going on under my nose for a while and I only just caught him out?

"Jess?" Mindy repeats. Kindly enough that I think I may have misjudged her.

I blink. Exhale. I've done well not thinking about Johnny so far, and I don't want to go there now. I fumble like crazy for something to say. "Oh! Sorry. I'm, um, just here to uh—"

"Get some new shoes," Conor finishes smoothly.

I look over at him in surprise, and he smiles at me. It's a small, secret smile that's meant only for me. A smile that makes my insides turn to Jell-o.

Mindy looks momentarily startled—which is fair, given the lack of context—but she recovers quickly. "Oh, I love shoe shopping. I can definitely go with you, Jess. Are you a boutique shopper or a 'visit the mall' sort of girl? Mall, right?"

As she speaks, she lifts one of her legs in a graceful arc, and runs a bare, glitter-toe nailed foot across Conor's leg. I don't miss the possessiveness in the gesture, the cattiness behind her seemingly innocent question. She's staking her claim so obviously, she may as well pee all over him.

Looks like my initial judgment was correct.

Or... maybe Conor and Mindy are together, and she's letting me know it. I mean, she's practically sitting on top of him. Over dinner, I didn't even ask Conor if he *has* a lady in his life. I just went along with what Aiden told me.

Conor shifts in his chair, trying to move Mindy's foot off him. Maybe they're not together, but she sure wants to be. That much is crystal clear. Maybe she's battling it out with Kayla/Marla for the prize.

I give Mindy a tight-lipped smile. "You're right. I usually shop at the mall."

I don't add that high-end boutiques make me feel both uncomfortable and unstylish, and the perma-smiling, hovering salespeople kind of freak me out. As a general rule, I avoid them like the plague.

What's wrong with Macy's, anyway? They always have great sales.

To avoid prolonging the painful shoe shopping conversation, I turn my attention to Pete Stevenson, the only person in the group I know. He and Aiden have been friends for years, and apparently they adopted an entirely new social group while I was gone.

I really should have visited more.

"How's Mia?" I ask Pete.

He lights up like the Fourth of July at the mention of his wife. "She's great. At home with Oliver tonight. Keeps complaining that she doesn't want to go anywhere because she feels like an elephant and none of her clothes fit."

He opens his phone and shows me a million pictures of two-year-old Oliver, and of Mia, who is currently eight months' pregnant and big as a house. I nod with a placid smile as an almost-identical series of photos flash before my eyes—Oliver at the beach, making a sandcastle, destroying said sandcastle, Mia dipping her toes in the sand, Mia laughing, and so on and so forth.

"Congratulations," I tell him. "Please send Mia my love."

"Will do, Jess," he replies. He takes a sip of his beer and wipes his mouth with the back of his hand. "It's good to see you home. Aiden misses you."

A smile crosses my face. "Thanks, Pete. I miss him, too."

"Alright!" Luke booms, grabbing my attention. "Who's ready to head out?"

A gorgeous brunette lets out a cheer. "Me!"

Across from me, Mindy slips her feet into a pair of killer heels and picks up her pink, sparkly phone. "I'll book the Ubers."

There's a flurry of activity as everybody gets to their feet.

I don't move, and when I look up, I'm surprised to find that Conor is watching me. I arch an eyebrow at him, asking a silent question.

"Everyone's headed to a bar in Midtown," he explains.

"It's Friday!" Mindy declares, sliding her arm into Conor's. "On Fridays, we party."

"Do you want to come?" Conor asks.

I hesitate.

I am *so* not a party person. Never have been. In fact, the closest I ever came to enjoying clubbing was my senior year of high school, when it was somehow considered "cool" to do the Cupid Shuffle in the Taco Bell parking lot on Friday nights. Right after we all got gee-d up on forty-ounce cups of Baja Blast Mountain Dew and chalupas.

Not that I'm going to admit any of that to Mindy.

I study Conor for a moment, unable to decipher the look on his face. I'm not sure whether he's asking me to join them out of obligation, or an actual desire for me to come. It seemed like he was flirting with me over dinner. Like he was enjoying himself as much as I was. But now, there's Mindy. She's a thing that exists.

Maybe he's just the guy who flirts as naturally as he breathes. The one who teases you and jokes around with you, but it always means nothing.

While I'm doing mental Olympics over what I'm sure Conor meant to be a simple, straightforward question, the exhaustion suddenly catches up with me. In one fell swoop, the effects of the painfully long drive and emotional roller-coaster of a day hit me square in the chest. I decide that it doesn't matter what Conor's reasons for inviting me are. Because what I actually need right now is to go to sleep.

"Nah." I shrug in what I hope is a cute, casual way. "I'm beat. Long drive today and all that. Have fun, though."

Conor looks at me for a second longer before Mindy tugs on his arm. "Come on, big boy."

I have to refrain from rolling my eyes, and I'm gratified to see that Conor appears to be doing the same.

"I'll see you later," I say, biting my lower lip to hide my amusement.

He smiles that slow, sexy smile. "Later... roomie."

By the time I drag myself into bed, I'm absolutely shattered.

After Conor and his friends left, I picked up the beer cans from the yard and tidied up a bit. I had a momentary dither about whether I should lock the front door, and I finally decided that I should. If Conor lives here, he must have a key. Or, at the very least, he should know about the gnome key.

Then, I went straight to the bedroom. Aiden's bedroom. Don't judge—his king-sized bed with a Casper mattress and 1000 thread-count sheets is very empty and available, and it called to me way more than the second spare bedroom's IKEA double ever could.

Today was a whirlwind of epic proportions, and I don't want to think about anything but how soft these cloud-like, Tempur-pedic pillows feel against my aching, tired head. Contrary to what I said before he left, I don't plan to see Conor later. My actual plan is to be fast asleep long before he comes home.

If he comes home.

Which is something else I don't care to think about.

Before I doze off, I decide to shoot Aiden a text.

Jess: Hey. Just wanted to say thank you for everything.

Aiden: Anytime, little sis.

Jess: Met some of your friends tonight. They seem cool. Caught up with Pete, too.

Aiden: Awesome. What are you guys doing now?

Jess: Everyone went out. I stayed home.

Aiden: Conor go with them?

I roll my eyes. Aiden's being about as subtle as a brick thrown through a window.

Jess: Yup. And I'm going to sleep now. Goodnight.

Aiden: You'd better not be in my bedroom.

Jess: Hahahahahahahahaha. As if.

I put my phone on the nightstand and roll over, closing my exhausted eyes. I'm just about to slip into dreamland when my phone buzzes again.

Am I busted? How does Aiden know I was lying? He's probably got security cameras rigged up, or some magic sibling telepathy, or something.

I reach for my phone, ready to deny, deny, deny.

But, it's not Aiden.

Unknown number: Sorry about all that. Your unexpected arrival made me forget I had plans tonight.

Warmth gathers in my stomach, but then I read the text again and frown. There's no way it could be Conor. I didn't give him my number. This must be a wrong number text; just another weird coincidence to end the weirdest day ever.

But, somehow, I *know* it's not a wrong number.

My fingers fly over my screen.

Jess: Who is this?

A response comes in mere seconds.

Unknown number: Conor, of course.

Unknown number: Unless you made an unexpected arrival at someone else's house today, too?

Unknown number: Is that a thing you do regularly?

I snort. Then, I smile.

Jess: I'm not answering that until you tell me how you got my number, you stalker.

Unknown number: May or may not have asked Aiden for it.

47

And suddenly, I'm wide awake. Because Conor is at a bar. With his friends. With Mindy. But he's texting Aiden, asking for my number.

I add his number to my contacts, then send a reply.

Jess: And he actually gave it to you? *surprised emoji*

Conor: Told him I needed it for emergencies.

Jess: Is this an emergency?

Conor: No...

Conor: *smiling emoji*

Butterflies gather in my stomach. He is *so* flirting right now. I study his message for a minute, then decide to play it as cool as I can.

Jess: Well in that case, goodnight, Conor.

Conor: Night, roomie. See you in the morning.

I fall asleep smiling.

7

JESS

Ever been on TikTok? It's not for the faint of heart, let me tell you. I have lost actual days to TikTok, and most of them have involved a rollercoaster of emotions. I've learned how uncool the crying with laughter emoji is, why my skinny jeans are no longer in fashion, and that I should basically just dig myself a hole and bury myself in it instead of even trying to be relevant.

In the app's defense, however, I now know how to make great feta tomato pasta.

And so, with that one little glimmer of cheesy goodness keeping my spirits high, I continue watching videos on the app. Repeatedly.

But, on my first sunny morning back in the ATL, there are only so many TikTok videos I can watch before my curiosity gets the better of me (Eighty-seven, in case you're interested).

I slide out of my deliciously silky sheet cocoon, then crack open Aiden's bedroom door. I was in such a deep sleep last night that a tornado crashing through the house probably wouldn't have woken me. And so, I have no idea when—or if—Conor came home.

I lean through the doorway, poking my head into the hall. No footsteps. No music. No clinking of pots and pans. And thankfully, no sign of Mindy. The house is deadly silent... but my nose perks up at a tantalizing aroma in the air.

Freshly brewed coffee.

My kryptonite.

I dither in the doorway for a moment, torn between my need for caffeine and the knowledge that my hair usually looks like I've been electrocuted first thing in the morning.

I don't really want Conor to see my scarecrow hair and regret texting me. *Not that I care about Conor texting me*, I remind myself sharply—between Mindy and Marla, he's already got his hands full of women.

It *was* nice of him to put a halt to Mindy's third degree, though.

And his texts made me laugh. A lot.

I step back into Aiden's room and close the door. The only reasonable thing to do is to go full "I woke up like this." You know, that age-old con beloved by women everywhere —the one where you spend hours getting ready in order to look effortless. Then, at the first compliment you receive, you shrug it off, looking innocently at your carefully chosen outfit to say, "whaaaaat? This old thing?"

I'm only making myself look presentable so Aiden's totally-out-of-my-league friend doesn't think I'm a total disaster. That's all this is.

And so, I spend the next several minutes rushing through a frantic hot wand styling session, while watching a YouTube tutorial on how to apply as much makeup as possible to make it look like I'm wearing none. Then, I slip into my cutest loungewear (so basically, not the giraffe onesie or stained UGA Bulldogs sweatpants I usually favor).

When my hair is finally somewhat tame, I step out of Aiden's bedroom and stride down the hallway. I turn the corner and the kitchen is bathed in a pool of golden morning sunlight. It's strange that I've been here less than 24 hours and feel more at home at Aiden's than I ever did in my own apartment in New York.

Conor is sitting on a stool at the island and, unless Mindy's hiding out behind the sofa, he's alone. He's sipping coffee and reading something on his phone, his workout shirt accentuating his broad, muscular shoulders. Mmm.

He turns around. Raises his eyebrows. "Mmm?"

Every drop of blood in my body rushes to my face and I panic. Did I really say that out loud? What is wrong with me? This one's on you, brain.

"Don't you mean, 'good morning, roomie?'" Conor continues, his lips twitching.

"I mean... mmm, coffee. That's it. I love the smell of coffee," I blurt in a sudden fit of inspiration.

Phew, nice save. Not obvious at all.

Conor's lips stretch into a lazy smile. "I take it you slept well?"

"Like a baby." I reach into the cupboard and pull out an oversized novelty mug that declares "World's Okayest Brother" (a delightfully thoughtful Christmas gift from myself to Aiden last year). I help myself to coffee, take a huge gulp, close my eyes, and say "mmm" again loudly. Just to reiterate my point.

"Thanks for the caffeine." I smile, leaning my elbows on the island. "How was your night?"

"Fine." Conor shrugs. "In all honesty, though, I'm not big into going out anymore. I prefer staying in."

I peer at Conor for a moment, my breath catching. This man just keeps saying the right things, and a statement like that is 100% my love language. The way his shirt is hugging his biceps doesn't hurt, either. Although, he probably wore that shirt on purpose, just to show them off.

"You were so quiet, I thought you might still be sleeping. Or, that you might not be home yet," I say and take an innocent sip of coffee.

Am I digging? Ah, who's to know.

Conor's eyes crinkle at the corners, and I'm suddenly glad my elbows are supporting my weight so I don't topple over in a Jane Austen-worthy swoon.

"I was being quiet on purpose so I didn't wake you," Conor says. "I felt bad for texting you so late when you were tired."

I'm so lost in his green eyes that I respond before I think. "Yeah, and it wasn't even an emergency."

Conor raises his eyebrows a touch and I curse my big mouth—WHY would I say that? I'm sure I meant it to sound flirty. I wanted to go for round two on our back and forth banter. Instead, I made it sound like I don't want him to text me.

I want to file a petition to retract my statement. Claim temporary insanity.

But, before I can do any of that, Conor grins again. "Would you prefer I didn't text you in non-emergencies, then?"

I shake my head a tad too eagerly, and his grin stretches.

"Text me when you need me," I say flippantly. "But, I'm very busy and important, so I'll get back to you when I can."

"Busy...and...important." Conor mimes writing something down. "Got it."

The twinkle in his eye catches me off guard and I shift. "And don't worry about waking me in the mornings, I sleep like the dead."

"Also noted." Conor quirks an eyebrow at me. "Anything else I should know about my new roommate? Allergies? Medications? Exotic pets?"

"Nope, nope, nope." I laugh and point to the Tupperware container on the island. "And it's just Fernie and me. You?"

"Just the one pet alligator. Her name's Susan."

He's joking... I think.

"What about you?" I decide it's best to ignore Susan and any questions surrounding her existence for the time being. "Anything I should know?"

"Well." Conor leans forward conspiratorially, and a lock of that thick, golden brown hair falls over his forehead. His eyes glint with mischief. "I'm pretty wild when it comes to scheduling."

"Color me intrigued." I mirror his movement reflexively. The man has a magnetic field, I swear. "Want to fill me in on this out-of-control schedule of yours?"

He laughs that rich, throaty laugh. "I'm a creature of habit. I meal prep on Sundays, vacuum on Mondays, clean the bathrooms on Tuesdays. Wednesday is laundry day and Thursday is garbage day."

His eyes are sincere, and I'm reminded of how he scrubbed the hallway yesterday before I could even get to the mess. He's serious.

Whoa. A neat freak who has a designated day for each household chore. *Why is that so sexy?*

Maybe because I'm the type of gal who never remembers to do laundry, resulting in frequent panicked rummages through my laundry basket to find socks.

"Well, either you are exceedingly OCD by nature or a woman has trained you well," I joke, expecting him to laugh.

But Conor's expression flattens, and the sparkle in his eyes dims.

"Something like that," he says, then gets to his feet. Like he's preparing to leave.

Shoot. Obviously, my comment touched a nerve. What if he actually has OCD and I just made fun of his medical condition?

"Do you want breakfast?" I ask quickly, hoping it's not too obvious that I'm trying to find a way to backpedal right out of that four-lane tunnel I call a mouth.

I watch his expression carefully, and I'm relieved when he smiles. He gestures to his outfit. "I have work at noon, I was going to go for a run first."

"A run!" I practically yell. I'm so delighted that he's not leaving because of my dumb comment that I can't control my decibel level, apparently. "Yes, of course!"

"You want to come?"

"Hahahahaha." I'm not really sure why I'm laughing. Hysteria, maybe. "A run? I don't really run. My car barely even runs half the time."

Good grief.

Conor pokes his tongue into his cheek and smirks. His ocean green eyes sparkle in this spine-tinglingly devious way that makes me a bit seasick. I turn my head and chug on my coffee, letting it scorch my throat.

"I can take a look at it for you," he says.

I bite my lip. "You can?"

"Sure. I'd be happy to."

I smile flimsily. It's nice of him to offer, but there's the teeny, tiny issue that there's actually nothing wrong with my car. Save for the broken AC. I think fast and change the subject. "You cook dinner, make coffee, *and* fix cars for all of your roommates?"

His smirk morphs into a cheeky grin. "Just the pretty ones."

A glow spreads from the top of my head down to my

toes, and I clench my fists to stop my arms from doing an impromptu happy dance. Conor thinks I'm pretty? No, he's just being nice, I'm sure. Trying to make me feel better about my recent breakup. Aiden probably asked him to be extra sweet to me, or something.

"Is there anything you don't do?" I keep my tone light, like I'm joking around.

But I'm serious. As a heart attack.

"Breakfast." He winks. "I don't do breakfast."

And with that, he gives me a little wave, puts in his airpods, and heads for the door.

Touché, flirtypants.

Conor goes off for his morning run (why couldn't I have been born with a gene that makes me want to hurl myself down city sidewalks in the name of health and fitness?), and I return to Aiden's bedroom. Never one to waste my hair and makeup efforts, I dig through my suitcase until I find a prim, white blouse and black slacks.

It isn't the most fashionable clothing in the world, but I hope my outfit is passably professional. As I have zero dollars to my name, I figure getting a start on job hunting can't hurt—I don't want to be squatting at my brother's place forever, and I have a list of galleries I want to pop into.

That's my master (mistress?) plan: get a job at a gallery, and then, once I'm in and pally-pally with the owners, I'll conveniently drop into conversation that I'm an artist. It's a foolproof plan.

Or, maybe, a plan for a fool. Either way, it's all I've got right now.

I add a pair of black heels to my ensemble, and wobble my way to the front door.

I am strong. I am confident. I am employable.

I repeat the mantra to myself as I strut down the front walk. And, when I say strut, I mean shuffle. Like a penguin. I've always been terrible at walking in heels.

I'm fumbling in my purse for my keys when I hear that booming voice again.

"BUTCH, NO!"

Before I know what's happening, I have an eighty-pound golden retriever on my person. And I literally mean *on my person*. The dog throws itself at me with such speed, I'm surprised I don't topple over seeing as I'm practically wearing stilts. Butch's paws are on my chest—he's almost as tall as me standing up—and a big, wet, pink tongue showers my face in slobbery dog-breath kisses.

"Hi!" I manage to remove my face from the line of fire and pat the dog on the back of the head, pushing gently. "Down, boy. That's a good boy, down!"

Down, he does not get.

"Sit?" I try. "Please?"

"DOWN!" Courtney barks the command and the dog immediately retreats, dropping down to lie at my feet obediently. He gazes up at me with a sweet, lovesick expression, his tail thumping loudly on the pavement. Despite the assault, he's cute as can be.

Courtney runs up the driveway with her other dog, Cassidy. Her backpack bobs up and down behind her, and she clutches a gigantic Tupperware. "I'm so sorry, once he's met you, he thinks you're best friends for life. He slipped right out of his collar."

"No problem," I say. Although the two, huge, grassy paw prints on my chest suggest otherwise.

Courtney hooks Butch back up to his leash and collar, then shoves the Tupperware into my arms with no small amount of force.

"This is for you," she says. "I baked you some cupcakes to welcome you to the neighborhood. And to apologize for getting us off to a bad start yesterday."

"Thank you," I say, softening towards my new neighbor. Baked goods truly are the way to my heart. "That's really kind, and totally unnecessary."

I pull the lid off the Tupperware and gaze at some very questionable-looking, lumpy cupcakes. Why are they green?

I snap the lid back on hurriedly, and tuck the container under my arm.

"Hopefully they're edible. If not, I'll bake you another batch," Courtney says brightly. Then, she eyes my shirt. "Although I may do that anyway, seeing as I also have to apologize for your stained shirt."

"Oh no, please don't," I yelp quickly. "This is enough. More than enough, thank you."

She gives me a very sudden, very sunny smile. "Are you staying for a while? Like that other guy?"

What is this, Neighborhood Watch? Courtney sure seems to keep tabs on everything going on in the house next to hers. I make a mental note to ask my brother what he knows about his nosy neighbor.

"Yeah, Conor and I are both living here temporarily." I'm wary of giving Courtney too much information. I have a distinct feeling that anything I say can and will be used against me. Hopefully not in court.

Courtney nods. "Is that redheaded woman Conor's girl-friend, then?"

"Who?" I blink.

"The one who's there all the time. She started showing up soon after he moved in."

Man, Courtney sure has a lot of questions about the females coming around Aiden's house.

I shrug, not sure what to say. None of the women in the

group last night had red hair. I've known Conor for less than twenty-four hours, but the one thing I know for sure is that there appear to be a lot of women in his life.

Courtney clearly misinterprets my shrug, because she shrieks so loud, her pups both leap to their feet. "Oh, sorry! Did I get it all wrong? Is he *your* boyfriend?"

"What?" My voice comes out all weird and high. "No! No, no, no. No sir-eeee."

Then, to make things worse, I laugh like a hyena.

She seems to sense my discomfort, because she rolls her eyes like we're in cahoots or something. "So, he's not your boyfriend, but you *want* him to be your boyfriend?

I startle worse than the dogs did. Courtney grins like she knows all my secrets with just a glance. It's rather unnerving.

"That's... kind of a personal question, Courtney."

"I like getting to know my neighbors." The woman is unflappable.

"No," I say decisively. "I don't want him to be."

She looks at me like I've just told her that the sky is green and grass is blue. "Why not? He's so hot."

Because I don't want to be added to Conor's long list of passing flirtations?

I purse my lips and bite my tongue. I'm not in the market for a fling with a player. I mean, I have to *live* with the man. We're roommates. And I need to treat him like a roommate. People who share a space, coexist peacefully and contribute equally.

But, Courtney does have a point—Conor is hot. And sweet. And funny. And a big old flirt who goes on lots of dates, according to Aiden. Which is why I can't let him cook me dinner, and make me blush and giggle like a schoolgirl. I can't let him fix my car and do nice things for me to make me swoon over him like every other woman.

And, right now, he has one up on me after cooking me dinner last night. That's going to have to change.

Yeah, two can play at that game, Conor Brady.

I realize I've been silent for far too long and there's a chance Courtney thinks *I'm* the weird one now. So, I roll my eyes and sigh. "Because I'm not into men who are more into themselves than the girls they date. He may be hot, but he sure knows it."

To my surprise, Courtney's face pinches and she nods in agreement. "I know a guy like that."

We share a small smile. Courtney may be a bit offbeat, but my new neighbor and I may have more in common than I first thought.

"I'd better go change my shirt," I say. "Thanks again for the cupcakes."

"No problem," Courtney smiles wide. Then, her brow crinkles. "Oh, and did you hear from Aiden about the fence?" Her lips twist over my brother's name like it's a four-letter word. "I know he wanted to get it replaced as soon as possible, seeing as he did all those renovations."

"No, sorry." I haven't heard about the fence from Aiden because I haven't mentioned it to him yet. Oops. Not wanting to be entirely unhelpful, I add, "Conor—the guy who's definitely not my boyfriend—did the renovations. Do you want to speak to him about it?"

An undecipherable look flits across Courtney's face before she smiles mischievously. "I'll wait until Aiden's home. All good. Nice to meet you again, Jane."

"Jess," I correct.

"Oh, I'm so sorry. Jess. I'm awful with names. *Jess Mess. Jess Guess. Jess Confess.*" She stops rhyming long enough to pull a face—tongue out, eyes crossed, like she's posing for a goofy prom picture. "I like to rhyme so I don't forget things."

Of course she does. And yet, I can't help but feel somewhat endeared by Courtney's bizarre antics. She's quirky... but she seems sweet. I have a feeling we'll be seeing more of each other.

Courtney and I say our goodbyes and I turn back towards the house to change my grass-stained shirt. As I walk, I think about her calling Conor my boyfriend and I snort aloud. Conor's a flirt, interested in nothing more. According to everything I've seen and heard about him, he should have told me earlier he doesn't do *relationships*, not breakfast.

I don't want any part of that. Plus, who's to say he'd want anything with me, anyway? He can have his pick of anyone.

So the odds of Conor and me getting together? Yeah, let's just say the chances are higher of me gluing every piece of Fernie's shattered pot back together.

CONOR

"I'm *very* impressed." A cool, manicured hand lands on my bare forearm.

She's flirting. Again.

"Thanks, Karla." I take a step away from my realtor and cross my arms over my chest as casually as I can, hoping to avoid any more unnecessary contact. "I think it should be ready to list in a couple of weeks."

There's an awkward pause as Karla registers my putting distance between us.

Flustered, I grab two sample tiles for the backsplash I picked out and hold them out to her. "What do you think?"

She wrinkles her nose at my question, so I give her a little more context. "The blue, textured mosaic will lend itself to the farmhouse feel, but the ivory fleur de lis will look more classic and elegant."

We went to visit my new purchase in Edgewood an hour ago, and now, we're standing in the kitchen of another one of my projects—a large Craftsman in Decatur that was a complete gut job. It's almost finished now, save for a few aesthetic details.

I bought this house at the high end of what it was worth.

The other interested party was a large developer who wanted to bulldoze the place and build condos. But, that damn sentimental side of me reared its insistent head, and I ended up paying more than I wanted in order to save the historic property.

The house always had good bones. And now, it also has raised ceilings, a chef's kitchen, and an enlarged master suite complete with walk-in closet and steam shower. The property is stunning, and I hope I did a good job capturing the essence and beauty of the house. But man, are the bills adding up on this baby.

Karla frowns at the tiles I'm holding, then waves an indifferent hand. "Whichever one will look more expensive."

I have to refrain from rolling my eyes. Taste and style aren't always about price. But, trying to get Karla to believe that would be like trying to explain string theory to a four year old.

"Speaking of expensive, though, let's talk money," Karla says, her face lighting up.

I chuckle dryly. Karla definitely doesn't beat around the bush. It's one of the reasons I work with her, to be honest—she's truly good at her job. She's been on this journey with me since my first flip, and I value her market knowledge. Over the years, she's given me lots of good advice—even if our priorities do tend to differ more often than not.

I bite my lip as I lean against the kitchen countertop, a little nervous. With house flipping, finding the perfect balance of spending money to make money is a constant battle. And I know I've overspent on this project.

I exhale and tell her what I'm in the hole for.

Karla confirms my fears when her eyes widen a touch. She shakes her head. "Decatur's on the rise right now, it's hot. We both know that. But, there's lots of inventory,

Conor, tons of family homes available. And, with the price point you're seeking, a house this size has got to have that extra touch of magic. That special something, you know?"

I nod. As much as I don't want to admit it, I do know. There's only so much value you can add by upgrading appliances and customizing bathroom tile.

"To get a premium on this place, you're going to need to sell the lifestyle that comes with this investment," Karla continues. She twists a lock of straight, red hair around a long, matching red fingernail as she speaks. "Which means..."

I shake my head. "My sister's about to pop, she's not going to be able to help on this one."

My little sister is usually my go-to for interior design and staging advice. After I've finished the renovations, she's the one who really makes each house come alive. She's always had that eye, and it's definitely come in handy over the years. But, she's also about a thousand months pregnant right now. I can't put this on her.

"Hire a designer then. Or a professional staging company."

"I'll think about it." Hiring a staging company is the last thing I want to do. I'm already in the red on this flip, and plus, I've gone out of my way to collect furniture and other staging items over the years. Which, with the help of Mia, makes all my houses look beautiful for a fraction of the price.

"You'd better think about it quickly," Karla simpers. "Because I'm scheduling the open house for two weeks from now."

I open the fridge and retrieve two Cokes. No such thing as a Pepsi preference here in Atlanta—that would be blasphemy. I hold one out to Karla, who shakes her head. I pop the tab off a can and drain half of it in a single gulp. It's still baking hot outside, and while the project site has power, I haven't hooked up the AC yet. I'm surprised Karla's not boiling alive in that suit.

"Face it, Conor." Karla smoothes an imaginary wrinkle in her royal blue jacket. "This was a risky investment to begin with, and I really think you need to take one last risk for this to pay off."

As she launches into her favorite risk vs reward speech, I down the rest of my Coke, then toss the empty can across the room. It arcs neatly into the recycling bin with a loud *clank*. Karla watches me, her keen blue eyes trained on my mouth. I wipe my lips awkwardly with the back of my hand.

On top of the constant "going for drinks" talk, she's asked me out twice in the past, and I've turned her down as gently as possible. She's whip-smart, and pretty too, but I'm just not interested in her like that. So, I keep muttering vague, dumb excuses about not mixing business with personal—that I like to neatly compartmentalize every area of my life and keep them separate. And, because I'm such a clean freak, it's believable.

I know I'm a hypocrite, though.

Since Jess showed up yesterday, I've done nothing but think about my buddy's little sister. Which I know is not cool. Especially because, when Aiden gets home, I'll have to live with both of them until my house is ready. Talk about blurring the lines.

But, there's just something about Jess.

Last night, I was having the best time getting to know her— until my friends showed up and popped our little bubble. Since then, I can't stop picturing her liquid brown eyes that narrow every time she's trying to work out if I'm joking. Her pale skin that reddens every time I tease her. Her soft, full mouth—possibly the most distracting mouth I've ever come across. A mouth that begs to be kissed.

This morning, I made the corners of that mouth turn down when I clammed up at the joke she made. I didn't mean to—she just caught me off-guard and it took me a moment to recover.

I could tell she was embarrassed, but I couldn't bring myself to explain my reaction. If I did that, I'd have to tell her the truth: that there's been no woman in my life for years, but lately, I've had this nagging feeling that I want more than casual dating. Maybe seeing my sister and her husband so happy triggered something within me, but I want someone I can have a life outside of work with. A relationship to share in each other's successes, and help each other through our failures. Not a "me" anymore, but a "we."

It's not exactly an easy, breezy conversation to have with the woman who just moved in with you. The one I just *had* to text last night, even though I knew better than to play that game. After a beer or two, I was convinced that a little harmless flirting was just that—harmless. Like friendly flirting.

Besides, keeping my growing desire to settle down and have a family to myself is an easier, less vulnerable place to exist. So, I went ahead and put my walls back up, keeping things in the friends-who-flirt zone.

Because that's totally a thing.

"Conor?" Karla's voice rips me back to the present. "Are you even listening?"

"Uh-huh," I lie.

"So-o?" She draws out the last syllable, pursing her artificially plump lips.

I blink, trying to recall what we were talking about before I so thoroughly tuned out.

She takes in my bewildered expression and laughs. "Liar, liar!" she sings. "You're so out of it today—late night last night, then?"

"Something like that," I mutter with a sheepish smile.

"I was just saying that I need to get to my next appointment. But, I'll ask around about options for affordable staging companies and check in with you this week."

"*Right*," I say. "Thank you, Karla. Sorry for the mush for brains today."

She pokes me in the ribs and it takes everything in me to avoid flinching. "You can thank me by taking me out for a drink when this house sells for over asking."

Great. I tune out for a couple of short, tiny little moments and, in that time, I've managed to secure drinks with Karla. There's nothing I can say to avoid looking beyond rude, so I simply nod.

I slip on my sunglasses and open the front door. I gesture for her to step out in front of me, and she waits for me to lock up. We walk down the tree-lined front path together and, when we get to the curb, she hovers for a moment.

"Thanks again, Karla." I stand as straight and businesslike as possible. Kind of hard to do when I'm wearing athletic shorts and flip flops, but so be it. Then, I walk to my vehicle as fast as I possibly can without it looking like I'm trying to run away (which I am).

As I unlock my truck, my phone vibrates in my pocket.

Jess: My turn to cook tonight.

A warm feeling gathers in my belly and my stupid face grins from ear to ear and at the thought of going home to a home-cooked meal after a long, hard day at work. Going home to *Jess*. When we talked about our routines this morning, Jess and I never discussed sharing the cooking. But, I have to admit I love this idea.

In my head, I'm picturing something out of a 1950s magazine. Jess looking adorable in a sweet, polka dot dress and I'd walk through the door and yell, "Honey, I'm home!"

I'd drop my briefcase so I could swing her around my arms, then dip her and kiss her hello.

Wait, what?

Since when does my brain go all *I Love Lucy* in my fantasies? I'd never want any woman in my life to feel like she has to stay home and clean all day. Obviously, because I'd want her to feel empowered to do anything she wants. But also, because *I* like cleaning.

There's nothing better than getting my emotions out by aggressively scrubbing countertops. It's therapeutic. Not that I'd ever admit that to Jess. To prove my point that I'm a normal-amount-of clean person, I even left a dirty mug in the sink this morning instead of putting it in the dishwasher. Take *that*, clean freak tendencies. I'm cool as a well chilled cucumber, see?

"Byeeee, Conor!" Karla's yodeling cuts through my jumble of thoughts like a knife. She's at the door of her white Lexus, waggling her fingers.

"Bye," I call before jumping in my truck. I lean my head against the headrest, then turn on the ignition. A sigh of relief escapes me as the air conditioning blasts my face. I watch Karla pull away from the curb, but instead of putting my own vehicle in drive, I type out a message.

Conor: It's like that, is it?

Jess: Least I can do. Get ready for some culinary excellence.

Conor: Oh yeah, whatcha making?

Jess: Waffles.

My heart speeds to double time as I'm thrown back to our little exchange this morning. Before I can reply, another message comes through.

Jess: So, get ready to do breakfast.

Oh, I'm ready.

9

JESS

"Could you keep it on file in case something does come up?" I smile tightly.

The fresh-faced receptionist, who looks like she's barely out of diapers, shoots me a sympathetic smile.

"Sure," she says, her voice colored with doubt. I glance around the hot pink and chrome foyer of Blend Creative, already knowing that I will never hear from anyone at this company.

"Thank you for your time." I turn on my heel and stride away. I'll show myself out gracefully. I may not have the experience any of these fancy design companies are looking for, but at least I still have my dignity.

Well, I do until I try to pull the front door open. It's a push door, so I end up face planting into the spotless glass.

"Are you okay, ma'am?" the receptionist calls after me, and I'm not sure if it's the goose egg forming on my forehead or the sting of the hundredth rejection of the week, but my eyes begin to smart.

Not needing to be humiliated any further, I pretend I've gone temporarily deaf and scuttle out onto the street.

Once I'm safely out of that nightmare of an office and back in the inferno that is downtown Atlanta, I use all my restraint to avoid having a full-blown meltdown.

It's been almost a week of pounding pavements and giving out resumes, speaking with snooty receptionists who refuse to connect me with the people I actually want to speak to. Let's face it, who wants to hire a washed up wannabe artist whose last experience in her field was working at a gallery right out of college? It was a good job, but after I moved to New York with Johnny, I was never able to find anything else comparable.

The sad thing is, it's not like I didn't try. I applied for a million jobs at art galleries and design firms in New York. I eventually got a volunteer position at the Museum of Modern Art two mornings a week, conducting tours with groups of students.

Middle school students, not art students.

Seeing as the rent on my cockroach-infested walk-up cost more than a mortgage payment every month, that didn't exactly pay the bills. So, I spent the last few years working long nights at *Cirque!*—an "avant garde experimental concept restaurant" that was basically a circus restaurant. Complete with waitress uniforms that featured top hats and red dinner jackets.

Yup. Nothing looks as good on a resume as four years spent as a calamari-delivering circus freak.

My long nights at work clashed with Johnny's nine-to-five so thoroughly that we were often ships in the night. And, apparently, we missed each other so many times that I ended up drifting out to sea aimlessly, while he docked in Sarah's welcoming port.

Ew. There's a mental image I never wanted.

I shake my head vigorously, attempting to expel all

thoughts of Johnny and his *mistress*. But all it does is give me a headache and earn me a concerned look from a mother passing me on the sidewalk. She takes her toddler's hand and moves away from me, pulling him into the safety of a Baby Gap.

Better run away before the crazy lady gets us!

What has my life become?

I check my watch. It's 3pm. On a Thursday afternoon. I've already wasted over forty hours this week being told I'm a failure, and now, I'm tired, sweaty and defeated. Plus, I'm pretty sure there's a blister forming on my big toe.

It's time for the only things that can help after a week like this one: wine and ice cream.

It's five o'clock somewhere, right?

I yank off my heels and stride barefoot to my car, calories calling my name.

After a quick stop at the grocery store for a whole pint of Ben & Jerry's Half Baked (okay, and a pint of Cherry Garcia, because everybody knows that variety is the spice of life), I pull up outside Aiden's house in a much better mood.

On the way home, I picked myself up and got my head in gear. Instead of collapsing on the couch with ice cream and wine, I decided that maybe I should start painting again (after I eat my ice cream, of course). If people aren't going to hire me to work at their companies, then maybe plan B is to start creating art again. In the hope that somebody might buy it.

Pigs do, occasionally, fly. Right?

Let's forget about the fact that I haven't painted in years. Johnny wasn't exactly encouraging of my art when we moved to New York, so, bit by bit, the little studio space

I'd set up in my apartment slowly disappeared. My paint brushes were packed away to make room for my circus uniform, and my easel was replaced with a bike. Because Johnny insisted we both buy bikes, so we could visit each other without taking the subway.

Only we never biked together once. I kept on taking the subway to Johnny's place (paying for parking in NYC is enough to bankrupt anyone), and Johnny continued to never visit me at my apartment, and upgraded to using taxis to get everywhere else.

But that was Past Jess. I want to be New Jess now. And, seeing as Conor won't be home for at least a few hours, I'm going to make the most of my time alone and do some painting.

Speaking of Conor, I've barely seen him in the past few days. He comes home from work every night later and later, looking more and more stressed. When I ask him if there's anything wrong, though, he just shakes his head. Then, he usually cleans the first thing in his path.

We haven't eaten dinner together since last weekend, when I cooked him waffles. Let me rephrase that—since I *tried* to cook him waffles. Turns out you can't make waffles without a waffle maker. Which Aiden did not have. Because, let's face it, who owns a freaking waffle maker?

And just a helpful Domestic Goddess tip—no matter how much Google may tell you otherwise, you cannot use a George Foreman Lean Mean Grilling Machine thingy as a substitute waffle maker. Especially if said Grilling Machine was found stashed at the back of a cupboard, coated in a thin sheen of stale grease.

My brother does not share Conor's neat freak, deep cleaning tendencies.

Honestly, I'm beginning to wonder if Conor's purposefully coming home late in an attempt to avoid my cooking.

To give credit where credit is due, Conor tried to eat the waffles. Even after his eyes widened in horror while he took in the batter-splattered kitchen and burger-scented smoke billowing from Big George. He sat down at the island, plopped a "waffle" (read: soggy pile of slop) onto his plate, and took a bite. Gagged. Politely pretended he wasn't gagging. He even went to take a second bite before I put him out of his misery and tossed the entire plate of waffles into the trash.

We laughed together, he helped me clean the kitchen, and then, we drove to the nearest Waffle House. There, Conor (the weirdo) forewent the smothered, covered hash browns and syrup-drenched chocolate chip waffles, and ordered a grilled chicken melt instead. I mean, who does that?

Guess Conor really doesn't *do* breakfast.

We sat in a sticky, pleather booth, drinking lukewarm decaf and chatting. Before I knew it, hours had gone by and, to my dismay, it turns out that Conor really does seem to be a good guy. With a pretty solid personality. We didn't touch on anything deep or personal, of course, but talking to him felt strangely comfortable—like there was an unspoken understanding between us to keep our conversation topics light and surface-level. Away from what may lie beneath.

It was pretty much a perfect evening. The kind of evening I'm sure is enjoyed by normal, non-flirty roommates everywhere.

So, why is it that, every day since, I find myself hoping that we'll spend another evening together? In a casual, not-a-date setting, of course.

I shake myself off and turn off the car. The places my mind goes after a long week. In any case, Conor will probably be working late tonight, meaning that nobody will be here to see my wine and sugar coma.

Eager to get the show on the road, I jump out of my car, pint of ice cream in each hand. I'm practically skipping towards the front door when—

"HEY!"

"Hey Court." I wave, then set my ice cream on the ground so I can pet the golden brothers, who are pulling on their leashes in a mad attempt to get to me.

Over the past week, Courtney and I have fallen into a bit of a routine—one where she basically accosts me whenever she sees me outside the house, and then we chat for a while. I've learned that she's a year older than me, an Atlanta native, her last name is Turner, and she has a dog-walking business called Life is Ruff. It doesn't pay the bills yet, so she works nights as a hostess at a fancy French restaurant.

To be honest, she's growing on me like a weed. A very pretty weed, though... like a dandelion—bright and unashamedly, unabashedly herself. I'm at the point where I look forward to seeing her, leashes in hand, blond ponytail and backpack bobbing behind her.

She's sweet. And kind. Plus, I don't have many friends in Atlanta anymore.

So, I could use a friend.

I just wish that she'd stop baking me cupcakes. My garbage is currently full to the brim with an array of rainbow-colored, entirely inedible treats.

Don't look at me like that—I appreciate the gesture, I really do. Unfortunately, I had to stop trying to consume the food after I nearly broke a tooth on what appeared to be an olive pit. In a chocolate chip cookie.

I can't afford a trip to the dentist right now.

Courtney, who's dressed in a paisley-print romper today and carrying her usual black backpack, eyes my ice cream. "Big plans for tonight?"

"No," I say decisively. "It's just me, Ben, and Jerry."

I'm not brave enough to tell her my real plan—to take out my paint brushes and get something on canvas.

"No luck on the job hunt?"

I shake my head.

"I'd invite you over to wallow with me, but your boyfriend got home a little while ago." Courtney does an exaggerated wink. "I'll bet you a hundred bucks that he wants to do something with you tonight."

Oh yeah, that's the other annoying thing about Courtney. No matter how much I protest, she's convinced that Conor is into me. Says he looks at me differently than he does the redhead.

I don't believe her.

"He's not my boyfriend, and I don't want to hang out with him tonight," I say fiercely.

There's an awkward pause. Probably because we both know I'm lying.

A beat later, Courtney tugs her leashes. The golden brother duo get to their feet, tongues lolling out of their side of their slobbery, smiley mouths.

"Whatever you say, Jess. I'll see you later." She shoots me a knowing wink and strolls away, humming to herself.

I watch her go, then pick up my ice cream. Which is practically soup by now. Sigh.

I let myself inside and my heart does a little skip when I see that Conor is, indeed, home. In fact, he's putting on his shoes in the entryway, a stack of reusable grocery bags at his feet.

"Good afternoon, roomie." He smiles wickedly. "I see you met Aiden's neighbor."

My eyes widen. *Please, please don't have overheard our conversation.* "A few times now. Do you know her?"

"Not well," Conor says. He pauses, like he's searching for the right words to describe her. "She seems a little..."

"Odd?" I finish.

He laughs. "I was going to say 'intense.' She's super intense the first time you meet her, but then she seems to relax... a lot like you, actually." Conor smirks at me. I pull a face at him.

"It's weird, though," he continues. "She warmed to both you and I pretty quick, but she really has her claws out where Aiden's concerned. Hates the guy. Like, hates him enough to gouge his eyes out."

"Why?" I blink.

"No idea." Conor shrugs. "It's pretty funny though, she's like a scalded cat every time she goes off at him."

Conor glances at me, sees my confusion, and smiles reassuringly. "Don't worry, the feeling's mutual. Aiden returns the dislike with equal fervor. It's like watching an old, married couple bicker. Good, cheap entertainment."

"I see," I say. Although I don't.

I'll have to ask Courtney about Aiden when I see her again. It's so strange that she hates him. Everyone loves Aiden.

"What are you doing home?" I change the subject, suddenly aware that Conor's standing not two feet away from me, and I am gross, sweaty, and clutching a day's worth of calories in liquid ice cream form.

Conor, meanwhile, is freshly showered and dressed in a fitted white t-shirt and light gray shorts that make him look extra tan. His hair is damp and mussed, and his strong jawline is all angles and designer stubble I'm dying to run my hands across. Or feel it scrape across my cheeks. Oh my.

Reel it in, Jess.

"Finished early. It's been a long week, and it's only Thursday." Conor's lips pinch slightly as he reaches for the bags. I feel his pain. "Are you okay, by the way? You look a bit—"

"I'm fine!" I interrupt. "Fine as a fine, fine summer's day."

What in the name of hobknocker am I talking about?

Conor's lips have unpinched and are now curling up in that naughty smile of his. "Okay, Miss Fine." His eyes travel over me, then land on my cartons of ice cream.

"Supper," I explain.

He shakes his head. "That's not supper."

"It's my supper," I say defiantly.

"Nope." He reaches over and plucks the cartons from my hand.

Uh, excuse me?

"Hey!" I protest as he carries them away. To the kitchen, where he stashes them in the freezer.

Conor gives me his dazzling smile, and my anger melts faster than my ice cream. "I was planning on making fajitas tonight, if you'd like some."

I would like some. Very much. Because not only are steak fajitas my favorite food in the world, ever, but I've been living off instant ramen all week and hiding the empty packages deep in the trash so Conor doesn't notice my awful diet. So yes, I want fajitas.

Plus, fajitas are casual. Friendly.

Especially if I eat at least three and don't use any silverware.

"Sure," I blurt before I can stop myself.

"Steak or chicken?"

Steak. Always steak.

"Um, chicken?" I choose the cheaper, less fancy option. Friends eat chicken together.

"Steak it is, then." Conor goes right ahead and reads my mind. What witchcraft is this?

"How did you—?"

"I like steak better, too." Conor pauses with his hand on the front door. "I just gotta run to the store, I'll be back to start cooking after."

He's going out to buy the food specially. Oh no, no, no.

"I'll come!" I throw myself towards the front door. The least I can do is buy some of the ingredients for this very casual roommate hang. I mean, I can't actually afford steak —my ice cream splurge was already not sensible—but Conor doesn't need to know that. And I'm sure my bank will understand that this was an emergency.

"Sure." Conor shrugs. "You could probably use a trip to the grocery store anyway. I can acquaint you with the things I like to call fruit and vegetables. Really good way to avoid scurvy."

Clearly, I didn't hide my ramen evidence well enough.

"Oh, haha. So funny." I cross my arms and fix him with a glare. "I'll have you know that I ate an apple earlier."

"Was it in a carton? In liquid form?"

FOILED AGAIN.

"Fine, so maybe I do need real groceries." I sigh. "Can you give me twenty minutes to shower and change before we go?"

Conor smiles that lazy smile that makes my entire body explode in goosebumps. He takes a step closer to me, so close that I can smell his clean, woodsy scent. His eyes twinkle with mischief as he drops the grocery bags on the floor beside me. "Ten minutes and you have a deal."

The combination of his closeness and the huskiness in his voice makes me want to pass out.

"Fifteen?" I wheedle, suddenly a little breathless.

He looks at me for a long moment. Holds my eyes captive with his. It's hard to think clearly with Conor's eyes on me. It's like he's physically touching me, the way his gaze makes my body react.

Then, very slowly and deliberately, he tilts his wrist. Looks down at his watch. "Nine minutes and fifty seconds..."

I sprint for the shower.

10

CONOR

Okay, so I *might* have asked Aiden what Jess's favorite food was.

And I *might* have skipped out on work early today so I could cook her favorite—steak fajitas—for dinner tonight.

But, in my defense, I saw the disgusting instant ramen wrappers in the trash. So, really, I'm just looking out for her health and wellbeing. Plus, Jess is obviously on a tight budget while she's looking for work, and this seemed like the easiest way to help her without embarrassing her.

And, yeah, there's also the fact that I've barely seen her since Wafflegate last Saturday. Most of my furniture and homewares are currently in storage, but the second I move into my new house and unpack my waffle maker, I'm going to gift it to her. As an act of public service.

Nobody should have to suffer through waffles grilled on a George Foreman ever again.

As Jess and I wander the aisles at the grocery store, I try not to glance at her too often. But, as I throw a bag of onions in the cart, I sneak a sideways look. Her face is wrinkled in a frown as she examines the selection of peppers, looking like she's doing a complex algebra equation. She's changed into short denim overalls over a white t-shirt, with matching white Converse. Her brown curls are tied up in a yellow scrunchie, and she's wearing thick, black-rimmed glasses that I haven't seen before. It's a good look for her. Like, a super good look.

Is it weird that I feel like I've missed her over the past few days?

Probably.

She sees me looking (not as sneaky as I thought) and shrugs. "Which peppers do you like?"

I reach past her and select a random bag. "The red ones?"

"Works for me." She laughs. "I'm too tired to think properly."

"I know the feeling." I offer her a little smile as I set the peppers in the cart. It's nice, walking around Whole Foods with Jess, pushing a cart we're both adding groceries to. Groceries that will be put into the same fridge, at the same house. "Rough week?"

She takes off her glasses and rubs her eyes. "Yup. I think I might be unemployable."

"I highly doubt that." I grab a box of kiwis that I saw Jess eyeing wistfully, and add them to the cart. "What did you do in New York?"

"Waitressed." She frowns. "By necessity, not by choice. And when I came back to Atlanta, the idea was that I wouldn't have to do that again. But, I guess I might have to."

"You'll find something," I assure her.

"You said you had a long week, too?" Jess diverts the conversation as we make our way out of the produce section and into the bakery, which smells like warm, sugary dough.

"Lots on the go right now."

"Do you always work so many hours?"

Yes. But how do I say that without sounding like a complete workaholic?

Which I'm not. Not really.

"Sometimes," I settle on saying. I watch Jess as she studies the bread and selects the cheapest loaf. I add another loaf of quinoa and flax bread. You know, for her health. Because Aiden would be happy to know that she's eating properly. "I'm definitely going to take this weekend off."

I mean, I might take Sunday off. We'll see.

"Any plans?" Jess smiles nonchalantly, but her eyes are focused on mine.

I grab a package of tortilla wraps. "I was going to head to Mia and Pete's for a barbecue tomorrow evening."

Jess's eyebrows shoot up in surprise. "Do you know them well?"

"I'd hope so." I laugh. "Mia's my sister."

"What?" She blinks, then pulls on a curl in her ponytail. "I had no idea."

"Yeah, she knows Aiden through Pete. When Aiden wanted his house renovated, she recommended me. I usually buy and sell the houses I flip, but it was really nice to work with a client, make their vision come to life. Aiden and I became buddies, and the rest is history." I explain as we walk. Then, I go for it. "Want to come with me tomorrow?"

She stops for a moment, her forehead creased. I watch her face carefully, my heart beating quicker than usual. I have no idea why I feel so nervous. I've never been nervous to ask a girl out. Not that I'm asking Jess out.

I'm just hoping she says yes. As any friend would.

"Mia said I should invite you," I add. See? Not even my idea. Just extending my sister's hospitality.

Jess's face relaxes a touch and she nods. "Oh, okay. That would be great. I'd love to see them."

Excitement flares within me, which is a bit ridiculous given that Jess only agreed to come when I extended Mia's invite. But still... It means more time together. Of which I am quickly becoming a bigger fan.

"Great. She'll be delighted." I hold out two jars. "Mild or medium salsa?"

Jess grins, putting two rows of square, white teeth on display. "Spicy."

She would say that, wouldn't she? I add two jars to the cart, because I'm not about to go and tell her that the mere thought of anything spicier than a jalapeño is too hot for me to handle.

I have a reputation to uphold, after all.

⚜

"Can you grab the buns for me?" Pete asks, casually flipping burgers with one hand while clutching his craft ale with the other.

I take a sip of my own beer and let the tart, crisp flavor sour my tongue before swallowing. It's a beautiful evening. The sun hangs low above the horizon, still angry hot despite the impending nightfall, and the heavy aroma of sizzling meat and freshly cut grass is almost intoxicating. I love summer.

"Sure thing." I set down my beer and walk towards the open patio doors and into the kitchen, where Jess and Mia are chopping up veggies for salad.

Mia and Pete's little boy, Oliver, sits in a high chair next to them. He and Jess are babbling and cooing sweet nothings back and forth, already completely in love with each other.

At two years old, Ollie already has better game than I do. Respect, little man.

I watch Jess as she passes Oliver a slice of cucumber. How she laughs when his eyes light up and he seizes it with one eager fist.

Jess's shower-damp hair hangs long and loose, and her face is free of makeup. She's wearing the same baby blue, floral sundress she wore for dinner the night I met her. Only tonight, she's ditched the matching sweater, leaving her arms and delicate collarbones on show (did I mention I love summer?) After a week in the Atlanta sunshine, she has a new dusting of freckles that dance over the bridge of her nose. I have the completely uncalled for, but almost insatiable urge to kiss them. All of them.

She's been smiling since we stepped into Pete and Mia's yard a couple of hours ago—a complete 180 from the frazzled, downtrodden woman who arrived home from job hunting yesterday. I guess it's been a long time since she's been here. Seeing familiar faces is probably just what she needed to cheer up after a week of fruitlessly looking for work. It's hard to believe she hasn't been home to see her friends and brother in two years, and once again I can't help but wonder what happened with that ex of hers. Why, exactly, did they break up? What really made her return home?

Whatever it was, I can't help but be glad that Jess is back in Atlanta. Last night, we ate steak fajitas in front of the TV, while watching the Falcons first preseason game. It was the most comfortable, unstressed and relaxed I've felt in ages. But, it also made me realize I have to be careful not to spend too much time getting too cozy with Jess. I can't go falling for her, because that would be dumb. Really dumb.

"Hey, Conor." Mia notices me hovering in the doorway and smiles, her hazel eyes warm.

"Hey!" I run a hand through my hair, embarrassed that I've been caught staring. "I'm just grabbing buns. Steaks are done and burgers will be ready in a minute."

"Perfect," she says and passes me a package of kaiser rolls.

"Come on then, buddy," Jess coos to Oliver. "Let's get you outside."

I watch her lift Oliver out of his high chair and place him on her hip. He giggles as she tickles his pudgy little tummy.

"Ready for your dinner?" Mia drops a kiss on her son's head as she glides by with a tray of caprese salad. "Uncle Conor made you a burger."

Although I'd never admit it aloud, it's still kind of cool to be called "Uncle." It's like I'm a member of some exclusive little club of doting adults. And I love Oliver, I really do. I guess I just like kids in general. They're so pleasingly uncomplicated.

"I don't know if Oliver is going to leave Jess alone long enough to try the burger I made him," I tease, smirking at Jess. "I should be jealous—I spend two years wooing that kid and then you turn up and steal my thunder in one afternoon."

Jess sparkles at me, grinning. "Oliver is smart enough to choose his favorite people. I think he might be gifted.'"

"Well, the gifted child just puked on your shoulder."

"EW!" Her face contorts with disgust as she swivels her head to survey the non-existent vomit. When she realizes I'm kidding, she swats me. I clutch my chest dramatically, pretending her little swat hurt.

Oliver laughs.

"He likes it!" Jess swats me again, and I stagger backwards, earning another laugh from Oliver.

I yelp in fake pain, and the kid just laughs harder. Little

bubbly, gurgling, joyful laughs.

Jess joins in.

And then, so do I.

I'm still laughing when we all sit down at the patio table together a few minutes later.

"To friends who feel like family!" Pete toasts, nodding in Jess's direction, and we all clink our glasses together as we repeat the sentiment. I notice Jess's voice is barely a whisper as she holds up her wine glass.

"Thank goodness it's almost dark out," Mia chuckles as she cuts Oliver's food into tiny, bite-sized morsels. "We can pretend we're eating somewhere nice."

"I like it here," I say without thinking, and Pete and Mia look at me with matching smiles.

I stare around their backyard, which is littered with plastic toys. A sandbox and paddling pool claim most of the prime real estate on the grass, but Pete and Mia have a great little bungalow. Inside, there are baby gates, child locks, and foam protectors on every corner, but every time I'm here, I can't get over how alive their place feels. Bursting with life and possibility and love.

Though I'm excited to move into my new place, there's a part of me that sometimes wishes I was twenty-two again, so it would be appropriate to live with roommates full time. Even before Jess came along, I enjoyed living at Aiden's. It was nice not to come home to an empty house every night.

"Ahh!" Oliver demands, opening his mouth wide for more food. He's sitting in his highchair between Pete and Mia, elbow deep in ground beef and ketchup. They share a tender glance over their son's head.

It's kind of cute (in a slightly sickening way) how in love they are after years of being in a relationship. Pete's that friend who has everything annoyingly together: wife he's head over heels for, an awesome kid, boring job with some big, corporate company he actually likes. He's the best brother-in-law I could've asked for.

Aiden and I used to rag on him for going home early on nights out, or skipping guys' weekend trips. I used to think it was strange that he never cared that we bugged him, or that he was okay with missing out on so much.

Lately, I'm beginning to think that maybe I'm the one missing out.

"Can you pass the corn, please?" Jess nudges me. She and I share a bench seat facing the happy family and, for a moment, it feels like I'm part of a different life entirely. It's such a cozy, domesticated moment—two couples and a toddler, cooking and eating and laughing together. Only Jess and I aren't a couple.

Which I seem to keep forgetting.

So much for harmless flirting.

If Pete's the one in our group with his crap together, I'm the bad friend... because I can't get my best friend's little sister out of my damn head.

I wonder if she'll join us when we go to the bar later tonight. Honestly, I'm kind of wishing it wasn't Friday, and we could just stay here all evening instead of heading out with our whole friend group. I didn't like the way Luke looked at Jess last week. Like he was on a strict, no sugar diet, and she was a vanilla cupcake with extra frosting and sprinkles.

"So, Conor, how's the house?" Mia leans over the table and forks a few spears of grilled asparagus onto her plate.

"Which one?"

"Decatur."

I sigh more heavily than I mean to, and her eyebrows shoot up. "That good, huh?"

This is the first flip that Mia hasn't helped me with—Pete and I jointly put our foot (feet?) down and insisted she rest—but her eyes still light up every time we talk business. I'm desperate to pick her brain, because, when it comes down to it, I'm better at building things than choosing mirrors and light fixtures. But, I feel bad talking about work when she's due to have her baby any day now. The conversation should be about her and her family. Not me.

"Karla thinks I'm in the red on Decatur." I shrug, hoping to end flipping talk. But Mia gestures for me to go on, so I continue, "A lot of family homes have gone up lately, it's a buyers' market. I'm two weeks behind on my own place, too, so Aiden's saddled with me for a little longer." I smile at Jess, who's watching the conversation with undisguised interest. "You are too, I guess."

"I don't mind," she says. A little too quickly. Which makes her blush.

"What are you in the red for?" Pete asks, shoveling coleslaw into his mouth. Gag. I hate coleslaw.

I focus on the nasty, slimy stuff on Pete's fork to keep from getting distracted by Jess's cute pink cheeks. "The house has all these upgrades I spent money on, but nothing to set it apart. Karla thinks we need to go above and beyond to stage it."

"How so?" Mia tilts her head.

"Karla's thinking that we need something cool and edgy to drum up interest at the open house, get enough people to come through that it justifies the list price—try to appeal to a trendier buyer willing to pay a premium. I don't really want to invest in using a luxury staging company, so I'm a little stuck on what to do."

"Sometimes it's as simple as some good art and unique textures," Mia says earnestly, adjusting her oversized glasses. She's the epitome of the cool, trendy young mom we're trying to appeal to, but I can't ask to work with her right now.

"What about Jess?" Pete asks suddenly.

"Ooh, yes," Mia chips in. "Jess is super artsy, she'd be a natural at staging."

I whirl to look at her. She looks like a deer caught in the headlights.

Jess blushes wildly. "I know nothing about flipping houses."

"Staging is only a part of flipping, it's like the lipstick after the facial reconstruction," Pete jokes.

Jess's brown eyes are wide and wild, and my mind races as I consider Pete and Mia's proposition. Jess *did* say that she studied Art History in college and then worked in a gallery. She could probably help with staging no problem. In any case, it would be better than anything I could do myself.

And if I hired her to do this for me, I could help her out. I know she's been struggling to find a job.

And you'll get to spend way more time with her, an annoying little voice in my head sings.

I know I said that I have to be careful not to spend too much time with Jess, but before I can stop myself, I'm speaking. "You know, I think hiring Jess is a really good idea, Pete."

"You'd have so much fun with it, Jess," Mia adds. "Conor has all the furniture and decorating stuff already— we've been collecting things for years. With your artsy eye, I'm sure you'll make it look amazing. Conor has zero eye for style."

"Hey!" I say. But, I don't mean it. She's right.

Jess shakes her head. "I couldn't."

I smile at her slowly. "Oh, but you definitely could."

"Surely, there are people available who are actually qualified for the job," Jess insists.

"I could teach you the basics." I shrug, keeping my eyes

trained on hers and silently willing her to step up to my challenge.

I know that this is a risk. That, if she's not right for the job, it will blow my project. Bomb the open house that we so desperately need to go well to turn a profit. But somehow, I don't seem to care right now.

"I couldn't," she repeats, her brows knitting together as she directs her gaze back on mine.

"Yes, you could," I say again. I widen my eyes, daring her to look away. Because whoever looks away first loses.

An electric current passes between us and I can physically feel the sparks heating my body.

Buzz!

My phone vibrates on the table, and I'm startled out of the moment.

I look around to see Mia and Pete staring at us like someone hit pause—Pete has his fork half-raised to his mouth, Mia, her hand clapped over hers. *Take a picture, it'll last longer.*

Then, Mia unfreezes and smiles a knowing, cat-like smile. I fix her with a glare before I sneak a glance at Jess, who looks as flushed and disoriented as I feel. What just happened between us?

Bewildered, I almost feel grateful that my phone was the distraction. I look at it and check the message.

Aiden: How's everything going? I've been meaning to thank you for being so nice to Jess. She's in a vulnerable spot right now, and she needs a friend.

I feel like a bucket of ice water has been thrown over me, extinguishing the fire I was stoking with reckless abandon.

That'll teach me to feel anything close to sparks with my best buddy's sister.

11

JESS

I have decided that I do not like Mindy. I do not like her stupid, smug face and her stupid, perfectly straightened hair, and her stupid way of backhanded complimenting me at every opportunity she gets.

Did I mention that I don't like Mindy?

Because she sucks.

And maybe, juuuuust maybe, because I've had a teeny, tiny bit too much to drink.

"Jess, your dress is, like, so cute. Precious. I love the *Little House on the Prairie* vibes." Mindy, who is unfortunately seated on my left, rotates between passive aggressive "girl talk" and flirting outrageously with Luke while glancing at Conor to see if he's noticed.

He hasn't.

But then again, he hasn't really paid much attention to me since we got here either, so I can't exactly gloat. He's been deep in conversation with a redhead—a fact that seems to be driving both Mindy and myself up the wall. So, I guess we do have one thing in common.

Earlier, I was so sure he was looking at me in a way that

was... more. Now, I'm not sure of anything at all. Except the fact that I want to go home.

"Thanks," I reply sourly, whirling my straw around my glass. "I'm sure Laura Ingalls Wilder would be proud."

"Who?" Mindy stares at me blankly.

I shake my head. "Never mind."

But she's already turned away—her question was apparently rhetorical. I pull a face at her back. Because resorting to acting like I'm five is currently the only thing making me feel better.

We're at this uber-chic bar downtown, the type of place that is just cool enough to attract a young, hipster crowd, and just expensive and pretentious enough to be frequented by those suit-wearing, vodka-soda swilling city guys who think they are God's gift to women—but have very little to say once they're done talking about their brand new iPhone and how much their car cost.

Either way, the bar is not my scene. The music is loud, it's so dark in here that I keep tripping over things, and the waitress is shockingly rude for someone who's relying on tips (of course, I tip her dutifully despite this).

Conor, however, looks to be in his element.

For the second Friday in a row, it had all been going so well until everyone else turned up. I'm sensing a pattern here.

Conor surprised me again over dinner—he's a doting uncle to Oliver, and he clearly loves Mia more than life itself. The way he cares for his sister reminds me of how Aiden is with me. And Conor has extended the same care and hospitality to me since I arrived in Atlanta, but that is the very reason that I can't possibly accept his job offer.

First off, because I don't know an iota about how staging works. It's not just about pretty, artistic design... it's about flow, and feng shui, and buyer psychology. Things I know nothing about. And secondly, because spending more time with Conor would be dangerous. A. Very. Bad. Idea.

The problem is that my pulse picks up every time Conor is anywhere close to me... more than it ever did when I was with Johnny. My break-up with Johnny was painful enough—even though our relationship hadn't been in a good place for a while, it still hurt to be cast aside. Imagine how much worse it would be to be hurt by a guy that makes my insides flip with a single glance. By a guy who, after only a week of knowing each other, seems to get me in a way Johnny never did.

I don't need my heart to break again, and that's what would happen if I let myself fall for Conor.

Because Conor's not serious about any girl, let alone someone like me.

Because Conor is my freaking roommate, and room-mates don't fall for each other.

I know this in my head. I *know,* logically, that we could never and would never be together. But, that doesn't stop the heart-stabs of jealousy and want as I watch women throw themselves at Conor. And I say women, plural, because there are a lot of them.

If this bar is a jungle, Conor's a roaring lion.

My irrational brain, however, is addled with two moji-tos, and wants Conor all to itself. Which is crazy.

I suck on my mojito loudly. He's leaning casually against the bar as he waits for his drink, and the woman next to him is tossing her hair so hard I'm worried she'll get whiplash.

Is this the same redhead Courtney was talking about? I hope not. This girl is stunning. She's wearing a tight, pink dress that shows off her—*ahem*—assets to perfection. I can literally feel my own butt expand as I stare at her pert, gym-toned derriere. This woman, along with every other female who's hit on Conor tonight, is an exotic bird of paradise. Together, they're a flock of long, lean legs and bright, colorful feathers.

I'm not exactly sure what creature I am.... Possibly a warthog.

Why did I even come here? I hate going out. All I want is to be at home, in my giraffe onesie, eating popcorn and watching trash TV. Preferably that reality dating show where a grown-ass man always ends up crying over the fact that he has too many beautiful women around him and it's so HARD for him to choose.

Pete and Mia had the good sense to bow out of this bar hopping excursion. I don't blame them. I'd way rather hang out with Oliver than Mindy, too. He has much better conversational skills.

I glance around the room, squinting into the dimness. Conor is looking behind him, and catches my eye. He holds up a finger, signalling to give him one minute.

Yeah, roomie, nice try. I'm not going to sit here and wait for you to be done flirting. Luke, Mindy and I are the only ones left at this table and, as Mindy is practically in Luke's lap, I have my cue to leave.

I grab my purse and slide out of the smooth leather booth. Nobody notices me go. Not even when I trip over a stray purse and fly towards the ground. I manage to put a hand out in time to hit the disgusting, sticky floor before my body does, which is fortunate. But, it also kind of makes me look like I'm playing a game of Twister with myself, which is decidedly less fortunate.

"Jess?" The incredulous voice speaks from somewhere above me. I stagger to my feet, cursing my utterly un-catlike reflexes, and come face-to-face with...

Mark Cuthbert. Johnny's best friend and college roommate, in all his abundantly hair-gelled, liberally cologne-spritzed glory. Of course, this would happen now.

"Hi!" I squeak, sticking out my hand awkwardly to... shake his? Why, oh why would I shake his hand?

Mark blinks, and then takes my outstretched hand. Yup, the same hand that was just on the gross, dirty floor.

As his warm, smooth palm slides into my sugary-drink-and-dirt covered one, regret flashes all over his features like a neon pawn shop sign. He recoils in horror, then looks at his Jess-soiled hand like it's on fire. He waves it in the air for a second, then lets it hang limply in front of him, obviously not prepared to wipe it on his thousand-dollar suit.

"Sorry," I mutter, not feeling sorry at all.

"What are you doing here, Jess? Is your main man here, too?" Mark does a weird little twirl, complete with finger guns and tapping feet, as he scans the room for his long lost bro.

Good gracious.

"Johnny and I broke up last month," I tell him.

At my words, his face morphs into a peculiar grimace, twisting and turning in all directions before finally settling into a flimsy smile coupled with eyes full of sympathy. No, not sympathy.

Pity.

It's an expression that tells me he knew all along that this would happen. An expression that says he's not at all shocked that it's over, but what he can't believe is how long it went on for in the first place. It's an expression that holds me in such low esteem, that reinforces what I should have known about Johnny all along but stupidly chose to ignore. I can't take it.

"I'm sorry, Jess," he murmurs, shaking his head. Like I'm some sort of grieving widow.

"I broke up with him," I blurt out of nowhere.

Mark's eyes widen with undisguised shock. He takes a big gulp of his (surprise, surprise) vodka-soda.

Propelled by the force with which the lie shot out of my mouth, I nod vigorously and keep on going. "You know how it goes. Gotta break a few hearts along the way to get to where you're going."

What am I doing? I have no idea what I'm saying right now.

Mark studies me for a few seconds, obviously confused. "So you broke up because you were... coming back to Atlanta?"

"That's right. Packed up and left him. Poor guy. Got a job offer I couldn't turn down."

"Oh yeah?" Mark says. A bit disinterestedly. Disinterestedly enough that I could have just replied with "yes" and left it at that.

But oh, no. Mojito-fueled, jilted-by-her-ex, desperate-to-prove-she's-fine Jess just doesn't know when to shut up.

"Yes. I'm a... house flipper."

WHAT FRESH HELL?

"Oh!" Mark looks as startled as I feel. Mojito-mouth has a mind of its own. I need to get out of here before I make things worse. "Where at?"

"Just finishing a flip in Decatur. I do the staging."

WHAT? NO.

"Oh yeah?" Mark cocks a smug, well-groomed eyebrow. Does he get them done professionally? If so, I'd love to get the name of his brow technician.

No. The answer is no, I was just joking. "Yup."

"That sounds like a blast," Mark says. The finger guns make another unfortunate appearance to accompany the word "blast."

Bury me now. "Oh, it is."

"Jess." Mark sets down his drink and places a hand on

each of my arms. The unwanted contact feels icky, and I have to resist squirming right out of his grip. "I know that you didn't break up with Johnny. You don't think my best friend talks to me once in a while? I know he's with Sarah, and that it's serious. You don't need to lie about breaking up with him. Or about house flipping."

"I *am* a house flipper," I insist. I suddenly feel a bit teary. "Wait, did you just say it was serious?"

Mark grimaces, then sucks in an inhale that whistles through his teeth. He releases me from his grip and pats me on the shoulder. Like I'm a little dog. "I heard he bought a ring."

I must have misheard him. It's loud in here. Dark, too. Which can also interfere with your hearing, I'm told.

"Ring?"

Mark nods. "He's planning on taking her to the Bahamas next month to propose."

He never took me to the Bahamas. Or anywhere, for that matter.

I take a step back foggily, eyes blurring.

I will not cry.

I will not cry.

I will not cry.

Instead, I will become the founding member of the I Hate Mark Club (#ihatemarkclub). I will plan to hold weekly meetings to talk about his stupid hair and make fun of his finger guns. Every year, I will host I Hate Mark Con in Vegas for the most enthusiastic club members. I'll make t-shirts and commemorative memorabilia and... okay, you get the picture.

Point is, I cannot believe he commandeered me like that with his "your main man here, too?" He knew all along what had happened.

What a dirty little hobknocker.

Why, oh why, did I not stay in the safety of Aiden's living room tonight? I could've been deep into two pints of ice cream and a romantic comedy where the weird, quirky girl gets the guy and lives happily ever after.

But, this isn't a rom com. It's real life. And, in real life, the girl gets cast aside for a newer, shinier, more successful model.

"Have a good night, Jess. Take care of yourself, okay?" I hear Mark speaking, but his voice sounds far away.

A tear threatens to slip out of my eye, and I don't hesitate a moment longer. Forget Mark. Forget Johnny, and Sarah, and Mindy, Luke and Conor. Forget everyone. I'm so, so done.

I spring into action and make a beeline towards the exit, only bumping into one table full of people on my way. I step into the street like a maniac, trying to hail a taxi.

And, only once I'm safely in a cab do I let the tears spill freely down my face.

My driver, who's about a hundred years old and has a face wrinkled like a raisin, shoots me a kind smile in the rearview mirror. Like I'm the first drunk girl who's cried in his cab all night. Which I know I'm not. It's almost midnight. There must've been many before me.

"Awh darlin', dry them pretty brown eyes," the cabbie drawls softly, his Southern accent thicker than molasses. "Whoever he is, he ain't worth them big ol' elephant tears."

He offers me a Kleenex. But, the old man's kindness has the opposite of its intended effect because I just bawl harder as I take the Kleenex from him.

I'm not crying over Johnny, per se. I know I'm not in love with Johnny anymore, and I know that breaking up was for the best. But, getting replaced so easily after six long years stings. Especially when those six years meant giving up all of my dreams in favor of his. Just so he could find someone else and drop me when he was done.

And a ring? Come on. Johnny wouldn't even entertain the idea of moving in with me.

I know, deep down, that he's the worst. I'm glad it's over, I really am.

I just wish that I didn't feel like a pathetic idiot left picking up a million pieces.

12

JESS

We pull up outside the house and I pay my lovely cabbie an extra twenty to make up for the mascara all over his back-seat ("Bless your sweet little heart, darlin' girl"). I can't get into the house quick enough.

My phone has been going off in my purse, but I don't dare look at it. No doubt Mark has already blabbed to Johnny about what I just told him, and I'm sure everyone is having a big old belly laugh at my expense right now.

I step into the dark house, not bothering to turn on any lights. Darkness suits my mood right now. I take off one sandal and fire it at the wall. It makes a satisfying *thunk!* So I do the same with the other.

Then, I feel bad and scramble around for them in the dark. After a few moments of fumbling, I set them neatly on the shoe rack in the hallway closet because I'm *such* a good, thoughtful roommate.

A warm shower and comfortable bed are beckoning me. I'm feeling my way towards Aiden's room, when—

BANG!

The front door flies open.

"JESS?"

The hallway light flips on, and I cover my eyes against the brightness. I peek through my fingers to see Conor standing in the doorway, his big, powerful frame practically filling it. His brown hair is mussed, his green eyes frantic.

What's he doing home? Doesn't he have some hot redhead to attend to? Unless... I glance behind him to see if he's got company.

But, he's alone.

"What?" I croak. "Why are you yelling?"

"What the hell, Jess?" He lowers his voice a touch, but it's still at a level I would classify as shouting. "Why did you run off like that? I was worried sick. I've been calling, I thought something happened to you."

I'm speechless as he takes a step towards me. When his eyes alight on my face, his furrowed brow clears and his voice drops to a soft tone that slides over me like silk. "Have you been crying?"

I know that there's no point in denying it—my face swells up like I've got a bee sting-allergy when I cry. It's deeply unattractive and I wish he didn't have to witness it, but here we are.

I give a small nod and Conor takes another step towards me. His hands tighten into fists at his sides, making the muscles in his arms ripple. He looks beyond pissed, but his voice is carefully—almost scarily—controlled when he speaks. "Did something happen, Jess? Did someone hurt you? You need to tell me."

I shake my head, mortified. "No! No, nothing like that."

"You can tell me the truth," Conor responds. All six foot three of him is vibrating with white-hot anger. The sight is simultaneously terrifying and breathtaking, like he's some kind of avenging angel. Looking at him almost hurts.

"I am," I stutter. "Seriously. I just ran into my ex's best friend, that's all..."

The second the words are out of my mouth, Conor visibly relaxes. His whole body breathes a sigh of relief and his fists unclench. The anger is immediately replaced with something entirely more terrifying—genuine concern and care. His gorgeous green eyes search my face intently. My breath catches once again. "Do you want to talk about it?"

I shake my head a second time, fresh tears forming. "I'm sorry for making you worry, I should've told you where I was going. I can't believe you followed me home. Now, your night is ruined. And you were with that girl—"

"Jess." He cuts me off abruptly. Takes a step closer. He's practically face to face with me now. Or, more like face to chest—he's got about a foot on me. "You have nothing to be sorry for. Not now, not ever. I was worried about you, so I came home. My decision. Okay?"

"Okay," I breathe.

I'm not sure how it happens, but next thing I know, his strong arms are around me, and my body melts into his. One big hand tightens on my back, while the other strokes my hair. It's the most tender, sweetest hug I've ever received.

And, I allow myself to give in, pressing my face into his chest and inhaling that delicious clean laundry scent mingled with pine. He's so warm and solid that, for a moment, I forget about everything that happened tonight. Forget about the state of my life. Forget about the past, the present, and what might happen tomorrow. I just let myself be *held*.

I don't know how long we stand in the hallway, arms wrapped around each other. But, when he finally breaks away from me, I feel better than I have in a long time. Like his hugs have magical properties.

As he steps away, his hands linger at my waist for a delicious moment. He leans forward a fraction, close enough for the warm mintiness of his breath to mingle in the air we're sharing.

"Better?" He whispers.

I smile a real smile, more than a little weak at the knees. "Yes."

"Good." Conor smiles too, and the whole room lights up. "Well, I guess we better get to bed."

Is it just me, or does it sound like he might not want this moment to end?

"I was going to watch a movie or something?" I say it like a question. "I don't think I can sleep yet."

Conor runs his tongue over his bottom lip, eyes trained on mine. "Want company?"

I shrug nonchalantly like I couldn't care less. But in reality, his company would mean everything to me. I don't want to be alone right now. "Yes."

"I'll see you out here in a few minutes." Conor steps away from me, and I miss his warm, slightly intoxicating, presence almost immediately. Then, he walks into his bedroom and shuts the door.

I stare at that closed door intently. Because currently, Conor is behind it. Getting changed. Like, taking off his clothes so he can put on new clothes.

That *is* how changing works.

Clearly I'm having a stroke—the mere thought of Conor taking off his clothes anywhere near me has sent me into a tailspin. That, plus my skin burns deliciously with the memory of his arms around me. Who would've thought that a friendly, casual hug from Conor Brady could be so satisfying?

I stand for way too long in the hallway, gazing at what is essentially a piece of white wood. My mind rolls over what he said when he slammed through the door. I still can't believe that he came after me. I didn't even think he'd realize I was gone, but he showed up moments after I got back. Which means he must have been watching me.

I slip my phone from my bag, suddenly curious. Sure enough, I have four missed calls and a few texts, starting right after I left.

My heart skips a beat. But then, I remember how kind his hug was. How his seething hot anger had morphed into something so platonically caring. Lacking all traces of his flirty, sexy smile.

Maybe he thinks of me like a little sister. Maybe he's being nice because *I am* his friend's little sister. Knowing Aiden, he probably asked Conor to watch out for me. Keep an eye on me.

What other reason on earth would make Conor leave that beautiful girl at the bar and come home after me?

The sinking realization hits me with all the force of the Titanic crashing into that iceberg. In my brain, the world's tiniest violin player whips out her fiddle and serenades me as my ship goes down.

I need to hit the brakes. Conor is being nice to me, nothing more.

I tear my eyes away from his door and stalk into Aiden's room. Where, yes, I am still sleeping. He never needs to know.

The bathroom mirror confirms my worst suspicions. My face is mascara-tracked and the color of beetroot. My eyes are swollen and puffy, like little mole eyes. Surely, no guy goes for the crumpled, weeping type.

He's just being a good guy. There for his buddy's sister. A friend to his roommate.

I scrub off all my makeup and take a quick shower. Then, in a fit of "friendly" defiance to my fantasy-filled brain—the one where Conor is Leo and I'm Kate, only I'm the one painting that glorious body and nobody drowns unnecessarily—I change into my giraffe onesie. I braid my wet hair, and stalk out of the bedroom makeup-free and ready to be the best roommate ever.

I walk into the living area to find Conor in the kitchen, popping popcorn. And, oh my giddy aunt's pajamas, does he look good. He's also taken a shower, and his skin is flushed, hair damp and tousled. He wears sweats and a navy hoodie that somehow makes his eyes look greener than ever. And since when have sweats been so attractive?

All of my friendly feelings go flying out the window as my eyes roam over him.

He catches me staring and his lips part slightly as he stares back at me.

Then, this really intense thing happens. His gaze locks on me, trailing tantalizingly upwards from my ankles. His eyes move slowly along my legs, over my hips, and then drag inch by inch up the line of my body. His gaze rests momentarily on my lips, my cheeks...

He's looking at me so carefully, so deliberately. It's as if his eyes are caressing every inch of my body.

Then, his gaze meets mine and I hold my breath.

"Nice onesie," he smiles.

I immediately look down to take in my orange and brown, fuzzy giraffe outfit, complete with a hood adorned with teeny giraffe horns. A blush explodes across my cheeks. I was so lost in the moment, I'd forgotten that I was wearing the least sexy outfit ever invented. An outfit so unsexy that it's a perfect cause for staring.

I curse myself for getting carried away by those stupid emerald eyes.

"Where did you get it?"

"Oh, it's kind of a *long* story," I reply.

Ughhhh why am I making idiotic giraffe puns now?

Can't my brain just be sensible for one second? It's really not too much to ask.

By some miracle, he laughs at my joke.

"You ready?" He nods towards the TV, where the Netflix homepage is already open. "Dealer's choice."

My heart flutters in my chest as I make my way to the plush, sectional couch. I curl up in the corner and pull a blanket over me. This is what I've been wanting all night. But, the unexpected plus of Conor's company makes me jittery.

I pick up the remote and start flipping, but I can't concentrate on any of the movies because my attention is on Conor.

"Sweet or salty?" he calls, transfering the popped corn to a huge glass bowl.

"Sweet, always," I smile.

"Good choice." He pulls a saucepan out of the cupboard, and throws in butter, brown sugar and syrup. "Oh, and Jess?"

"Yeah?" I look up distractedly and his eyes bore into mine from across the room.

"For the record," he says slowly, his voice low. "That girl I was with? She's my realtor, Karla. We were talking business because *someone* doesn't want to help me with my staging."

He says it so flippantly, so casually, that he could've been talking about the weather. Then, without waiting to gauge my reaction, he turns his attention to the pan on the stove.

He hums softly, stirring the mixture. Then, he turns off the heat, pours the syrup over the popcorn, and frowns in concentration as he swirls the bowl. The scent of caramelized sugar fills the air and my mouth waters.

And all the while, I stare at him, my mind going a

million miles per minute. Because I could actually make my stupid lie to Mark into the truth, prove that I'm not pathetic enough to lie to my ex's best friend in a bar about what I'm now doing with my life.

"I'll do it!" I blurt.

"Do what?" He feigns innocence as he walks across the room and plops down right next to me on the eight-foot long couch. Close enough that I can smell his shampoo. But not quite close enough to touch.

Tingles erupt throughout my body.

"The staging," I stammer. "I'll help. I'd love to help. I mean... I hope I can help."

Conor reaches into the bowl and scoops up a handful of sweet popcorn. Pops the handful in his mouth and chews. I can't tear my eyes away, I'm sitting there fixated, watching the muscles in his jaw as he eats.

He takes his time. Chews slowly. Swallows. Takes a sip of water.

Dread churns in my gut. What if he doesn't want me to help anymore? What if he thinks it's a terrible idea?

Just as I'm ready to crawl under the blanket, never to be seen again, Conor smiles. A real, big, genuine smile.

"I'd love that." His voice is soft, almost sensual, and shivers roll up my spine. I have the sudden urge to leap on him.

"Really?" I say instead.

"Really, really." There's a loaded pause as we stare at each other. Then, Conor's eyes glint mischievously. "Now give me that. I'm picking the movie."

He reaches over to pluck the remote out of my hand, and I yell in mock-protest, my grip tightening. His fingers brush against mine, and the tension that crackles between us is undeniable. Conor's eyes widen at the contact, and I let go of the remote. Drop my hands to my lap.

No touching the wildlife. Because that lion could easily bite your hand off.

Quick as a flash, Conor points the remote at the TV and starts flipping through movies.

But, he makes no moves to shift away from me.

If anything, he moves a little closer.

13

CONOR

My resolve can only take so much. I'm a strong man. A man of principle (mostly). But Jess is driving every single piece of me absolutely crazy right now.

She's agreed to work with me. Help me stage Decatur. Which means that we will be spending even more time together.

It's practically the middle of the night, and she's sitting on the couch beside me, dressed in weird giraffe pajamas that shouldn't be in the least bit sexy. But, every so often, her delicate hand dips into the popcorn bowl balanced in my lap, or her laugh fills the air in response to the stupid romantic comedy we finally settled on watching, and it's like all logic goes flying out the window.

I can't explain how I felt earlier when I saw her with that greaseball in the bar. I was watching them talking out of the corner of my eye, and I could sense Jess's discomfort all the way across the room.

It took me exactly two seconds to pin the guy—I know the type perfectly. An overgrown, frat boy dude-bro who's nearing thirty but still acts a decade younger. There's always groups of them on the prowl at the bar, acting like the world is a Brazilian rodizio restaurant and women are the meats they can sample when and how they like.

Anyhow, I digress. One moment, I saw the guy with his hands on Jess's arms. I turned for all of thirty seconds to pay the bartender for my drink, and when I glanced back, they were both gone. Nowhere to be seen.

I assumed she left with him. Which, maybe, was a little short-sighted, but man, I was already fired up at that point. Not just jealous—although the green-eyed monster was certainly stirring—but something more than that.

Concern. Proper, real concern. I saw the way she spoke with dude-bro, the way her shoulders caved in and she smiled that smile I already knew was fake as blue raspberry flavoring. She had her arms crossed—like she wanted to protect herself.

And so, even though Jess is a strong, independent woman who can make her own choices—even though she is just my roommate and she can leave with whoever she wants—I texted her. I wanted to see that she was okay.

When she didn't reply to that text, or the next one, or answer any of my calls, I booked it. Straight home. To find her crying.

In that moment, I was ready to hunt the guy down and murder him. I'm not an angry guy in general, and I know that violence is never the answer. But right then? Yeah, violence seemed like the obvious solution. I calmed down when I found out he hadn't hurt her... although I still have an intense desire to muss up his stupid, shellacked hair.

Being around Jess is unlike anything I've ever experienced. She's gorgeous, but she's feisty and funny and, quite frankly, different from anyone I've ever met—which is possibly the most endearing thing about her.

My heart breaks that someone so wonderful is so vulnerable right now because of the way her ex's best friend made her feel tonight. And, even though I know she's strong, everything in me wants to take care of her. Make her smile. Keep her safe.

Which is exactly why I know I should keep a careful distance. She doesn't need a guy to complicate things for her, especially after her ex. She needs a good friend. Like Aiden oh-so-kindly reminded me earlier.

But, she's making it difficult. I can't help but notice the way her eyes flare when she looks at me, pupils dilated, face flushed, lips parted. So, unless she's experiencing autonomic hyperreflexia every time she looks at me (yeah, yeah I watch a lot of *House*), I'm beginning to think that the attraction between us might just be mutual.

As if reading my thoughts, Jess suddenly looks at me. "Hey, Conor?"

"Mmm?" I say, as noncommittally as I can manage.

"Thank you."

"For what, Jess?"

She smiles tentatively. "Caring."

I want to put my arms around her again, but I resist. "Of course I care." *If only she knew how much.* "And I know you said you didn't want to talk about what happened tonight, but I'm here if you ever change your mind."

Jess closes her eyes, wrinkles her nose, and lets out a sigh. A sigh so loud and forceful that it sounds like it's been locked in there for weeks. "My ex is getting engaged."

I freeze, caught off guard. "What?"

She screws up her face and shifts slightly, laying her head on the couch's armrest. "To Sarah. She has nice hair."

"I'm sorry," I murmur, wishing I had something more original to say. Something that was actually comforting. Maybe I could offer to rough the guy up a little? The thought gives me way too much pleasure.

"Don't be. I know it was for the best. I really do. That guy I met tonight..."

She trails off so I pick up her words. "He made you remember all the good times with your ex?"

Jess snorts. "Yeah, no."

I wish I didn't feel so happy at that reaction. But, like I said, my resolve can only take so much. "What was it, then?"

She sighs. "He's the one who told me that Johnny bought Sarah a ring. That he's planning to propose."

Sympathy balls in my gut. Poor Jess.

She looks at her hands and picks at a chip of pink nail polish on her thumb. When she speaks, her voice is quiet, resigned. "We were together for six years. Six. And he never wanted to commit to anything. But, he bought Sarah a ring after six weeks. So yeah. Guess I'm pretty replaceable."

I gently set my fingers over hers and squeeze her hand. "I find that hard to believe."

She gives me a weak smile. "That's nice of you to say."

I mean it, though. She's incredible, and has no idea. And yet again, I wonder if there's more to the Johnny story than she's letting on.

"Jess, what you must be going through—"

"I told him I was a house flipper."

I tilt my head to the side. "Pardon?"

"The guy I was talking to tonight—Mark. He asked why I came home and I said that I have a new career in house flipping." Jess's chocolate gelato eyes are wide and unblinking, like she's confessing to a terrible crime. "I don't know why, I panicked."

I stare at her. "Let me get this straight. Your ex's best friend told you that your ex was getting married and you responded by telling him... you were a house flipper?"

"Pretty much."

I nod slowly. "So that's why you changed your mind about the staging job."

She bites her bottom lip, looking indescribably sad. For a moment, I think she's going to cry again.

What I am not expecting is the snort of laughter that escapes her mouth. "How's that for a job interview?"

I take in all her giraffe-pajamaed glory. "You're hired."

Jess snorts again and, before I know it, we're both cracking up laughing. Real, deep belly laughs that feel so, so good. Tears prick at my eyes and Jess leans against me as she collapses into laughter, the sound filling the house so beautifully.

It occurs to me that I'd do anything to make Jess laugh like this.

After we finally calm down, she peeks up at me. "Tell me the truth. Is it really okay that I work with you?"

I smile as an idea forms in my mind. Something I think can actually help her. "It's more than okay."

14

JESS

BANG. BANG. BANG.

I roll over in bed and moan, "noooooooo" into my pillow.

What is happening right now and why won't it go away?

"Jess, wake up," Conor calls.

Wait, what?

I bolt upright in bed. Where I check my surroundings to confirm that yes, I am in bed. And also that yes, I am alone. Conor's voice is coming from the other side of my bedroom door. A door which he appears to be banging on for no good reason.

I'm a bit blurry on what happened last night. After I spilled the guts of my sad saga about being dumped (a saga longer and much less interesting than the Twilight Saga) and admitted my big, fat porkie-pie about being a house flipper, Conor had not run away screaming. Which was weird.

Instead, he'd laughed his head off and told me the job was still mine. Which makes me vaguely question his hiring skills, but so be it.

I have a job! Of sorts! I have no idea what I'll actually be doing, because I know precisely zero about staging, or anything to do with house flipping. Apart from what I've learned on TV, of course, which is that it's pretty darn easy —your makeup always looks perfect, and you make squillions of dollars just to get divorced, remarry an English guy, then divorce him, too. Then, the network gives you your own show that's mostly about working out and driving up the coast in a convertible.

But somehow I don't think that's entirely accurate in real life.

Anyhow. We laughed, watched the movie, ate popcorn... and then, I'm pretty sure I fell asleep.

I have a vague memory of strong arms gathering me up and carrying me to bed. Gently laying me down and pulling the covers over me. And then—unless I was dreaming, which let's face it, I may well have been—I seem to remember a hand tracing my cheek for just a moment.

That must have been a dream.

A very good dream at that.

"Jess, wake up!" Conor calls again. I glance at my phone —8:30. What does the man think he's playing at? We didn't fall asleep until late, this has got to be a sick joke.

"No, I'm sleeping!" I yell back, flopping into my sheet cocoon and burrowing like a little mole. A very tired mole.

"No, you're not. You're talking to me."

"Nope, I'm sleep talking. I talk in my sleep."

"Yeah, you do." His voice softens fondly as he says this and my heart plummets into my stomach. Please, please, pleaseeeee for the love of all that is holy, tell me I didn't sleep-talk to him last night.

I am a sleep talker. I've also been known to dabble in the occasional sleepwalking session. As a child, I used to bring Aiden pieces of cheese in the middle of the night. Like, literally steal cheese out of the fridge and bring it to my brother's room like a thieving house mouse. When I was twelve, my mother found me trying to walk out of the front door of our family home at 3am. I had a fully packed suitcase in my hand, and apparently, I told her to eff off so I could go to LA to meet Oprah.

First of all, I never swear. Secondly, I have zero recollection of this as I was FAST ASLEEP at the time. But, somehow, I still got grounded for two weeks for using foul language.

So all bets are off when it comes to what on earth I could have said to Conor last night. Knowing my luck, it was probably something along the lines of "I had thirty-six cellulite dimples on my butt last time I counted" or "I want to eat your shirt."

Conor raps on the door again, softer this time. "I have something to show you."

My stomach drops. Something to show me?

"I mean, some*where* to show you," he corrects with lightning speed. "A place to show you."

I'm on my feet in an instant. I don't care where he's taking me. I just know that I want to go with him.

"Can you give me twenty minutes to shower?" I ask through the door. Then I get a glance of my reflection in the mirror. I have electric shock hair, a pillow crease on my cheek and I can smell my own gross morning breath. "Actually, can you make that thirty minutes?"

"You have ten minutes." I can hear the teasing smile in his voice, and I roll my eyes at the memory of the last time we bartered over getting-ready time.

"Fifteen?" I try my luck, just like last time.

"Nine minutes, fifty seconds...."

Twenty-three minutes later, I'm sitting in the passenger seat of Conor's truck, drinking a cup of coffee he made me. My hair is in an unruly knot, and I dressed how Conor instructed: in something I didn't mind wrecking (so, a t-shirt I stole from Aiden's drawer and an ancient pair of black leggings that have a hole in the thigh).

Conor drives with the windows down and the radio up. Soft country sounds and the scent of sweet honeysuckle fill the cab of the truck. He has one big hand on the wheel, his darkly tanned arm taut with muscle, and the other dangling out the window. I take in his profile greedily, along with the fitted t-shirt and the jeans that hug his butt (yes, I allowed myself a glance or three as I followed him out of the house earlier). My gaze lingers on his backwards Brady Homes baseball cap and the line of stubble across that strong jaw. His Ray Bans hide his gleaming green eyes.

Right now, he could say we were going on a tour of the local sewage treatment plant and I'd probably be down. Those biceps are practically hypnotizing me, and for the first time, I'm allowing myself to give in. After what happened last night, the way he hugged me, a girl's allowed to look at her roommate's biceps, right?

"Stop staring," he says without taking his eyes off the road. *How did he know?!* "It's not going to make me tell you."

I flush, and in a fluster, take a huge gulp of hot coffee. The rich, dark liquid practically scorches my tongue and I yelp aloud.

Conor tilts his head. "Doing okay there?"

"Yes, yes, fine as—"

"A fine, fine, summer's day?"

Oh, for goodness sake. Does this man have the memory of an elephant or what?

"Yes. That." I nod my head staunchly. "And if you're not telling me where we're going, do I get a clue at least?"

"Nope."

He's way too smug right now, with his secrecy and using

my own stupid quotes against me. I decide to try another tactic.

"Pleeeeeeaaaseeeee," I wheedle.

"No!"

I reach out to tug his shirt like a kid who wants candy. He bats my hand away playfully.

I go in for a second tug. I'm just playing, goofing around. This is not at all an excuse to get near those perfect abs or anything, no way.

Conor laughs. "Okay, okay. One clue."

Victory! I'm about to gloat when he says, "goggles."

That stops me in my tracks. I blink. "Come again?"

"Goggles," Conor says a second time.

What?

"That's not a clue."

"Sure is." Conor takes his eyes off the road for a moment so he can turn and smirk at me.

I crinkle my nose. "Like swimming goggles? Ski goggles? ...*Night vision* goggles?"

Conor laughs. "Something like that."

He pulls off the main road and into a beautiful residential area. We've only been driving for a few minutes, we can't be at our destination already?

Conor parks in the driveway of the sweetest single-storey ranch house I've ever seen. The house has lemon-yellow siding, a slate roof and a huge, wraparound porch. Lush greenery and flower beds surround the exterior, and there's a huge white oak tree in the front yard with a wooden swing hanging from one, thick branch. White shutters adorn the windows and the front door is London bus red—a perfect pop of color welcoming you to the most perfect little house.

"What are we doing here?" I say, a little breathless.

Conor smiles at my reaction. He pulls the keys out of

the ignition, then takes off his sunglasses, giving me the full, blinding effects of that oh-so-green stare. "Come on, I'll show you. Oh, and put this on."

He reaches into the back of the truck, and pulls out an oversized red and blue flannel shirt. Before I can ask any more questions, he leaps out of the truck and walks towards the house, shrugging on a second flannel shirt as he goes.

I pause for a moment, and then put on the shirt. It's massive on me, engulfing my body, and I roll up the sleeves at the cuffs. It has Conor's clean laundry and pine scent, mingled with hints of sawdust and bleach.

Resisting the insane urge to just sit and inhale, I climb out of the truck and hurry after Conor, my short legs struggling to keep up with his long strides. When I finally catch up, I defiantly hang back, walking a couple of steps behind him on purpose. I don't want to look *too* eager about his surprise. And definitely not because I want to give that backside another appreciative glance.

What? I'm only human. It's not like my admiring his muscled self means anything.

"Is this one of your flips?"

"Not exactly." Conor climbs the steps to the porch and fishes a ring of keys out of his pocket. He unlocks the front door, then grins at me like a schoolboy, the dimple in his left cheek popping. He pushes the front door wide open, then gestures for me to go first. "This is my house."

I stop dead in my tracks.

That was the *last* answer I expected.

This sweet, adorable ranch house belongs to Conor? I'm beyond enamored.

I'm charmed. Infatuated.

Enchanted.

And then, I step through the front door.

If the exterior of this house is the perfect combination of

stylish and classic, homey and impressive, then the inside is... The polar opposite.

The walls are plastered with wallpaper that's salmon pink. The ceilings are salmon pink. Geez Louise, even the window trim is salmon pink. Thick, shag pile carpet in—you guessed it—salmon pink, runs wall to wall. It even smells fishy in here. Like old cat food. Bleughh.

"Conor," I stammer, my mind struggling for a compliment. What am I supposed to say to this? "Oh my gosh! It's..."

Conor chuckles at my expression as he welcomes me into Fancy Feast headquarters. "It's really something, isn't it?"

My mouth opens and closes again—I'm doing a pretty great impression of a salmon myself. I'm floundering (pun very much intended) for any words that can be said to describe this place.

"It's... pink."

"That, it is," Conor agrees with a wink. He beckons me to follow him, and we walk into a small, boxed off kitchen with orange wood cupboards and a pink and gray speckled countertop. He jumps up to sit on it, dangling his long legs. "The lady I bought it from hadn't renovated the interior in about half a century."

I laugh. "That much is clear."

Conor flashes me another deliciously dimpled grin as he explains how he bought the house with the intention of flipping it. He decided to keep it for himself after he drew up the plans for the renovations and fell in love with his vision for the place.

"It's a total gut job, but it's going to be worth it." Conor's face is animated as he speaks. "Thank goodness for Aiden letting me crash in the meantime."

I look around, then frown. "Wait, what does this have to do with goggles?"

"Well, I've been spending any extra time I've had in the past few weeks cleaning out this place and getting it ready for demo." Conor's eyes twinkle. "It's finally ready."

I purse my lips, not understanding.

He passes me something—a pair of goggles.

Safety goggles.

"I know you're hurt right now, Jess. But, sometimes, when we get hurt by people, it makes us really angry. And you know what I like to do when I'm angry?"

My heartbeat picks up a touch. "What?"

Conor jumps off the counter, puts on his own pair of safety goggles. His eyes are intent on mine and I almost forget where we are. He takes a step towards me. And.... holds out a crowbar.

"Smash things up," he says huskily.

HECK TO THE YES.

I grab the crowbar out of his hand, heart beating wildly. I might not have watched enough home reno shows to know the ins and outs of staging, but I definitely know what's going on right now. "Are you telling me today is demolition day?"

"I'm telling you today is demolition day." That slow, sexy smile is forming on his face again. He picks up a sledgehammer and bounces it in his hand, making those arm muscles ripple. "What do you say, Jess?"

I glance around, but my decision is made. "Where do I start?"

"Anywhere. This whole room is getting destroyed."

He flips on the old radio in the corner. A shrieking, ear-bleeding scream reverberates around the room, followed by the clash of guitar chords as a rock song blares at a deafening level.

I clap my hands to my ears, and Conor cracks up.

"It's just a little mood music!" he yells over the roar. He brandishes the sledgehammer in one hand and lifts it over his shoulder. His broad back muscles tense before he slams it full force into the wall.

Boom!

Chunks of drywall fly everywhere, spraying the air with salmon-colored confetti. A huge, gaping hole is left in the sledgehammer's wake. Conor grabs the edge of the wall hole with his free hand, ripping a whole piece off in one go.

I can't look away. My eyes are fixated on him and my mouth is dry. Not only is it wildly sexy to watch him with the sledgehammer, but seeing this is like unwrapping a whole new piece of candy in the box of chocolates that is Conor. Gone is the carefully controlled man with suggestively glimmering eyes and a slow, deliberate smirk. In his place is this completely undone, untamed, *powerful* force of destruction.

And forget restraint, because I am HERE FOR IT.

After he's torn down about half the wall, Conor glances at me. A trickle of sweat dribbles down his temple and I have to bite my tongue to stop the urge to lick it.

He smiles at me and gestures a hand towards the kitchen. "Your turn."

He doesn't need to tell me twice. Filled with a strange, heady mix of anticipation, fear and burning attraction, I seize my crowbar with both hands and charge at a kitchen cabinet. I swing. Hard.

Crack!

The crowbar connects with the glass front, shattering it into a million pieces. My stomach leaps, and my head spins deliriously. This feels *good*. Like the sweet relief of jumping into a cool ocean in the hottest heat of the day. The first bite of chocolate cake after a juice cleanse.

I feel strong. Reckless. Completely out of control in the very best way.

"Woooooo!" Conor yells, throwing his arms in the air. "Again!"

My heart thrums in time to the raging, angry rock song, pumping blood and adrenaline through my veins.

"AGGHHHH!" I give a war cry that would put the Spartans to shame, and charge at the cabinet again, crowbar above my head.

I bash the bar on the cabinet over and over and over. I'm vaguely aware of Conor laughing and cheering me on, of the pain in my arms from the effort. But, all I can focus on is how good this feels, how splinters of wood and glass are raining down around me with my insistent pummeling.

When the rock song clashes to a screaming end, I stop for breath. Conor is leaning against the counter, watching me, and his eyes are smouldering with something new. An emotion I've never seen in his gaze before... Pride?

I redden under his scrutiny. "Did I do okay?"

"Well, how do you feel?"

I exhale happily. "Lighter."

"Then, you did amazing."

I nod at the sledgehammer in his hand. "Think I can have a go with that?"

A hint of a smile tugs at his lips. "Sure."

"This house flipping business is a cakewalk! I'm practically a professional on my first try," I gloat as Conor extends the sledgehammer towards me. I reach for it, filled with confidence. I am strong, I am capable, I can do anything I put my mind to.

I am Woman, hear me roar!

I grab the weapon out of Conor's hand eagerly...

And, it immediately hits the floor.

"Oof!" My shoulder is practically pulled out of its socket. The thing weighs about a hundred pounds.

"Heavy?" Conor quirks an eyebrow, eyes dancing. He knew that was going to happen. Jerk.

"How were you swinging that around, making it look so easy?" I demand.

Conor's tongue runs along his lower lip, a mesmerizing sight. "Practice."

I'll bet.

I gingerly wrap both hands around the handle of the sledgehammer and lift it off the ground about an inch. Yup, it weighs a ton. There's no way I can swing this thing by myself.

I'm about to admit defeat and let my confidence be taken down a few pegs when Conor is suddenly right behind me. Electricity crackles through my body.

"Want me to show you?" he says quietly, his breath warm on my neck.

I shiver involuntarily. "S-sure," I stutter, my heart leaping like a salmon. Which is appropriate, given our surroundings.

He takes a step closer so that his chest brushes against my back. Slowly, he circles his arms around me, and places his strong hands over mine. They're calloused and rough in the *best* way. He gently moves them to clutch further down the handle, one directly above the other. "Like this, see?"

I nod dizzily, my head full of Conor's clean smell. My nerve endings tingle where he touches me.

"Now," he breathes. "We just pull back, like so."

With Conor's hands still covering mine, we lift the sledgehammer together and swing it backwards. My heart thunders, beating like a drum as I lean into him, letting his large frame envelop me as we drive the sledgehammer into the wall.

123

Bang!

The sledgehammer connects with so much force that my arms tremble. A dusty cloud of drywall erupts around us and I shakily sink further into Conor as I take in my—our —handiwork.

We pause for a long moment, both silent. I can feel his heart beating against my back. Strong and reassuring.

"Again?" he asks, his voice gruff.

"Yes," I practically gasp.

Together, we raise the sledgehammer again and do more damage to the wall. But, I'm no longer thinking of how good it feels to smash things up. Instead, all I can think and feel is how good his body feels pressed against mine. How down-right *sensual* this entire experience is. I'm an absolute mess.

All too soon, he lowers the sledgehammer, slides his hands off mine, and steps away. He puts enough distance between us to help clear the fog around my head, but my body unashamedly yearns for his. *Come back!*

"Nice work." Conor grins. "Destruction successful."

And then, something awful happens. He holds up his hand... For a high five.

A high five.

A high *freaking* five.

I'm rudely ejected from my trance, reality catapulting towards me and splatting me in the face like a cowpat. I raise a hand and slap his limply.

There I was, fantasizing about this being a sensual experience... and he wanted a high five. Ain't nothing sensual about a high five.

15

JESS

After our unfortunate little high five moment, I return to the safety of my crowbar, and we smash and crash the kitchen to smithereens. All while maintaining an appropriate, non-head-fogging distance from each other.

By the time we take a break—around noon—I'm a dusty, tired, sweaty mess and I can't feel my arms. I'm going to suffer for this tomorrow. This is the most I've worked out in... well, in forever, actually. Working out has never been my thing.

Conor shrugs off his flannel, throws down his safety glasses and gives me a dazzling grin. His t-shirt is damp and clings to his muscles in a way my brain can't quite handle. *That chest was just pressed up against me.*

"Come on." Conor leads me out the back door and into the yard, clutching a cooler in his hand.

It's another scorcher of a day, and the sun sizzles overhead, searing everything in its path.

The back of Conor's house is just as gorgeous as the front—a world away from the salmon skin roll monstrosity inside. The yard is bordered with magnolia trees, and the air is still heavily fragrant with remnants of their recent bloom.

There's a large patio with built-in bench seating, and a gigantic oval swimming pool.

"Wow," I croak, my throat dry as the Sahara.

Conor smiles. "I re-landscaped the back yard and re-did the pool the second I got the place. Didn't want it to go to waste this summer."

"Can I?" I ask, looking up at him and tipping my head towards the pool.

He raises his eyebrows. Nods. "Go nuts."

I run towards the water, kick off my shoes, roll up my leggings and plunge my feet in. A rush of cold laps at my ankles and I lean back on my hands, enjoying the contrast of the cool water and the hot sun on my face.

Conor drops down beside me and rolls up his jeans. He dangles his feet in the water next to mine. "I thought you were going to jump in."

"Maybe I should have," I reply.

He cracks open the cooler. "Thirsty?"

"Very." I accept a can of icy soda and press it to my fore-head, savoring the stinging shock of the cold on my skin. Then, I pop it open and practically drain the entire thing in a single gulp. The sweet fizz soothes my dry, cracked throat and I moan with pleasure.

Conor watches me carefully, smiling. "You need to stay hydrated in this heat."

I raise my chin a touch in acknowledgment, trying to keep my mind off the fact that he's all sweaty and mussed up and oh-so-sexy from all that physical work.

I set the can next to me and take off the flannel shirt before reaching forward to dip my hands in the pool. I splash the water up my arms and onto my face.

"Do you mind?" He gestures to his t-shirt.

My brain drops right out of my head and I can't respond coherently. All I can do is give my head a little shake, then try—and fail—to avert my eyes as he strips off his t-shirt and chucks it over his shoulder.

I haven't seen Conor with his shirt off since I ran right into his bare chest on the day we met. The sight is even more majestic than I remember. I can barely drag my eyes away as he reaches into the pool and splashes water over his face.

His skin is smooth and tan, his arms strong and perfectly muscled—but in a way that tells you that he's the type to hit the gym regularly and look after himself, but not shoot up steroids or post workout videos on Instagram. He's not just buff, he's powerful and masculine with his big, calloused hands and broad shoulders decorated with thick bands of muscle that narrow down to a tapered waist and... *holy cow, Batman!* Those abs.

All eight of them.

EIGHT.

I counted. Twice.

How on earth did he think I would *mind*?

I pick my jaw off the ground long enough to re-engage my brain and ask a decoy question. You know, so my abject staring won't be quite as obvious to everyone within a hundred mile radius.

"When do you think this place will be ready?"

"Can't wait to get rid of me, huh?" Conor smirks, and takes a sip of his soda.

Yeah, no. Definitely not that.

Even though I know he's joking, it's a stark reminder that Conor will be moving out at some point in the near future. Will he still want to hang out with me when we don't have the forced proximity pushing us together? Because I've really come to like hanging out with Conor as a friend. A very hot friend, yes. But still, a friend.

"Noooo," I say slowly. "It just seems like a lot of work."

Conor laughs and kicks his right foot, splashing a misty spray of water across the surface of the pool. "A lot of these places involve this much work. You generally get a better return on your investment when they're total gut jobs."

Well, if he's doing work like that all day, every day, that explains the octo-abs.

"Why this one?"

"Hmm?"

"What made you decide to keep this house for yourself instead of flip it? Out of all the houses you flip, what's different about this one?"

Conor considers this for a long moment, his eyes crinkled in thought. When he finally speaks, his voice is serious. "I liked that it looked so perfect outside. It was the house I never knew I wanted, and I fell in love at first sight. Then, I stepped inside and it was the biggest disaster I'd ever seen. But, I looked beyond the mess. I saw how perfect it could be. I just needed to put in the work."

He looks at me and shrugs, and it's such a sweetly vulnerable gesture that my heart squeezes. "I guess, sometimes, everything's gotta get broken before you can start fresh and build what you want."

Despite the heat, my skin tingles with goosebumps. Conor might be talking about his house, but to me, his words cut deeper.

I thought that losing Johnny, giving up my apartment, having no job, and slinking home in defeat meant that I had a million pieces of my life to pick up. But, maybe I don't need to. Maybe I just need to sweep up those heart-breaking, life-altering pieces and throw them away. Start over. With a blank foundation to build the life I *want*.

With the things that mean most to me.

This sinks in and I feel breathless with the thought of

what this could mean. For my life, for my future. And, for the first time in a long time, I see possibilities.

"You okay?" Conor places his hand next to mine, just close enough that his pinky grazes mine. I shiver involuntarily. Twice. First, at the delicious sensation of his skin against mine. Second, at the fact that he doesn't take his finger away. It remains pressed against mine. "You look lost in thought."

I shake my head as a smile slowly creeps over my face. "Not lost. Not at all, actually."

16

CONOR

Jess is beautiful. I already knew that.

Everybody knows that. I'm sure that, if I was blind, I'd still know that.

But, what I didn't know was that seeing Jess in my house—falling in love with the same details that made me love the place—would become the most beautiful thing I've ever seen in my life.

After a morning of demolition (where I took the very opportunistic chance to give her a hands-on demonstration of how to swing a sledgehammer) we're sitting by the pool. The soothing, cool water laps around my ankles, but that sensation is overtaken by the fact that our fingers are touching. Pinky fingers, to be specific. Just that one tiny point of touch ignites a thousand flares all over my body. I know I should pull my hand away, but I don't.

"Did you have fun this morning?"

"So much fun." Jess smiles broadly. "Better than therapy, I imagine."

I laugh. "Cheaper than therapy, too."

"I don't think I'd ever smashed anything before." Jess

wiggles her feet back and forth in the pool, creating ripples that lap at my calves.

"Uh, your plant pot would beg to differ," I tease.

She immediately goes a cute shade of pink. "Thanks again for saving her remains. And, um, for buying her a new pot. It's beautiful."

I'm immediately gratified that she likes it. A couple of nights back, I went to Lowe's Garden Center after work to pick one out, and spent ages poring over the selection. I finally chose a grey concrete pot with a white stripe around the middle and a gold lip—simple and classy, yet interesting and pretty. Just like Jess.

But instead of saying any of this, I shrug. "Ah, I was at the Garden Center anyway, to get some stuff for the yard at the Decatur flip."

We chat about Decatur for a little while, and I tell her about how I understand staging to work, and what she'll be doing to help. The conversation then turns to my plans for my house, and we talk easily, ideas ebbing back and forth. Jess is brimming with suggestions, and most of them are fantastic—some, I would have never thought of. Jess understands light, color and balance so well that it makes me even more excited to have her create something really special at the Decatur flip for the open house.

"You know so much about design," I tell her, impressed.

Jess tucks a strand of hair behind her ear. "I love art, so I guess I look at everything with an artist's eye."

"You studied Art History, right?"

She nods, and the breeze catches in her hair.

"Did you ever do any art yourself?"

"Used to. I haven't for a while. I'm hoping to start again when I get my feet back on the ground with work." She flushes. "Which I have now, thanks to you."

"I'd love to see some of your work."

"Ah, maybe one day." Jess gives a non-committal wave of her hand. Then, she shifts, picking up the fabric of her ridiculously large t-shirt and shaking it to create a breeze on her body. "I'm hot."

Yeah, you are.

A bead of sweat drips down her neck and I want to taste it. In fact, I'm aching to reach over and kiss her. Tell her how I can't stop thinking about her. How, when I saw her crying last night, all I wanted was to protect her from everything that could hurt her.

But, friends don't kiss friends. Jess just got out of a relationship, and she's Aiden's little sister. Who I live with. There are so many reasons why I shouldn't fall for her.

I'll admit it, though. I'm falling anyway.

Clearly, my harmless flirting plan is not harmless at all, because all it's done is remind me over and over of what I can't have. That I can't go for what I want. Which is, overwhelmingly, to kiss Jess.

"It's hotter outside than usual," I say, rather stupidly. Anything to stop my wayward thoughts.

Jess laughs and the sound is like music. "It is."

The laughter in her eyes draws me in. Before I can stop myself, my head dips instinctively towards hers. My mind is a blank blur of static—all reason and logic have evacuated in the face of those endless, hypnotizing brown eyes.

Sorry, lights are on but nobody's home.

I've moved a few inches towards her before I finally get a hold of myself and kick my brain back into action. I don't know if it's adrenaline from being so close to her, or if I've come down with a sudden case of heat stroke that clouds my rational judgment, but what I do next has no explanation. None at all.

Because I continue to move towards her... But, instead of kissing her, I push her in the pool.

Like, shove her. Fully clothed.

Into the pool.

SPLASH!

Jess topples in like a bowling ball and hits the water with enough force to send a spray of drops all over me.

I stare, openmouthed and shocked. What did I just do?

One second passes.

Two.

Three.

Four... *oh dear Lord, what if she can't swim?!*

Now I've done it. The thought hits me like a punch in the gut, and blood pumps in my ears. I scramble to a stand, ready to dive in and save her.

But, like Moses parting the Red Sea, two arms emerge from the pool and Jess pulls herself up to the surface. She places her elbows on the side of the pool and I wince, waiting for her wrath to be unleashed. Instead, she throws her head back and laughs. Laughs and laughs.

So, I laugh too, a cacophony of emotions clashing within me—relief that she's okay, happiness that I made her laugh, and pure shock at my thoughtless action.

"Okay, okay," Jess says, smiling up at me and extending a hand. "Now I'm no longer hot. Help me out?"

I crouch forward and hold out my hand, ready to yank her out of the water. Jess gives me the sweetest smile. "Thank you."

Then, her hand closes around mine and she pulls. Hard.

KERSPLASH!

I go flying, headfirst, into the pool. Which is exactly what I deserve. But, as I'm not in the least bit prepared, I inhale a lungful of chlorinated water. When I breach the surface, I'm coughing and spluttering.

Jess laughs even harder. "That's what you get, you jerk."

"I'm"—*cough, cough*—"sorry!" I tilt my head, gasping and wheezing for breath.

Jess, merciless and vindictive, attempts to dunk me. In my spluttering state. So much for that butter-couldn't-melt sweetness.

When I catch a glimpse of her face, she's smiling like a villain. A really cute villain.

"Hey!"—*cough*—"You are SO asking for it!" I grab her arm and twist her away, trying to dunk her back. In response, she moves like a tornado, twirling in the water with one arm skimming the surface. The motion creates a tsunami of water that hits me in the face.

"Okay, now you're really getting it!" I've recovered enough to spring into motion, pouncing on her so we both go tumbling back beneath the surface.

We spend the entire afternoon like this, play-fighting in the pool like a pair of kids without a care in the world. I don't think about boundaries, or what I should or shouldn't be thinking or doing, I just let myself enjoy being with her. Making her laugh. Being myself.

It's beautiful. Perfect.

Every damn second of it.

17

JESS

"YOU LIKE HIM, YOU CHEEKY LITTLE MINX!"

"Speak louder Court, I think a few people in Timbuktu missed that," I hiss, glancing around to quadruple check that nobody is listening.

My new friend wriggles in glee, her eyes glittering in a slightly manic fashion. "Tell me everything. Spill the tea."

"Listen to you! You're so down with the kids," I tease. "And, there's no tea to spill. There isn't anything to spill."

"Lies."

I shake my head.

Courtney points an accusing finger at me. "Terrible, awful, wicked lies."

I pull my sunglasses down onto my face instead of answering, and sit up on my lounger. Courtney and I have been spending more time together lately, and I'm growing very fond of my neighbor. Today, we're in Aiden's backyard, tanning in our bathing suits and sipping Courtney's "famous homemade pina coladas."

To buy myself some time from inevitably having to talk about Conor, I take another tentative slurp of my cocktail. I shoot Courtney a big smile to avoid gagging.

"Good?" Courtney says.

"Mmmm." I nod as convincingly as I can as I set my glass down. As far away from me as possible.

Calling this a cocktail would be extremely generous. Even calling it a drink might be pushing it.

It looks, and tastes, like toxic waste.

But, Court went out of her way to pick up the ingredients for the pina coladas, just to share them with me. Her hospitality means so much to me, I don't have the heart to tell her the truth.

"Remind me what you put in these again?" I ask through my smile as I attempt to swallow the slimy mush.

"Secret recipe." Courtney waggles her eyebrows. "And stop trying to change the subject, missy."

"Fine."

I flop back on the lounger and adjust my bathing suit. Usually, I'd feel frumpy next to a tall, tan, lean creature like Courtney. She's got one of those rangey bodies like a gazelle, all sharp angles and graceful limbs. And perfect, normal-sized perky boobs—she can probably wear those itty bitty triangle bikini tops without worrying about her chest having a mind of its own and trying to make a desperate bid for freedom.

Yes, that is based on a real story.

And no, I don't want to talk about it.

Anyhow, one of the nicest things about Courtney is that, even though she's tall and slim and gorgeous, she is totally non-judgy. For the first time in my life, I don't find myself wanting to compare. We're different, and that's okay.

Courtney rolls on her side and looks at me expectantly. "Tell me."

I let out a happy sigh. "I dunno, Court. There's nothing going on between us. Nothing's happened. He's never made a move. But there's, like, this... *chemistry* when he's close to me. Like, he has a force field that I'm being sucked into."

I pause for breath, realizing how stupid this must sound. I don't think I'm imagining it, though. The way he looked at me by the pool last week, I could have sworn he was about to kiss me... right before he shoved me in the water.

Courtney, meanwhile, fans herself with a *People* magazine, pretending to swoon like some sort of heroine from a Victorian novel.

"Can I live vicariously through you?" she asks wistfully between fans. "Take pity on this poor spinster who only has love for her dogs."

I fish a piece of ice out of my drink and chuck it at her. "Oh, please. One disastrous Tinder date and you're acting like you're going to run off and join a nunnery."

Courtney went out with a guy she swiped right on last week who turned out to be Mr. ALL Wrong. Martin looked great both on paper (well, phone screen) and in person—he's a successful attorney with classically handsome looks. Lover of books, baseball, and vintage cars, according to his profile. I helped Courtney pick out a stunning, low-cut pink cocktail dress and she went off to meet him at a beautiful restaurant on the river, which was a great start. But, it all went downhill from there.

To recap:

He told Courtney that it was "his treat" but then ordered the house white before asking what she wanted to drink (which happened to be scotch on the rocks). He then suggested they order food from the appetizer menu to share. So, basically, a cheapskate. Strike one.

Then, with a leering smile, he proceeded to check out every female in the restaurant. And, he had the nerve to make a backhanded compliment about how Court's dress was nice, if you're into that sort of short, tight thing. So, both pervy and misogynistic. Getting worse by the second.

Strike three—and the cherry on top of the dumpster fire —came when Martin passed gas at the dinner table. Like, the man farted while on a date. Loudly. As Court so delicately pointed out afterwards, if you have the urge to pass gas on a date—or anywhere in public—you should go to the bathroom and do so in private. Nobody takes risks like that.

"Forget Farty Marty," I tell my friend. "He was a total dud. That date was zero reflection on you as a person, you could have your pick of any guy. And, like I told you, there is nothing for you to live vicariously through when it comes to Conor and me. Because nothing's happening. Period."

"Why not? You're both young, single and hot. And, he's just a bedroom away." Courtney smiles a Cheshire Cat grin and I stick my tongue out at her.

"Oh, gee, thank you so much for pointing that out, Court. I'd never realized." I roll my eyes at her. Then, I sigh. "But the thing is, I think he sees me as a friend. He barely even flirts with me anymore. Plus, guys like that always know when a girl thinks they're hot. Which means that he could've made a move at any point and tried for the full roommates-with-benefits experience. Which I would have turned down, obviously."

Courtney snorts a laugh, which she promptly attempts to disguise as a cough. "No, you wouldn't."

But I'm not lying. I would have turned down any proposition like that. Because I like Conor as a person. A lot. And I don't want to be anybody's casual fling—my emotions can't help but get involved. Plus, I'm not into that sort of thing to begin with.

But, despite my words to Courtney, I'm beginning to think Conor isn't into that sort of thing either. I've never seen him do anything more than talk to another woman, and he's not the big flirt I originally pegged him for, either.

He's been nothing but super sweet to me lately. A good roommate, and a good friend. Who pushed me in the pool, instead of kissing me like I thought he might. Which leads me to my second point...

"But I haven't had to turn him down because he hasn't tried anything. Which makes me think that he's probably just not attracted to me."

I sigh, deeply disappointed in myself for caring this much. I can't believe it's been almost a week since Conor took me to his house for demolition. Almost a week since he followed me home from the bar, held me as I cried, and made popcorn for me.

The day of the demolition, I was sure there was something building between us. The mere memory of his hands on mine as we swung the sledgehammer makes my body tingle. But since then? Nada.

He's been busy at work all week, and we've only seen each other briefly here and there—although I still wake up to a freshly brewed pot of coffee every morning. The most time we've spent together in days was when he took me to see the house I'll be working on, which is stunning. While we were there, he gave me my written offer to contract for Brady Homes as a stager—for more money than I used to make in a month at *Cirque!* I told him it was way too generous, but he insisted it was the going rate for staging.

That afternoon, I sped to the library and checked out every book they had on home staging.

"Think about it, Jess. You're fresh out of a break up, living with him, *and* he offered you a job—which means, technically, you now work for him. Maybe he's just a good guy and he doesn't want to cross any boundaries."

Was that why he pushed me in the pool when I was sure he was going to kiss me? Boundaries?

"Or, maybe he's just worried about upsetting your stupid brother," Courtney continues with a shrug.

I cock an eyebrow at her. "Remind me why you hate Aiden so much?"

Courtney, for all of her forthcoming brashness, is surprisingly mute on the subject of my brother—unless she's ranting about something he supposedly did wrong.

"I don't hate him."

"I don't believe you."

"This isn't about Aiden. It's about Conor. Who is clearly blind if he's not attracted to you."

"Smooth conversation diversion," I tell her. But, I drop the Aiden subject, which is clearly touchy.

I'm thankful for Courtney's support, but she's being too nice. I'm not the girl who gets the guy that everyone wants. I'm the girl that gets left for someone else.

"Blind or not, it doesn't matter. I need to stop thinking about the fact that it's never going to happen, and move on. The important thing is that he's nice, and he's really helping me out with giving me work." I smile to myself. "Which is more than any guy's ever done for me."

Courtney's cat-like grin is back. "And that, my dear, is exactly my point."

After Courtney goes home to attend to the loves of her life— Butch and Cassidy—I decide that there's no time like the present to get to work on doing some painting. I've been putting it off for days now, battling with nagging self-doubt and thoughts of failure. I've conveniently used my staging books to procrastinate, telling myself that I was too busy reading to make any of my own art.

But the job with Conor is a one-off, temporary. I'm going to need further employment down the line, so I've got to bite the bullet sometime. I've decided to ease myself into creativity by doing a painting for Aiden. Something to thank him for letting me stay at his place rent-free. There's a spot above the couch where I'd love to hang it.

I hum to myself as I retrieve the supplies I bought at a local art store and set myself up in the backyard—I'm not going to risk getting paint on the pristine floors of Aiden's renovated house. I spread the dust sheet on the lawn and prop my canvas on a makeshift easel assembled from old plastic garden chairs I found in the shed. Obviously banished to exile after the patio makeover.

I'm still in my bathing suit, but as said bathing suit is an ancient and saggy purple one-piece that does nothing for my figure, I'm not too worried about getting paint on it. Besides, Courtney would be delighted for an excuse to take me bikini shopping. When I appeared outside to sunbathe with her earlier, I got a ten minute lecture about embracing my inner sex kitten and flaunting what the Good Lord gave me.

Pfft. Inner sex kitten, my butt. Try old, overweight, flea-bitten tabby cat with half an ear missing.

Anyway, despite the innate unattractiveness of my bathing suit, I feel pretty secure in the fact that no one's going to see me prancing around in the yard with my paint brushes. Courtney's safely ensconced at home, Aiden is tucked away in LA, and Conor's working late again today. I made sure to confirm over text.

Which means that it's just me, my canvas, and, hopefully, inspiration.

I set out my paint brushes, mixing palette, and tubes of

paint, and then put my headphones in. May as well bring out the old "Heartbreak Playlist Part 2"—the Taylor Swift edit.

With the bitter breakup sounds of "I Knew You Were Trouble" blasting in my ears, I circle the blank canvas, studying it. I nod to myself, my adrenaline building as creativity starts to flow through my veins like a drug. It's been too long since I painted, and now that I've worked myself up to this moment, excitement vibrates through me.

I've missed this.

I seize my paint brush, splash dollops of seafoam green, burnt ochre and navy onto my palette, and get to work.

Something funny happens when you get lost in creating. It's like your mind and body become one, moving in tandem to chase a vision. You make something conceptual become tangible before your very eyes. Space, and time, and worries—things you have to do, or say, or be—all just melt away. When I paint, it's just me and the paint brush, dancing in our very own world of color, movement and beauty.

There's just one tiny potential downside to entering this special world: You lose all sight and track of the real world. Which can be wonderful.

But, can also be not-so-wonderful.

Like, when you're bleating along to Taylor Swift, prancing around in a bathing suit that's lost all elasticity around the butt, and your hot roommate shows up.

With his equally hot realtor in tow.

"Urghh!" I make a strangled sound and drop my paint brush as Conor and the redhead from the night at the bar—*Karla*—stare at me. The brush clatters to the ground, sending a spray of seafoam splatters all over my legs in the process.

My very bare, very pale, very unshaven legs. Frick, frick frick.

"Conor, Karla... hello! " I squeal. My voice is so loud, I can hear it over my blaring headphones. I rip them out and drop them on the ground next to my paint brush. I cross my arms over my chest. Cross my legs. Uncross my legs when I realize I must look like I need to run to the restroom. Finally, I settle for smiling way too brightly. "What's up?"

All the while, the two of them simply stare at me like I'm some exotic animal in a zoo.

A hippopotamus, perhaps.

And what's with me and all the nature comparisons lately?

Karla's perfect features twist in horror as her eyes move over me, while Conor's beautiful face contorts in undisguised amusement.

"Hi Jess," he says through his *you-know-what*-eating grin. His green eyes hold my gaze, glinting with silent laughter. He's clearly getting way too much enjoyment out of this. "We just dropped by to grab paperwork before we check out a few listings for upcoming projects, and thought we'd say hi. What's up with you?"

"Oh, you know." I shrug nonchalantly. Or, as nonchalantly as is possible when red-faced and wearing the world's most unflattering one-piece. "Painting."

"In a bathing suit?"

"Yes," I say smoothly. Move along, nothing to see here. "It's a technique that lots of artists use."

"Is that so?" Conor takes a step towards me. "And what's this *technique* called?"

"Stippling." I take a step away from him. Mostly so I can think better. Because I have no idea why I said that.

"Stippling," Conor repeats slowly. That dratted grin

tugs at his lips again. The one that makes me want to slap him in the face but also scream "have my babies!"

I go an even more alarming shade of beetroot. All the way down to my legs. Which, on the bright side, means that they're not so pale anymore.

Karla frowns. "Isn't stippling when you make lots of tiny dots?" She holds up a perfectly manicured hand and mimes the process.

Of course. Not only is Karla the epitome of business chic in her white pantsuit, patent leather stilettos and matching handbag, but she knows that I'm lying. She has absolutely no paint on her person, her makeup is flawless, and she probably shaved her legs this morning even though she's wearing pants. Who does that?

"It can be." I nod, trying to look casual.

Conor is still smirking. But then, his gaze lifts as he focuses on something behind me.

My painting.

My lungs constrict, and for a moment, I forget my apparent determination to consistently embarrass myself. I whirl around so I can see my work through Conor's eyes.

You know that thing that men do when they see a Ferrari or a fancy speedboat? Where they circle the object slowly, almost reverently, tilting their head to look at it from each and every angle, studying it like it's the eighth wonder of the world?

That's what Conor does with my painting.

As he approaches the canvas, I realize I'm holding my breath, waiting for his reaction. I also realize how important his reaction is to me. And yet, a warm, fuzzy feeling gathers in my stomach and spreads through my entire body. Nobody has ever given my art this kind of consideration before.

Johnny barely even glanced at my paintings. My

parents thought my dreams of being an artist were just that —dreams.

But, Conor is looking at my work like it *means something*. Like it matters.

"Jess," he finally says, looking at me. My breath catches as I see the fire in those green eyes. "This is incredible."

"You think?" I don't know where to look, so I stare at the ground. I'm not used to receiving such compliments.

Conor takes another step towards me. And another. Heat prickles the back of my neck at his closeness. But, this time, I don't step backwards.

"Jess," he says again. His voice is low. "Look at me."

Slowly, I tilt my head up to meet his emerald gaze. Every nerve in my body sizzles as we stare at each other.

"It's fantastic," he says gravely, his eyes sincere. "I mean it."

It takes me a moment to accept that he's serious. Actually serious. He's not trying to humor me or make me feel better—he really likes it.

My heart soars.

"I'm so glad." My voice is so throaty, it sounds like I swallowed a swarm of bees.

There's a moment of heaviness between us—a moment of aching anticipation that takes my breath away. It feels a little like the moment by the pool when he (maybe) almost kissed me. No, it feels a *lot* like that moment.

My body buzzes and my brain goes out the window. My conversation with Courtney suddenly fades far, far away into oblivion. Right now, I can believe that Conor might want to kiss me. Right now, all I'm aware of is the intense attraction I feel towards him.

Not only because of the magnetism he projects, but because, somehow and for no apparent reason, he believes in me. Seems to see something in me that feeds my soul.

I think he must feel it too, because, still staring into my eyes, he touches his hand to the corner of his bottom lip.

"You got a little..." he murmurs, then he leans forward. Moves that same hand towards my face.

And my heart stops.

Time stops.

Everything stops as he grazes the pad of his thumb across my mouth. Electricity sparks on my lips at his touch. I inhale sharply, and his pupils dilate.

His face is only inches from mine, and I feel my breath quickening.

Is he going to—

"Paint on your face!" Karla's squeal finishes Conor's sentence, murdering the moment. And for a moment, I want to murder her, too.

We spin around and Conor jerks his hand backwards, blinking like he's just remembered where he is. He breathes out shakily. "Yup. You had some paint on your chin."

"It's in your hair, too," Karla adds.

I reluctantly move my eyes towards Karla and, above her oh-so-helpful smile, she's glaring daggers at me, her eyes narrow and cold.

The tension in the air is thicker than molasses. And I'm suddenly desperate to get out of this sticky situation.

Now.

"Oh, silly me." My nervous giggle makes me sound like a schoolgirl. And not the *Hit Me Baby One More Time* type of schoolgirl. More like a teenager fangirling over Justin Bieber. "I'd better go wash up."

Karla's dagger eyes never leave mine as she snakes a possessive arm around Conor's bicep and gives it a squeeze. "We'd better go anyway or we're going to be late." She shoots me a fake apologetic smile. "Sorry we've got to jet, but business calls. Conor won't have any houses to flip if we stand around and chat all day. You know how it is."

I don't know how it is. And I'm pretty sure she's aware of that.

Judging by the glint in her eye, she also knows she's done a great job of making me feel small and unimportant. Just a dumpy, paint-splattered idiot in a saggy bathing suit next to a willowy, beautiful, successful *businesswoman* in a power suit.

This feels uncomfortably familiar...

Karla's hand is still wrapped around Conor's arm and I want to swat it away. Until I turn my eyes to him.

Because, despite the fact that Karla has the upper hand in every single way right now—both physically and metaphorically—he's looking at *me*. Intently.

"See you later, Jess," Conor says in a voice that sends shivers down my spine and makes me want to start counting the minutes until "later" arrives.

18

CONOR

We're halfway to the car when I change my mind. "You know what, Karla?"

She turns, tilts her head. "Hmm?" She jiggles her car keys in her hand, not really listening.

I extend the paperwork towards her. "I don't think I need to see the new listings."

Karla's forehead creases in a deep frown. She's suddenly paying attention. "What? Why?"

Because I work too much as it is. I don't need more projects on my plate.

Because Jess is in the backyard right now, covered in paint, and against all of my better instincts, the only thing I want to do right now is join her.

Because I'm done trying to stay away from her.

I shrug, trying my best to sound casual. "I want to slow down a bit, get a couple of projects out of my hair before taking on anything new. Plus, I've had an idea for the staging in Decatur."

It's not a lie. Now that I've seen the art Jess creates, I've had the best idea in the world for the open house. And, I don't want to waste another second.

Karla looks at me skeptically. "What is this big idea?"

"It's a... surprise."

"I hate surprises." Karla purses her lips and sucks in a breath through her teeth. "How about if we go to your storage unit together later? I can help with staging, too."

My thoughts race. "I'd prefer to go alone because, um... your outfit will get dirty?"

I know I'm a terrible person and a big fat fibber to boot, but I'm not dumb. At least, not dumb enough to tell Karla my real plan. Plus, if anything will give Karla reason for pause, it's the thought of mucking up her designer clothes.

Karla dithers for a moment, stepping from one stiletto to the other as she assesses her white pantsuit. "Okay—"

"Okay, that's settled then." I force a bright, innocent smile.

Yup, terrible. But right now, I don't care. I just want to get back to the yard. Back to Jess.

Karla's face pinches in, but she doesn't argue. She clatters off to her car in a bit of a huff, shooting me glances over her shoulder. I stride towards my truck and jingle the keys in my hand. But, the second Karla pulls out of her parking space, I double back on myself.

Go back in the house.

I can see Jess through the patio doors. She's still in the backyard, standing a few feet back from her painting. She stares at it intently, like it'll reveal all the secrets of the universe if she studies it hard enough.

And I can't take my eyes off of her, causing a weird sort of *Inception* scenario, but with staring.

What's going on behind those chocolate truffle eyes of hers?

It's been almost a week since I took Jess to my house. Almost a week since I came *this* close to kissing her by the pool and, effectively, ripping to shreds my vow to be nothing but friendly with her. We've barely seen each other since—a combination of my busy work schedule, and the fact that I've been trying to put some distance between us.

I had to. Because I know that, next time, I won't be able to control myself. Won't have the strength to stop from claiming those beautiful lips.

So, instead, I channeled all of my self control into being the best friend I could be to Jess—which meant staying as far away from her as possible. Which is no easy feat when the person you're trying to stay away from sleeps in the next bedroom.

But, my plan was working. Or, at least, I thought it was.

And then, I saw her in the yard today. Wearing that ridiculous bathing suit that looked like it was designed for the very, very elderly... Not that it did anything to hide her incredible curves. My only real complaint was that the monstrous garment covered way too much of her tan, freckled skin. Her hair, hands and arms were streaked in a rainbow of paint, and when she turned to me, wide-eyed and open-mouthed, a smudge of paint adorning her lower lip, all of my steely resolve fizzled away to nothing.

Poof! Gone.

Like I'd taken a Magic Eraser to it.

And now, all of a sudden, I have a new plan. Well, calling it a "plan" is a bit of a stretch. Basically, I've decided that I can't stay away from Jess anymore. Whatever this thing is between us, it's worth whatever risk it may entail to find out. Because when it comes to Jess, I've realized I'm pretty much powerless to restrain myself. Which means that my careful, five step pasta program has been replaced with a single resolution: throw caution to the wind, and let the chips fall where they may.

I open the French doors and step onto the patio. "Jess?"

She snaps out of her statue-like state and whirls around.

"Conor?" A delicious smile flits on her lips and I'm an absolute goner. Remind me why I was trying to stay away from her again? Jess tilts her head. "Did you forget something?"

"Yes." I nod. "You."

Her eyes widen a touch, the liquid brown darker than usual, like fresh espresso. Her mouth is slightly open, and after a long moment, her eyelashes dip, fanning her cheeks as she averts her gaze downwards.

Warmth bubbles in my chest and my new game plan suddenly seems like a winner.

"What about Karla and the new listings?" Jess mumbles, but something that looks like hope creeps over her expression.

"Forget Karla." I shake my head, wanting to keep the conversation on Jess. "What's that painting for?"

"I was thinking of hanging it in the living room, in that bare spot above the couch," Jess says quietly, wringing her hands in the frumpy fabric of that awful bathing suit. "I wanted to thank Aiden for letting me stay here, and I didn't exactly have the funds to get him something nice. So..." She gestures lamely towards the painting, then chuckles dryly. "It's stupid."

"Your painting is way better than anything you could buy," I say seriously, meaning every word.

Jess fiddles with the lid of a paint tube, chewing on her lower lip. I watch her hands, small and delicate, her finger-tips twisting back and forth. I wonder what those fingers would feel like tangled in my hair, running down my arms...

I take a deep breath. "Jess, I have an idea. Can I show you?"

She pauses for a moment. Then, she nods.

Twenty-six minutes later (yes, I timed her again), I'm driving my truck to my storage unit with a freshly showered and paint-free Jess in the passenger seat. The truck cab fills with the heady scent of citrus body wash and shampoo, mingled with her warm, damp skin—she smells so much better than any fancy perfume.

She wears jean shorts, flip flops and a black and white striped t-shirt, and her hair hangs loose and wet around her shoulders. She's got her sexy, thick-rimmed glasses on again, and the whole look makes me want to drive somewhere private to park like we're teenagers.

But, Jess deserves so much better than that.

We pull up at the storage facility, and she follows me to Brady Homes' storage unit. I unlock the garage door and slide it open.

Jess lets out a squeak and I slide a sideways glance her way. She puts her hands to her cheeks in sheer delight as she peers inside.

"This is SO cool. Like that *Storage Wars* show!" She turns to me, all white, smiling teeth and sparkly eyes. Karla hates coming here—too dusty—and I'm enamored to see how much Jess digs it.

I laugh. "I bought a storage locker once, like you see on that show."

"You *did?*"

"Yeah, it looked like there were a couple of good couches in there. But, it turned out they were just hiding a marijuana grow-op. We had to turn the whole thing over to the police."

Jess's eyes are like saucers. "That's wild! Better than anything I've seen happen on the show."

"Not really... they wouldn't even let me keep my new couches!"

Jess giggles as she bounds inside. She runs her index

finger over the edge of a vintage mahogany vanity, then places a palm on a padded king headboard. "Where did you get all this stuff?"

"I've been collecting furniture for years. From garage sales, auctions, thrift shops, estate sales—you name it. Mia helps me, she loves this stuff"

It was one of my better ideas—one that's not only been a ton of fun, but has saved me a fortune on staging over the years. And Mia has been invaluable when it comes to styling the old, cheap pieces to look good in my homes.

"So, what's your idea?" Jess asks now.

I put a gentle hand on her soft shoulder, and turn her towards the right wall, where the art collection is gathered. And I say "art" with a serious pinch of salt.

"Look at these." I gesture in the direction of the plastic-wrapped canvases. "Tell me what you think."

Jess takes a few minutes to study the mish-mash of geometric line art, bowls of fruit, prints of nameless, generic beaches, and black and white cityscapes.

She pauses for a really long time, then eyes mine. "Umm..."

"Do you like them?" I push.

"Well, I... um, yes."

"Liar," I say quietly, and take a step towards her. Goose-bumps pepper her skin as I move closer, and I enjoy every second of her discomfort.

"I, uh—"

"You don't like them?" I repeat seriously.

Her eyes are wide and her mouth twitches open and closed. She glances around, looking anywhere but at me. Then, she appears to give in, shaking her head. She tucks a stray strand of hair behind her ear, making her stud earring flash as it catches the light. "Sorry, I don't mean to be a snob. It's just..."

I can't hold my expression a moment longer, and I burst into laughter. Her mouth pops open and she punches my arm. Hard.

"You jerk!" She yells. Hits me again.

I circle my fingers around her delicate wrist, holding it between my thumb and index fingers to stop her attack.

"I'm sorry, I'm sorry." I release my grip on her wrist and wrap my hand around hers instead. "I couldn't resist."

"That was mean." She pouts, but she keeps her hand in mine. It feels so perfect there, small and warm in my grip. I tighten my fingers a touch, and I'm rewarded with feeling her shiver.

"What I was trying to get at, is that collecting nice paintings and such for staging has been tough. Art is such a personal thing, and a space needs to showcase the art that hangs in it—whereas all the art we have kind of just fills spaces on walls. Doesn't add anything."

"You want me to help you find new art?" Jess asks, and I almost laugh at her sweet expression.

"No, silly. I want *you* to make something new. Fill the Decatur house with your paintings, your vision. That way, you can pick out staging pieces that will make your art pop. That house needs something special, Jess. And your art is special."

She shivers again, and I resist the urge to wrap her in my arms. One step at a time.

"I'll pay you extra," I add.

"I don't know, Conor." She frowns. Bites down on her bottom lip again. "What if prospective buyers hate it?"

"They won't." I smile at her. "Your painting amazed me, I had no idea how talented you are."

Her eyes search my face intently, like she's looking for signs of sarcasm.

I frown as something clicks into place. My eyes scan her face. "Has nobody ever told you how talented you are?"

She flinches. Removes her hand from mine and sinks onto a particularly gaudy orange velour loveseat. Her jaw clenches and I get the impression she has something to say.

I take a seat next to her. Wait patiently, giving her time to talk if she wants to.

"Aiden always tells me how much he likes my art. To be fair, he has to, he's my brother," she starts slowly, and then smiles at the thought. I love how close they are—just like Mia and me. Then, her face darkens. "But, Johnny... Well, Johnny used to act like he was indulging me, like it was a stupid hobby that wouldn't go anywhere."

She stares at her hands, her shoulders slumped, and my heart actually aches to see her this way. She tucks a strand of hair behind her ear and then goes on. "I guess, over time, his words began to sink in, and I started to believe them, too. Started to believe I was wasting my time. That there were better things for me to be doing..."

She trails off and I can't help it anymore. I shift closer and look directly into her eyes. I push that same stray lock of hair back from her face, letting my fingertips linger by her temple. Her pulse jumps beneath my touch, and I swallow hard before I can get my next words out. "Jess, believe me, you're not wasting time with painting. You have real talent. Johnny's an idiot for not seeing that."

"Thanks," she says, but she doesn't look up from her hands.

I gently tilt her chin so her eyes meet mine. "I mean it. I want your artwork to lead on the staging. Paint what you want and pick out the furniture and decor that will work with your vision."

Her gaze becomes anxious and worried. "I know how

much your work means to you, though. Are you sure you trust me to do this?"

I smile, not even having to consider my words. They're simply the truth. "I'd trust you with anything."

She smiles wanly in return. "Why are you so nice?"

"I was born this way."

She shoves me. But, her smile widens into a real grin.

"Okay," she says slowly. Then, she jumps to her feet. Nods. "Let's do this thing."

Jess spends the next hour poring over furniture, collections of vases and various plant pots. She rifles through boxes of drapes, bedding and throws. And, as she touches leather, wood and cotton, it's like she can somehow summon ideas from their textures. She lights up, her face glowing, whenever she finds something she likes.

It's incredible to watch her move through the space. I'm captivated as she chatters, thinking out loud. She describes how she can pair certain items to make a statement, how she envisions a cozy, mid-century modern living room, a kitchen where everything is based around showcasing the natural sunlight that fills the room. I've never seen her talk this much, never seen her buzz with so much life and vigor.

I hang on to her every word, stepping into her vision alongside her. If I close my eyes, I can almost pretend that we aren't working on a flip, but shopping for the actual house I own.

And, for the first time, I begin to imagine my house actually feeling like a *home*. That's part of what makes Jess so beautiful, though—she has the incredible ability to bring warmth and life and excitement to something as mundane as furniture shopping. She makes it possible to envision a home.

I realize with a jolt that I'm going to miss her presence more than anything when I move out of Aiden's place. I'll no longer get to see her in the mornings, with her dishevelled hair piled up on her head and her glasses on. I'll no longer get to sit next to her on the couch at midnight, our hands brushing as we eat popcorn.

If I know one thing to be true, it's that I want to keep living these moments with her.

"Conor?" Jess looks at me, head quirked and amusement dancing over her features.

I blink, coming back to earth. "Sorry, I missed what you said."

"You were far, far away there for a minute." Jess laughs.

I don't ever want to be far away from Jess. I want to be *with* Jess, as close as possible, at all times. But, if I want to do this with her, I need to do it right.

Starting now.

"Are you hungry?" I blurt.

She frowns. "Sure... you want to go home, then?"

Not at all.

"I was thinking we could grab some dinner."

Jess's brow wrinkles. "Like, at a restaurant?"

"That's usually where people go to eat, yes."

"Me and you?" Jess fumbles, looking adorably uncertain. But those wide eyes aren't just nervous, I also see a hint of... desire.

And, in that look, I know. She wants me, too.

I smile slowly. "Jessica Shaw, would you like to go to dinner with me?"

She exhales shakily. "Yes."

"It's a date."

19

JESS

Code red. CODE RED.

This is not a drill. I repeat, NOT a drill.

Conor Brady and I are on a REAL LIFE DATE.

At an actual restaurant. With tables and food and wine and... *oh my gosh, shut up brain!*

My nerves are on high alert and electricity zips through my body. We're seated on the patio of a beautiful rooftop restaurant, decorated with soft, billowing canopies, intimate booths, and a rich array of tumbling vines and ivy. There's even a trickling water feature!

It looks like something out of some prestigious "World's Best Rooftops" magazine (if there is such a thing), but the relaxed vibe ensures it isn't pretentious or forced. I don't feel like I'm sticking out like a sore thumb in my shorts and t-shirt combo.

Johnny never took me anywhere like this—he preferred the kinds of ritzy places that try too hard. You know, the ones that always have overpriced spinach dip and tons of dark wood panelling.

Conor smiles softly at me, his features even more chiseled under the glimmering fairy lights. I feel like

I'm in *A Midsummer Night's Dream*. Though hopefully I'm not that character who ends up turning into a donkey.

"Do you like it?"

I nod, breathless. "I love it."

I'm about to ask how he discovered this hidden gem, but then, I remember who I'm on a date with. Of course Conor knows about the best date spot in all of Atlanta.

"Do you bring a lot of girls here, then?" I blurt.

Conor reacts surprisingly well to my complete lack of grace, and he laughs, emerald eyes glinting. "No. I've never brought anyone here. Unless you count Mia. Which would be weird—so please don't."

I bite my lip to hold back a smile. "Why not?"

He shrugs. "This place is special to me."

Special. My heart picks up speed, leaping around my chest like a rabbit gone rogue. He's taken me somewhere special.

"How so?" I prop my elbow on the table and rest my chin casually in my cupped hand.

Conor swirls the water around his glass, frowning. He pauses for a moment and I watch him keenly. It occurs to me that I could watch his face for hours, pick out the tiny details and make a list of them.

Then, he sighs. "My parents went through a really bad divorce when I was in high school. My mom moved us to Atlanta, and we lived in a little apartment in a crappy neighborhood."

I sit back in my seat. That wasn't the answer I expected. "I didn't realize you weren't from here."

"I've been here for long enough that it feels like I am."

"Where did you move from?"

"Durham."

I nod slowly and continue to watch Conor. He's still

swirling the liquid around his glass. "So how did you find this place?" I ask gently.

"Mom worked nights, so she wasn't around much. At the time, I was in tenth grade, and Mia was in eighth. She was struggling at her new school, had a hard time fitting in. So many nights, she'd come home sad, and there was nothing I could do to make her feel better. The middle school was separate from the high school so I couldn't even have lunch with her."

Conor takes a deep breath, his frown darkening. I'm silent, just watching him.

"I'd pick her up after school," he continues. "And we'd drive downtown and spend hours walking around, exploring. It always felt so sparkly and fancy compared to where we lived. For a few hours, we could forget about the problems of our real lives. Especially after we stumbled upon this place. The owner used to let us sit in the back corner. He'd make us vanilla milkshakes and we'd do our homework."

My breath catches and my heart expands a little further for Conor. With every moment I spend with him—every little thing I learn about him—my heart makes room for him. Wants him more.

Before I can reply, though, our heavily tattooed waiter appears at our side, and refills our water glasses. "Can I get you two anything else to drink?"

"We'll have two vanilla milkshakes," I say decisively.

The waiter glances between Conor and me, and a flash of confusion crosses his face. I just stare right back at him, as if to say—that's right, we're two full-grown, thirty-ish year old adults, and we want to drink milkshakes.

He recovers quickly enough and takes down our order. "Uh—sure. Coming right up."

When I turn back to Conor, he's grinning.

"Where does your mom live now?" I ask, diverting the subject a bit. I'm sure he doesn't want my pity.

He looks dreamy for a moment. "The first house I ever flipped was for her. She didn't like living in the big city, so I bought a cottage in the far suburbs, and made it into the home she always wanted."

My heart groans with the new stretch mark that appears after that comment.

"She must be so proud of you."

"Her and Mia are my world."

I nod, understanding. Because it's how I've always felt about Aiden.

I smile and lean forward, happy to be learning so much about Conor's past and hungry for more. Hungry to know everything about him. "So, that's where Brady Homes started. How did you end up growing your business to where it is today?"

Conor reaches for his napkin and runs the material through his fingers. "I met Karla while doing that first flip— she was the selling realtor for the cottage. We got to talking and I told her about my vision. She wanted to take another step in her career, and with her knowledge of the market, it made sense to partner up and use her for every project. Well, back then it made sense."

I'll admit that the selfish little brat inside me did a happy dance at his use of the past tense.

Bad Jess.

"What changed?"

"Karla's, um, priorities are a little different than mine sometimes." A shadow crosses Conor's features. "I care a lot about restoration, Karla more about... other things. She thinks I should be taking on investors, but—"

"Two vanilla milkshakes!" The waiter interrupts brightly, setting down two huge glasses practically overflowing with creamy white liquid and whipped cream. "I'll be back shortly to take your food order."

"Thank you." I accept the treat and swirl the straw in the glass before taking a big sip. It's delicious—rich and frothy and sweet. "Mmm."

I open my eyes to see Conor watching me, his eyes hooded and glinting. "Good?"

"*So* good." I wipe my mouth with the back of my hand. "Why don't you work with another realtor if you don't like the direction Karla's suggesting?"

"I don't know." Conor's frown deepens as he wraps his fingers around the frosty glass. "Karla and I have worked together for years. She's been a bit of an advisor, but this time, I'm not sure I want to take her advice."

"I love that you care about restoration. And people appreciate the care you put into things, I know they do," I say more passionately than I intend. "It was the first thing I noticed when I stepped into Aiden's house. You really managed to preserve the character of the place."

Conor smiles, his lips parting slightly. Then, without warning, he reaches across the table for my hand. His fingertips are icy cold from where they cupped his glass, and a shudder travels all the way up my arm. The good kind of shudder. The kind that makes the hairs stand up at the back of your neck and your stomach plummet into free fall.

He gazes at me with such intensity, such sincerity, that my breath catches. "Jess." His voice is low. "Why don't you believe in yourself like you believe in other people?"

My smile fades as I get lost in his eyes. "Hmm?"

He leans closer, so close that I can feel the heat radiating off his skin. Smell that pine and clean laundry scent that makes me want to pounce on him like a starving tiger on a raw steak.

"You don't believe in yourself, but you believe in

162

everyone else," he repeats, and I'm hypnotized watching his lips moving around the words. "You should be thinking about how *you* could start your own business selling your art. You could be so successful."

His words sink in and I shift in my chair, chuckling nervously. How is it that this man—a veritable stranger until two weeks ago—can see inside me to my deepest desires, greatest fears, and strongest doubts? He seems to know me in a way that my boyfriend of six years never even began to discover.

Conor waits for me patiently, his eyes scanning my face.

"Oh, I don't know," I finally dither, uncomfortable.

"You should." Conor's tone is firm, like he's stating a well-known fact.

And maybe it's the confidence in his tone, his clear belief in me, or the oncoming sugar rush, but for the first time in years, I begin to entertain the thought that I might actually want to pursue painting. For real.

The thought is fleeting, and is quickly followed by layers of self-doubt and uncertainty. But Conor's words light a fire in me that I'm not sure will be going out anytime soon.

We spend hours on that rooftop, as he and Mia used to do every day after school. We talk, and laugh, and share our hopes and dreams like we've known each other forever, but want to spend forever getting to know each other better. By the end of the evening, I haven't had a single sip of alcohol— favoring a second milkshake over a glass of wine—but I am well and truly drunk on Conor Brady.

We leave reluctantly when the restaurant closes for the night, and the whole way home, we're silent. My pulse hammers in my throat, and I keep stealing glances at Conor. Sometimes catching him in the act of stealing glances at me.

I've never been on such a perfect first date.

But, I've also never been on a first date where our final destination is the SAME HOUSE. Where the person I am on said date with, lives in the NEXT BEDROOM.

The air in the cab of the truck is crackling, full of static, and my head swims.

By the time we get home, my insides are a jangle of nerves. I jump out of the truck too fast, almost face planting on the sidewalk.

Conor is at my side in an instant. He extends an arm to steady me. "Whoa."

"I drank too much," I joke weakly.

He chuckles. "Vanilla milkshakes have that effect on you often?"

"What can I say? I'm a lightweight."

"In that case, you're cute when you drink too much." Conor smiles.

We walk up the—*our*—driveway together, his hand on my arm, and I swear I see the curtains moving in Miss-Busy-body-Next-Door's window. I'm sure my phone will start blowing up any minute, Courtney texting me madly to know what's happening with Conor and me right now.

Which is probably nothing. Nothing is going to happen.

But, regardless, I plan to keep her guessing until tomorrow, at least. Serves her right for those naughty assumptions I know she's making.

Because nothing's happening.

Right?

Conor opens the front door and gestures for me to go inside. "After you."

We stand in the entryway looking at each other. He's close enough that I can smell the clean scent of his shirt. Close enough that I can hear him breathing. Close enough that I'm sure he can literally see my heart pounding through my t-shirt.

Every inch of my skin is begging to be touched by him. So much so, I'm almost reconsidering my stance against a roommates-with-benefits situation.

No!

BAD Jess.

"So, usually, I walk a girl to her front door after a first date." Conor shoots me this sexy, lopsided grin and I could swear my ovaries scream aloud at me. "But, since we both live on the other side of the front door, maybe I can walk you to your bedroom door."

OH MY GOSH. This is it. He's going to stick some moves on me, and I'll be helpless to his charms.

He reaches a hand towards me, and I jump with anticipation. Then, I realize he's indicating for me to hold his hand. I giggle a little too loudly, rattled, but he just keeps smiling that amused, sexy smile.

We walk up the hallway. Slowly.

My mind is in overdrive. How on earth can I tell him that I'm not into casual stuff? That I'm not that girl? That... maybe he actually likes a very different sort of girl than me.

Before I can blurt out any of my jumbled thoughts, we reach Aiden's bedroom door (yes I'm still sleeping there). Conor faces me and gently disentangles his hand from mine. "I had a really nice time tonight."

"You too." I clap a hand over my mouth. "Uh, I mean, um—me too."

"Goodnight, Jess." Conor half-smiles, then leans forward. My mind goes blank with desire. I want nothing more in the world than for him to kiss me right now.

And, this is it.

It's finally happening.

My pulse picks up and my skin flushes.

He grazes his lips against mine for one, heart-stopping

second. Fire blazes through my body at the sensation of his mouth on mine.

But, instead of the deep, passionate kiss I'd built up in my head—where I grab him and pull him closer—he steps back. Smiles knowingly, like he can hear every one of my embarrassing thoughts. Then, he turns and leaves, shutting his bedroom door behind him. Leaving me standing alone in the hallway, stunned and craving more.

I stumble into Aiden's bedroom, stars and butterflies spinning in a halo around my head. My entire body feels like Jell-O. I touch my fingers to my lips, replaying the painfully short-lived kiss.

I want more. More kissing. More time with Conor. More everything with Conor.

But, he respected me enough to treat me like a princess on the first date—from the beautiful restaurant, to the intimate conversation, to the most chaste, gentlemanly kiss. A kiss that was only a split-second long, but somehow felt more sensual than a heated makeout session.

That is how my being responds to Conor Brady, apparently. It's unlike anything I've experienced with any other man. And, it appears that the sweet, sensitive, sexy guy I'm falling for is not the player I thought he was.

Because it's true, I'm well and truly falling for Conor Brady. Hook, line and sinker.

My phone lights up on the bed next to me, and I reach for it, suddenly all too eager to tell Courtney everything.

But, it's not Courtney.

Conor: Hi

My heart flutters wildly and the goofiest smile possible spreads across my face.

Jess: Hi back

Conor: I'm just checking you got home safe.

I laugh out loud. Maybe he's not a player, but he's definitely a charmer.

Jess: I did, thank you. And, isn't there some rule where you wait three days before texting someone after a date?

From down the hallway, I swear I hear him laughing, too. My phone lights up again a beat later.

Conor: Yes. But you're worth breaking the rules for.

Jess: Oh please. If you were a real rule breaker, you would have let me pay for dinner.

We'd argued over the bill until Conor grabbed it, put down his credit card and sent the waiter off with it. Effectively putting an end to my insistence that we at least split it. Johnny always wanted us to go Dutch—which I didn't mind, per se, as I can pay my own way.

But, in saying that, there was something really nice about Conor's persistence, saying that paying for dinner was the least he could do to thank me for helping him with the house. Even though we both know he's paying me for that, too.

Conor: That's one rule I always follow. Non negotiable. Now that's established... Are you up for letting me pay for dinner again sometime?

My breath catches and my skin grows warm. If I was in one of those kids' cartoons from the 90s, my eyes would be heart-shaped.

Jess: Conor Brady. Are you asking me on a second date?

His reply comes through less than a minute later.

Conor: I am.

I fist my hand in the bedspread in victorious joy to avoid squealing out loud. A second date!

Be cool Jess, be cool.

Jess: I think I can fit you into my very busy and important schedule.

Conor: I'm glad to hear that.

Conor: Oh, and Jess?

Jess: Yeah?

Conor: I don't kiss like that on the second date.

OH. MY. GOSH.

His words send a fresh flame of fire through my body, and my only coherent thought is that this second date cannot come fast enough.

20

JESS

Over the last week, I've learned a lot about restraint.

And when I say restraint, I mean that it has taken every single, teeny weeny ounce of my self-control not to launch myself into Conor's arms every time I see him. But, the man seems to have an iron will, and he's beyond determined to keep our date very separate from our roommate situation.

Which is really sweet, I know. But, it's also really freaking frustrating when all I want to do is grab him by the shirt and demand he kiss me. Not that I'd ever do anything like that IRL—maybe in my fantasies, I'm a wicked, wanton woman who grabs what she wants by the shirt. But, in reality, I'm a massive chicken who's way too scared of rejection —and way too burnt in the past—to try anything of the sort.

Plus, we've both been up to our necks in work all week. Between my painting and staging, and Conor's last minute finishing touches on the build, we haven't had a chance to go on that promised second date yet.

I feel like a little kid at a carnival, standing in front of the cotton candy cart. Starving and craving a sugar high that nothing else in this world will satisfy. Only, the cotton candy costs $1.99 and I've only got a dollar in my pocket.

So close, and yet, so far.

In the evenings, we've hung out, cooked, and watched movies together. The times we're at the Decatur house, working together, we've chatted as normal. And, every morning, I wake to a fresh pot of coffee in the kitchen. It's been wonderful in every way, as spending time with Conor always is.

But, there's been no more kissing. Or even a hint of a suggestion of kissing.

And it's enough to drive any sane woman crazy.

"Ready?" Conor quirks a grin at me and I swallow. Hard.

We're in his truck together for the first time since our date last week, and the proximity to him is wearing my nerves thin. I'm hyper-aware of his hands on the steering wheel, how his muscular arm rests so close to mine.

"Mmm-hmm." I mumble, as we park outside of the Decatur house. The flip looks phenomenal. The cute house has been beautified within an inch of its life with fresh white paint, a butter-yellow front door, and flower troughs in the windowsills overflowing with red petunias. A newer, better version of its character-filled self.

I smile as I take in the cheerful flowers, which were my idea.

The open house is in just a few hours, and I'm nervous as all heck to see what everyone thinks of my work. All these people looking at my art hanging on the walls, the way I've arranged the furniture to play off the paintings...

I open my door and slide to the ground, but as I'm about to step away from the vehicle, Conor appears in front of me. Like, right in front of me. Mere inches between us. He puts a gentle hand on my arm and I suck in a breath.

"Hey, Jess."

"Hey," I squeak.

"What are you doing tonight?" Conor's tone is maddeningly casual and conversational.

I force a laugh. "Well, depending on how long the open house goes, I'm guessing cleaning up and sleeping?"

"No."

"No?"

"Not that." He draws a lazy circle on my bare arm, making my head spin.

"What were you thinking?" My voice is more breathy than I'd like.

"I was thinking about that second date." His eyes bore into mine, and that thumb of his keeps on drawing circles. I bite down on my lower lip to stop from making a noise in my throat, and his eyes flicker to my mouth. "In fact, I haven't stopped thinking about that second date."

"Me either," I manage to reply. Unmistakable desire flares in Conor's green eyes and my legs almost give way.

"Good. It's a date, then." His eyes may be alight, but he sounds casual as can be. He releases my arm, steps back, and strides down the driveway to the house, jangling his keys as he goes.

I lean against the truck, not trusting my legs to carry me until I've caught my breath.

Conor glances back over his shoulder with that wicked smile. "Come on, we don't have all day."

I walk behind him on wobbly baby-deer legs. The time that stretches between now and tonight seems like a vast, endless chasm.

I take a huge gulp of coffee. I'm going to need all the help I can to get through this one.

For the next couple of hours, Conor and I bustle through the house, fluffing cushions, arranging flowers into vases, lighting scented candles, and making up the beds in the bedrooms with fresh linens.

In the end, I went for a contemporary feel in the house, with just a touch of boho chic. So, comfortable, neutral-colored living room furniture, a gorgeous maple wood dining table with contrasting modern chairs, white linen drapes, round vanity mirrors, and jute rugs. Then, I brought in rich color and texture through a multitude of jewel-toned throw pillows, cable knit blankets, and a veritable green-house-worth of plants in adorable ceramic pots.

I even found a little lemon button fern for the coffee table.

And, craziest of all, my paintings adorn multiple walls. A series of slightly abstract, warm, desert oasis scenes that tie the entire design together. I can't help but feel that little leap of hope in my chest. To me, it looks beautiful. Conor has told me a thousand times that he loves it.

But, I'm still dead nervous that I'm somehow seeing something everyone else won't see. That the prospective buyers and Conor's potential investors will hate the place. Proving, once again, that it isn't worth taking a chance on my art.

That I should probably go back to circus-freak wait-ressing.

"What's on your mind?" Conor asks from behind the stack of sheets he's carrying. We walk into the master bedroom, and I'm highly aware that this is the first time we've been inside a bedroom together.

The realization makes my already blended insides liquify further. "Just nervous."

He sets the heap of white cotton on the bed and looks at me. "For the open house or for our date?"

"Both."

"No need to be nervous for the open house, this place is phenomenal."

I bite my lip, but can't disguise my hopeful smile. "Do you think?"

"I know." Conor nods firmly. "Did I ever tell you that, on my first open house, the fire department had to evacuate the place?"

"What?"

Conor laughs and sits on the edge of the bed. "I read online that you should fill the house with homey smells to help people envision their lives there. So, I threw a loaf of bread in the oven. And promptly forgot about it. Fast forward an hour or two, and there was so much smoke billowing out of the oven, it set the fire alarm off." He snorts at the memory. "Karla was so choked."

"What happened then?"

"One of the attendees called the fire department, even though I was taking care of it. It was just a loaf of smoking bread. They showed up with the sirens blaring, in full gear, prepared for a structure fire. I thought Karla might murder me. But, it all worked out in the end, because one of the fire-fighters loved the house so much, he bought it."

I burst into laughter. "That's amazing."

"It was," Conor agrees with a small, nostalgic smile. "So, no need to be nervous about the open house today. If you can top that disaster, I'll just be flat-out impressed."

I smile back, reassured. But then, I realize what he's left unsaid.

I tuck a strand of hair behind my ear. "So, I have reason to be nervous for the date?"

Conor grins. "Of course. The second date is when women fall deeply, irrevocably in love with me. There's no going back."

He's kidding.

I think.

"I doubt that's going to happen." I toss my hair and attempt to stare him down. Which I realize was a very, very bad idea the second I meet those eyes.

"Oh no?" Conor's voice comes down a notch. "Not even if I kiss you properly?"

I shake my head as vehemently as I can.

"I want to kiss you right now," he adds.

My eyes sweep his face and I gulp. Audibly. Did someone crank the thermostat up to a thousand in here?

"You do?" I croak.

"I do." Conor looks straight at me and I draw in a sharp breath. "But I won't."

The frustration must be evident on my face because he smiles.

"Not yet, anyway," he amends. "But, on our second date, like I promised."

"Fine by me," I say defiantly, although my entire body is protesting otherwise, not wanting to wait another moment. So much for restraint...

"Unless you want to move things forward... I have time in my schedule to make that happen." Conor glances at his watch, then back at me. "Two hours until the open house starts. Maybe there's time to squeeze in a second date."

Conor takes a step towards me and my mind takes a little ride on a tilt-a-whirl. My anxiety for the open house is already sky-high, and Conor's closeness, while intoxicating, is not helping my nerves right now. I need to get through this open house before I can even think about what kissing Conor Brady on our second date might feel like.

And so, knowing that my brain will jump off the tilt-a-whirl and head straight for the vertical drop ride if he comes any closer, I pick up a decorative ceramic elephant and brandish it at him. "Stay there, buddy."

"Buddy?" he repeats, his mouth pulling at the corners.

"You heard me." I wiggle Ellie in front of him. "Stay back. My attack elephant bites."

"You've upgraded from an attack fern to an elephant?" Conor laughs. "Am I that dangerous?"

Yes.

"I can't go falling in love with you until after the open house is over, so you'd better stay back."

"I don't think I can wait until later." Conor's gaze is so fiery, his tone so intense, that I almost drop Ellie and smash her to smithereens.

My heart does a series of backflips as my eyes lock on Conor's. The tension in the room crackles like static electricity. All of his jokes and teasing and sarcasm are gone, and he's just looking at me. Really looking at me.

And my resolve fizzles away to nothing. "Me either."

Conor darts towards me, and it's like we can't get close fast enough. The world spins as I tilt my chin up. Close my eyes. Eager for his lips to meet mine...

"AUNTIE JESS!" Hurricane Oliver swirls into the room in a tornado of Osh Kosh denim overalls and sticky fingers.

I open my eyes with a start and step backwards, almost overbalancing.

Oliver's big, round eyes light up. "A HEFFALUMP!"

He throws himself at me and somewhere from deep, deep inside me, my nurturing instincts kick in. I catch the little boy in my arms. Swing him onto my hip.

Motherhood abilities unlocked—yesss!

I let out the shaky breath I didn't know I was holding. "Ollie! Hi! Where did you come from?"

"Mama's here," he mumbles, curling one pudgy arm

around my neck and petting Ellie with the other.

"Your mama's here?" I ask.

"Downstairs."

"*Auntie* Jess? One meeting and you're already family, huh?" Conor says, but his voice is light and teasing.

"Hi, Uncle Conoww." Oliver looks at Conor seriously. "What you doing?"

Good question, little man. Very good question.

I finally dare look at Conor, too curious to care how embarrassed I must look.

A delicious little smile plays on his lips as we make eye contact.

"I don't know what we were doing," Conor says. "Auntie Jess here seems to make me forget all of my rules."

Ollie looks at me, disappointment etched all over his tiny features. "You and Uncle Conoww being bad?"

I laugh. "Yes, I think we were, Oliver. Good thing you stopped us."

Conor looks at me over the child's head. "Until later."

A thrill zips down my spine.

Downstairs, Mia is standing in the middle of the living room. She's wearing a button-front sundress, the buttons of which are straining desperately over her watermelon-like bump. Which she's cradling as she examines one of my paintings.

She looks up when she hears us. "Oh, hey. Thought I'd drop in and check out the place. Hope Ollie didn't interrupt anything."

"Auntie Jess bwoke the wules," Oliver sings.

Little brat.

I flush like a child who's been caught with her hand in the cookie jar, but Conor smiles easily. "Nope, not at all."

He moves to his sister and gives her a kiss on the cheek. "How are you feeling, do you want to sit down?"

176

"I'm not an invalid!" Mia rolls her eyes, then pauses. "But yes, I do."

She sinks—with no small degree of difficulty—into an oatmeal-colored armchair, letting out an "oof!" as she takes the weight off her feet.

"I'm just going to check on the yard," Conor says. "Coming, Ollie?"

"Yay!" Oliver cheers as Conor deftly scoops him up and deposits him on his shoulders. The toddler's chubby fists bunch in Conor's thick hair, and I'm momentarily jealous of little Ollie.

As Conor and Oliver head outside, Mia turns to me, shifting her weight awkwardly. "I can't wait until this child is out of me."

"I'll bet." I sit primly on the edge of a couch, scared to mess anything up. I take a look around the completely staged living area. Then, I take a deep breath. "So... what do you think?"

My stomach twists into a nervous knot as I watch Mia's face carefully. I realize that her opinion means a lot to me.

Because she's an artist herself, or because she's Conor's sister?

"Jess, this place looks incredible." She shakes her head, her eyes wide with awe. "You've outdone yourself."

"Thanks." I blush bright red at her praise. "I'm so nervous."

"You shouldn't be." Mia grins. "This is better than anything I've ever pulled off. You're really talented."

"Thank you," I say again, hugging a pillow to my chest. The silky tassels tickle my bare arms.

"So, tell me something."

"Sure." I lean forward, expecting a question about one of the design elements.

But, Mia shoots me a wicked smile—one that makes her

look exactly like her big brother. "What's going on with you and Conor?"

My blush deepens.

"I'm... not sure." I answer. Honestly.

Mia lifts one delicate eyebrow. "He looks at you like Ollie looks at his Goldfish crackers."

"Like he wants to crush me?" I shudder at the memory of Ollie "eating" Goldfish by the crunched up, drooly fistful.

Mia laughs. "No. Like you're a snack."

"Oh." My words fail me as heat rises to my cheeks.

"He likes you, Jess. I can tell."

Her words give me buoyancy, like I'm drowning in a lake and she just threw me a life preserver. And, somehow, for the first time in a long time, I feel like I can say how I truly feel.

"I like him, too," I say, shyly.

"So, when's the wedding?" Mia wiggles her eyebrows at me and I laugh.

I feel lighter, freer after admitting the truth to her. So much so, that I want to hold the throw pillow over my face and squeal into it like a lovestruck teenager. But I don't. Because of all the restraint I've developed this week.

"Have you told Aiden?"

Aiden.

No. I have not told Aiden. Because what would I tell him? *Oh, hey bro, guess what? Your roomie and BFF took me on a date, then walked me to my bedroom door. He kissed me, but the kiss was shorter and more chaste than the ones I've endured from Great Aunt Mildred. That was a week ago. Nothing has happened since—even though we live under the same roof—but I've never experienced tension like this in my life, and if something doesn't happen soon, this pressure cooker is going to explode. And nobody wants to deal with cleaning up that Jess mess.*

Yeah, Aiden would be on the next plane to Atlanta to check me into the nearest asylum.

For the criminally lovesick.

I shake my head and Mia laughs again, then winces. "Shouldn't laugh so hard. I don't want to pee on your chair."

I blink. "Sorry?"

"Pregnancy bladder. It's a thing. And don't let me change the subject... Aiden's going to love hearing about what's happened in his house while he's been away."

"Nothing's happened between Conor and me," I tell her. "I think he's just being nice."

Mia smirks, her eyes glinting. "I know my brother. And whatever is going on between the two of you... it's not that, believe me."

I seize the opportunity to find out more. "What about Karla?"

"What about Karla?" Mia sits back and strokes her bump absentmindedly.

"Hasn't anything happened between them? All that time spent alone in abandoned houses?" The mental image fills my mouth with bile, but I have to know.

Mia snorts, then makes a pained face. "Oops. No sudden movements. And no, nothing has happened between them. That woman is as bloodthirsty as a great white shark. I'm sure Conor sees it. He's not blind."

A tentative glow of warmth gathers in my chest. No, not warmth. Hope. Hope that Conor might actually be one of the good ones...

"Why do you ask?"

The glow dissipates as quickly as it arrived. I look at Mia, at her uncomfortable posture, her kind, genuine eyes. Her face looks way too much like Conor's when I stare at it too long.

I can be honest with her, I decide.

I look down at my hands, chipping the nail polish on my pinky finger, which I always tend to do when I'm nervous. "My ex left me for a woman like Karla," I admit quietly. "A woman who was going places, had it together. It's... hard for me to imagine that Conor wouldn't do the same. Wouldn't go for someone so poised, elegant and successful."

Mia's brow furrows as she considers my words, considers the gravity of my confession. Then, her hand stops the circles on her belly, and she sits up to look at me sincerely.

"Jess, I'm so sorry that happened to you." She shakes her head, the action full of sympathy. "But, Conor's not your ex. Don't ever tell him I said this, but he's a good guy. And, even if he doesn't always act like it, he knows that he wants to make a woman really happy one day. Under all the flirting and confident persona, he's just a nice guy looking for a nice girl. For life." She stops. Smirks again. "At least, he *was* looking for someone. I think he may have stopped the search."

"Stopped what search?" Conor's voice comes from behind us, and we both just about leap out of our skins.

I wheel around to see him looking at us, amused. Oliver is clutching his hand.

Mia recovers quicker than I do. "The search for my bladder control. Now, help me up before I wet your armchair."

"I am begging you, please keep your bodily fluids to yourself," Conor responds, but he's at his sister's side in a flash. His touch is gentle and caring as he helps her to her feet. "Mia, are you sure you should have driven here alone?"

"No!" she says cheerfully. "Now, can someone tell me where the bathroom is?"

21

CONOR

It's going... well.

Really well.

In fact, as far as open houses go, I'd consider this one to be a home run. Knocked right out of the park.

All afternoon, a steady stream of young families, professionals and a few older couples have moved through the house, ooh-ing and ahh-ing in every room. The sounds give me hope that this project won't be a money pit after all, that I might actually have a chance of turning a profit on this thing.

Karla brought along her bigwig investor friends—a pair of elderly men with perma-tans, very white teeth, and immaculate, matching three-piece suits who I've nicknamed Chaz n' Chad—and even they look impressed.

But the best part is, I've arranged a silent auction at the end of the open house for Jess's paintings and she has no idea. When I asked her what she wanted to do about the paintings once the open house was over, she was all too quick to say that she'd give them away. But, I can't let that happen. Her paintings are worth more than that, and I can't wait to see what they go for.

Jess has spent most of the afternoon in the backyard, pacing by the pool and smiling at people as they come through. Her smiles don't fool me, though—her eyes are wide and wild, fear etched clearly in her velvet chocolate irises.

She seriously has no idea what an incredible job she's done. No idea that I haven't been able to focus on anything else all week now that I know how she tastes—warm and sweet—and how soft her full lips feel against mine.

I want to speak to her more than anything, but I'm currently being held hostage in the kitchen by a sweet couple in their late thirties—a plump, rosy-cheeked woman and a bespectacled, overly serious man. They're chatting about wanting a house big enough for their six cats.

"We plan on adopting a seventh soon," purrs the proud cat mom. She has an angry red mark on her cheek which looks remarkably like a cat scratch, but I decide it's safer not to ask.

"Congratulations?" I murmur, wishing the word hadn't come out sounding like a question.

"Thank you." Cat dad adjusts his glasses. "We're very excited about this place. We will definitely be making an offer."

I give him my best professional smile and handshake. "I'm so glad to hear that. We look forward to hearing from you."

As the couple toddle off (and I can't help but notice the woman plucking cat hairs from her sweater as she walks), Karla swoops in next to me. She's decked out in a navy suit and crimson stilettos. Her crisp, white blouse has just one too many buttons undone, and her red hair is scraped back in a tight chignon. Which makes her fore-head look unnaturally rigid. Although that could just be the botox, I guess.

She clutches two martini glasses, and extends one to me. "Here."

"No, thanks." I never drink on the job. Better to keep a sharp mind.

"You deserve one," Karla objects, pressing the glass into my hand with so much force I'm surprised it doesn't shatter. "This is actually going well."

I nod, and set the glass on the island behind me. "Yeah. Jess did amazing, didn't she?"

I love my sister, and Mia does incredible staging work, but whatever magic Jess has woven in this place is just next level.

"Very nice, yes." Karla's tone becomes pinched and she lays a hand on my arm. She leans in to say something else, but I don't hear a single word she says because I'm focused on the front door. Well, not so much the door as the person who's just walked through it.

The man is about my age, his hair slicked back with enough gel to bathe in. He's got mirrored sunglasses on, sports a gold signet ring on his pinky finger, and he's wearing one of those really annoying trendy suits where the pants legs are a bit too short. Paired with suede loafers, no socks.

The two inches of bare, hairy ankle is not a good look.

But, that's not what bothers me about this city slicker. What bothers me is that I know him from somewhere... I can't place him, but I have a bad feeling in my gut looking at him. Is he a realtor I've dealt with before?

The man whips off his shades and gazes around the room, an arrogant smirk on his face. He takes out his cellphone and starts snapping pictures. What the?

"Excuse me," I tell Karla, and stride towards the front door.

"Conor Brady, of Brady Homes." I extend my hand to

the man. I'm hit by a wall of Axe body spray and I have to hold back a grimace. Who is this joker? "How can I help you? Are you a potential buyer?"

The man laughs derisively. "In Decatur? No."

He clasps my hand in a shake and I'm gratified to see that his hands look small, soft and pale in my grip. I squeeze a touch too tight, just because I can. Then, I look him dead in the eye, daring him to show weakness.

I have no idea why my feathers are so ruffled right now. There's just something about this guy.

"I'm looking for Jessica, actually. Jessica Shaw." He's positively smirking now as he peers around the crowded room.

I drop his hand like I've been burned, realization smacking me in the face.

It's that douche canoe from the bar.

The one who made Jess cry.

Her ex's best friend.

Suddenly, all my angry, territorial instincts make a little more sense. I paste on my biggest, falsest smile. "Oh, how do you know Jess?"

At the casual use of Jess's name, the man seems to snap to attention. He looks at me properly for the first time, taking me in. I feel the air around us change, cooling ten degrees in a single heartbeat. "We go way back. You?"

I remember Jess saying that she lied to this guy, told him she was a house flipper. As of now, it isn't a lie, but I make sure to embellish. Just a bit. "She designed this *entire* place. Incredible, isn't it?"

Douche canoe's jaw drops open. Too bad there's no hair gel designed to keep a shocked expression firmly in place. "Wow."

"I know. She's amazing, the best in the city." I'm really warming up now. "She's in such high demand, she has a months-long waitlist. Come on, I'll take you out back. She'll be delighted to see an old friend, since you guys go *way back* and all."

I can see that he wants to make an excuse to leave, but he doesn't really have a choice at this point. He's backed himself into a corner. In fact, he looks downright ruffled. Judging by the way his arrogant smirk is nowhere to be seen, he obviously stopped by the place simply to catch Jess in a lie. Humiliate her further.

What a little—

"How do you know Jess?" the man asks as he follows me across the room.

I give him an even bigger smile, and lower my voice conspiratorially. "After asking for her help for weeks, she finally agreed to do this job with me. But, I'm hoping it'll lead to more. She's in high demand in more ways than one, If you know what I mean."

I do the whole wink-wink-nudge-nudge thing to really rub it in, and for a moment, I think I may have gone too far. Acting was never my strong suit.

But, an Oscar might be in my future yet, because some-how, the guy buys it. And judging by the way his eyebrows practically shoot off his face, it appears that he isn't *just* here for Johnny. He clearly has some ulterior motives with his good buddy's ex-girlfriend.

Classy dude.

I give him a faux-apologetic look. "Oh! Sorry! Did you guys used to be involved?"

He shakes himself off. "No, I, uh..."

I pat him on the shoulder, full of pity. "Hard luck, bro."

By this time, we're outside and Jess is just a few feet away, chatting with Luke and Pete. Which couldn't have worked out better, judging by the way this cretin's face darkens.

"Jess!" I call, striding forward.

She looks up, and a million emotions cross her face as she sees who's trailing me.

"Someone's here to surprise you." I turn back to the man, and in the most ambivalently pleasant, sincere tone I can possibly manage, add, "forgive me, I've forgotten your name. Dick, was it?"

Jess splutters, almost spraying a mouthful of her drink all over poor Pete, who's watching the scene unfold in bewilderment. Luke's mouth drops open.

"I never gave you my name," the man says crisply, his cheeks reddening.

"Mark, what are you doing here?" Jess asks. Her voice is calm but I notice the way she fists her hands in the hem of her little black dress (which she looks incredible in, by the way).

"Oh!" I slap *Mark* on the back. Harder than necessary? Yup. "My bad, Marky Mark."

Dick suited him better, I think. But, maybe that's just me.

Mark flinches and I almost—*almost*—feel bad for him. But then, I remember Jess crying and I don't feel bad at all.

Meanwhile, Pete and Luke make hasty excuses and start backing away. I'll have lots of questions to answer later, but for now, I don't care about that. I look at Mark expectantly and he scrambles for something to say.

"You've done well," he stutters, the arrogant expression I'm sure he's perfected is gone without a trace. "It's a nice place, Jess."

Jess's face is dark. "Thanks. Is that all you stopped by to say?"

"I—well—uh, can we, maybe, talk in private?" Mark shoots me a sideways glance and we both look at Jess.

She folds her arms across her chest. At that exact

186

moment, a warm breeze circles us, lifting her hair off her shoulders. She looks like a poster for Bad Ass Women Not To Be Messed With.

And, I am here for it.

"Anything you want to say to me, you can say in front of Conor."

Mark scowls and glances between the two of us. "What —are you two some kind of a *thing*?"

"I wish," I say staunchly. "I'd be lucky to have a girl like Jess in my life. Anyone would be lucky. Don't you think, *Mark*?"

Mark goes a highly unhealthy shade of puce. Jess, meanwhile, looks at me with the most meaningful expression I could ever imagine—gratitude. Grateful that someone has finally taken her side, stood up for her. But the crazy thing is, the last thing she needs to feel is grateful. I'm telling the truth... anyone would be lucky to have Jess in their life.

And I realize, in that moment, that I want to be the lucky one. Badly.

I want Jess to look at me like this—I want to make her smile like this—every single day of my life. 'Til we're gray and old and have to wear diapers.

Okay, well, hopefully not the diapers part, but you get the picture.

For the first time, I'm highly, acutely aware that some-thing has been missing in my life. Lately, I thought it was just a family, someone to settle down with. But, that wasn't it. At least, not completely...

I was looking for Jess. *She* was missing in my life. And, with her by my side, I feel whole, complete.

Home.

"Mark, I think you'd better get going," Jess says coldly, continuing to come into her own power and strength. I watch her, impressed and slightly mesmerized. "I'd tell you to send my best to Johnny, but it wouldn't matter. I'm sure you'll be reporting back to him the second you walk out the door."

Mark coughs, but he at least has the good grace to look placated. Like a little boy being told off for saying a naughty word.

I barely notice any of this, though, because I'm looking at Jess. Looking at the woman who's changed everything for me.

I'd call Aiden right now to tell him I want to be with his sister, but Jess might have something to say about that. So, tonight, I'm going to tell Jess that I'm all in. That I want to do this for real, whatever happens. That I'll fight for her, and never let her down like her moron of an ex did. That she's special and worth it.

"Don't let the door hit you on the way out."

Jess's sweet voice cuts through my thoughts and, when I look up, she's smiling at Mark, a devilish twinkle in her eye.

I want to kiss her more than ever.

22

JESS

Exhausted is an understatement.

I am bone-weary, drained, knackered, fatigued, shat-tered, dead-on-my-feet tired. And yet, I've never felt so energized in my life.

Because the open house was a roaring success. People loved the design, the staging. Even the art. Plus, I managed to stand up to stupid Mark when he showed up snooping for my even stupider ex, and best of all, Conor had my back every step of the way.

He said he'd be lucky to have me.

And then, the biggest surprise came at the end of the event, when Conor announced a silent auction was taking place for the artwork on the walls.

My artwork on the walls.

And even though I insisted again that I was happy to give my paintings away, that they were worth nothing, Conor had looked at me fiercely and said, "no, they're not." He went on to reveal there were already multiple bids.

It was more than I could have ever asked for, and I'm beyond grateful for his belief in me.

A surge of happiness shoots through my body as I load

the last box of leftover snacks into the back of Conor's truck. I set it down, turn away, have second thoughts, and turn back, cracking the box open to swipe another cookie. I cram it in my mouth.

Mmm. Warm chocolate chips melt on my tongue, mingling perfectly with the thick butter and brown sugar flavors of the batter. We may have gone a bit overboard on the food, but who doesn't like chocolate chip cookies? Karla, apparently. Because I didn't see her eating any.

I lean against the truck and pluck my phone from my purse. Courtney's been texting all afternoon, asking how everything is going. I finally have some time to reply.

Courtney: How did it go?

Courtney: Sorry I couldn't be there, I had six dogs today and I didn't think your lover boy would appreciate me turning up with the motley crew.

Courtney: Jess, answer your phone. I'm dying over here!

Courtney: Are you mad I called him your lover boy? If so, I'm sorry. But if you're not mad, I'm not sorry.

I cackle with laughter and text my bestie back.

Jess: Not mad. Also not my lover boy. It went super well!

Courtney: Pina coladas at my place to celebrate?

I cringe a little, suddenly very glad to have an excuse to get out of drinking Courtney's "famous pina coladas" again tonight.

Jess: Can't, sorry. I have a date.

Courtney: LOVER BOY'S TAKING YOU ON A SECOND DATE?

Jess: Still not my lover boy. And yessssss.

Courtney: I'll be there at 7am tomorrow. Sharp. Because I'm going to need every detail in person.

Courtney: Unless you want me to come over later tonight. I'm not sure I can wait til morning.

Jess: See you tomorrow *sticky out tongue emoji*

Courtney: Be good. Or not. *kissy face emoji*

I'm grinning at my phone like an idiot when Conor's sexy voice distracts me. "What are you smiling at?"

My head jerks up to see that he's standing in front of me, arms stacked with boxes.

"Oh, I, uh..." I stutter, then I smile flimsily. "Never mind. Not important."

He steps around me to pile the last of the stuff in the truck bed. Then, he holds out his hand. I stare at that big hand for way too long. Does he want me to hold it? High five it? Shake it?

"Take my hand, Jess," he says. But not in a bossy way. In a smooth, silky way that makes me want to do anything he asks.

I slide my palm into his warm grip, and he gives my hand a little squeeze. His smile makes my knees weak and his clear eyes gaze into mine. "Today was great. You did amazing, and I can't thank you enough."

My mouth is dry and I feel like I might just float away on a cloud. Because I'm clearly in heaven.

But then, his expression becomes wickedly playful. "Now, are you ready for tonight to start?"

No.

Yes.

Could I ever actually be ready for a date with Conor Brady?

I settle for a casual nod, heart beating fast. "Where's Karla?"

Conor smiles as we walk up the pathway and back into the empty house.

"Gone," he says. "Everyone's gone. It's just you and I."

Chills erupt on my skin. It's finally time for our second date.

Conor brings me back into the house, and I expect him to turn off the last light in the living room before locking up the place. I sigh happily as I look around, thrilled and relieved with how the day went.

Conor flips off the living room light, but then, instead of getting ready to leave, he tugs gently on my hand, leading me towards the stairs.

I frown, bewildered. "Where are we going?"

"To our date."

He starts climbing the stairs and disappointment bubbles in my chest, bitter and sharp. I know what lies up there—a ton of furnished bedrooms with freshly-made beds.

I stop fast, red alert signs flashing in my mind. "Conor Brady, I am not going to the bedroom of a strange house with you... that's *not* what I would classify as a date."

Conor turns to me and his green eyes spark with what looks like... annoyance. The disappointment grows, burning and heavy in my chest. Have I completely misjudged him this whole time? Was I unable to see the forest for the trees? Has Conor been doing nice things for me just to try to get me into bed—a notch on a bedpost to forget tomorrow?

And now that I've said no, is he mad?

If so, he's the worst type of guy. The worst.

A flash of anger sears my veins and I yank my hand out of his grasp. I make for the front door without looking back, my head spinning uncontrollably. I came here with Conor in his truck but I'd sooner walk home than be stuck with a guy who doesn't understand the concept of "no."

"Jess. Wait. We're not going to the bedroom." Conor's voice speaks from behind me. "Just look at me, Jess. Please."

There's an edge to his voice that I've never heard before. And, for some reason, it makes me turn around.

His eyes burn as they zero in on my face and, when he speaks again, his voice is clipped and matter-of-fact. "I was taking you for a picnic dinner on the rooftop. Not for a quickie in a strange bedroom. Which I don't do with anyone, for the record. Despite what you may think of me, I actually feel like sex is better when it's saved for someone special."

I frown, anger and disappointment still lighting a fire in my veins. But then, I notice the way his brow crinkles, the way his lips turn down at the edges. His eyes refuse to meet mine, and the world stops spinning.

Conor doesn't look annoyed or frustrated. He looks... hurt.

All at once, the fiery anger I felt evaporates into thin air. A heavy wave of mortification washes through my body. "Conor, I'm so sorry, I..."

I trail off, lost for words. I'd clearly made a terrible assumption about him. I felt awful.

"Don't be sorry." Conor shakes his head and offers me a small smile. "I just want you to know that I'd never use you like that. I'm not that guy. You deserve so much better than someone who's just after one thing."

I tilt my head, narrowing my eyes. "So... you don't want to get me into bed?"

He laughs. "Of course I'd like to get you into bed, Jess. I'm only human. But, I want to get to know you better even more. And, I want to start the get-to-know-you-better process by taking you on a nice second date."

"Oh," I say dumbly.

He takes a tentative step closer to me. "You're worth getting to know, Jess. I want to spend time with you, hear your thoughts, find out what your favorite color is, when you had your first kiss... what you think the meaning of life is."

Conor focuses his gaze on me, all traces of laughter gone, as he comes to stand directly in front of me. He reaches out and tucks a strand of hair behind my ear, brushing my cheek as he does so. My skin lights where he touches it, and I can't help but fixate on his face, mere inches from mine.

His voice drops to barely above a whisper. "I want to know all of it. Everything that makes you the person you are. Okay?"

"Okay," I say. My voice is shaky and my heartbeat skitters wildly.

Conor grins that slow, sexy grin of his, and I just about melt into a puddle. "Now that that's cleared up, would you like to come upstairs? To the *roof*?"

I nod. Smile too. "I'd love to."

He takes my hand again and leads me upstairs, past the bedrooms, and to the rooftop patio. When I step outside, my breath catches and I blink a few times, hardly believing that this is reality. Conor Brady has blown all of my expectations out of the water for what feels like the thousandth time.

It's a blissful evening—not too hot and not too cold. The warm summer breeze carries the smell of hydrangeas and the woodsmoke of a nearby barbecue. The entire patio is decorated with flickering Chinese lanterns, the light warm and cozy. Beyond the patio, the cityscape of Atlanta makes the most mesmerizing backdrop. On the floor, a checkered picnic blanket features a cheeseboard, a bottle of champagne, and two glass flutes. Next to those, there's a tub of what looks like chocolate gelato.

I look at him, openmouthed, and he just shrugs.

"See? Picnic."

I have no words, so I settle on hugging him. I lock my

hands behind his neck and bury my head in his chest. The fabric of his t-shirt is soft and warm against my skin. He laughs and wraps his arms around me, hugging me back. And, for a few minutes, we stand in each other's arms, swaying to the soundtrack of the city pulsing in the distance. He holds me tight, like he never wants to let me go, and my heart glows.

When we finally break apart, he's smiling. "I didn't mean to mislead you, or make you think I didn't respect you, Jess."

"You've been nothing but a gentleman," I tell him. Well, an extremely flirtatious, sexy gentleman. But, I'm not telling him that. "I think I'm just on edge about what happened earlier with Mark."

Conor sits on the picnic blanket and gestures to the spot next to him. I collapse on the ground, glad to rest my tired legs.

"What's that guy's deal anyway?" Conor busies himself pouring me a glass of wine, but I don't miss the shadow that crosses his face.

"He's Johnny's little errand boy. And I know they're both pathetic, but still, it gets under my skin that Johnny wants to keep tabs on me." I rub the back of my neck as I speak, tired and weary. "In all honesty, I'm surprised that Johnny hasn't texted me. He loves interjecting when he finds out that I might actually be happy without him."

"What do you mean?"

I flush and look at the ground. I'm not one to share this kind of information lightly. To this day, very few people know this about Johnny and me. But, there's something about Conor... though we've only known each other a few weeks, I feel like I can trust him.

I take a deep breath. "We broke up once before. He didn't call me for two months and I heard he was dating around. Then, I went on a date with a guy I really liked and, all of a sudden, Johnny was calling and texting and sending flowers."

"And you got back together?" Conor swirls his wine in his glass, gazing into the whirlpool he's created.

"Like an idiot." I shake my head as shame overcomes me. "I'm such an idiot."

I squeeze my eyes shut, remembering that time. It was a couple of years ago now. Despite my striving for independence, my desire to be strong and confident, it turns out that I'm just another sob story. Guy breaks girl's heart. Girl breaks up with guy. Girl takes guy back and he ends up breaking her heart all over again.

I mean, I took back my lying ex. Let him hurt me twice. Who does that?

"You're not an idiot," Conor says sharply. "You're a human being and you guys had a history together. It's understandable why you'd try again. Especially if he tried so hard to win you back."

"Maybe," I venture. If only he knew everything that happened.

"Do you think he'd try to win you back again now, even when he's engaged to someone else?"

"I don't know." I pick at my thumbnail, frowning. "One of the reasons why I left New York in the first place was to put enough distance between us to make sure we were done for good this time. But, even now that he's engaged, he's still sending Mark after me to check up on me. Like, he doesn't want me, but he doesn't want me to move on."

Conor sets his glass down with a clatter. "He's the one who's an idiot, if that's the case."

Despite the heaviness of my confession, I love how much Conor dislikes Johnny simply because he knows he hurt me. His concern fills me with that special kind of light you get when the people you care about care for you too.

"Um, tonight, I—I wasn't scared of the physical, uh, part of everything," I stutter. "Like, when I thought you were taking me upstairs." I swallow awkwardly. Pause.

Conor takes my hands in his. "Go on," he says gently.

Unable to bring myself to look in his eyes, I stare at our clasped hands, my cheeks warm. "It's more that I was scared that it was all you wanted me for. That you were being nice to me for that reason only. After Johnny, my confidence is a little... lacking."

"You should be nothing but confident, Jess." Conor's thumb traces the edge of my hand, and the movement makes me dizzy in the best way. "You should be confident in yourself first and foremost. Only then can you be confident in anyone else. In me, and my intentions. And, for the record, we don't need to do anything physical until you're completely ready. As long as that takes. Like I said, I want to get to know you. Everything about you."

I peek up at the beautiful man in front of me, telling me to believe in myself. That I'm worth believing in. He sits patiently, his eyes gazing openly at my face, and I realize just what's so special about Conor—not only does *he* believe in me, but he's giving me space and confidence to grow my belief in myself. He's not demanding that I tear down my walls, he's simply asking me to open a window. Take a breath of fresh air.

And, all of a sudden, I want nothing more than for him to know me... And I want to know him, too. Every little piece of what makes him who he is.

"Purple. Trevor Newton, tenth grade. At the movie theater. I had a piece of popcorn in my mouth when he leaned in, and I was so surprised, I swallowed it whole. He almost had to give me the Heimlich Maneuver." A small smile crosses my lips. "And I don't necessarily think there's one meaning. More that we're here to do good, make things better. Be happy."

Conor blinks. "Huh?"

I almost burst into laughter at his baffled expression. "You had questions for me, and those are my answers." I smile, delighted to have caught him off guard. "How about you?"

Conor bites on his bottom lip, an innocent gesture that sends a swirl of butterflies through every one of my internal organs. "Blue. Rebecca Sanderson, seventh grade, on a dare. I had no idea what I was doing and I knocked my teeth against hers. Luckily, I've improved my technique over the years."

"And the meaning of life?"

Conor's eyes meet mine. "Finding someone you truly care about, and waking up every single day wanting to give them the world. Building a home with that person."

Energy rushes through my being at his words, at his sincere expression. He's right, I might not be ready to fully let him in yet, but I am 1000% sure I'm ready for one thing.

He sees me staring, and he tilts his head. "What?"

"I was just thinking about how I was promised a proper kiss."

Flares appear in his eyes and he pulls his hands from mine. My stomach drops deliciously as he slowly, painstakingly, begins to slide his hands up my arms. I inhale shakily, breathing in his woodsy, warm scent. One of his hands tangles in my hair, while the other cups my chin.

He moves towards me, and my heartbeat quickens. I take in his strong, angular jaw, his sexy stubble and mussed up hair. He's the most gorgeous man I've ever seen.

And he wants to kiss *me*.

"Is that so?" Conor says quietly.

He moves a touch closer. Still not close enough.

I make an impatient noise, and he smiles. That sexy, sexy smile. He lowers his head towards mine and his lips skim my cheekbone.

The sensation sparks fire on my skin and I suck in a sharp breath.

"Should I kiss you here?" he asks, teasing.

I shake my head, try to twist my mouth to meet his. But, his hands hold me steady.

He drops his head further, his lips pressing little kisses along my jawline, making my head spin. I bite my lip to stop from yelping out loud.

"Here?" he asks again, his voice lower. The obvious desire in his tone stirs a fresh wave of desire in me.

"Please," I say softly.

It's the magic word.

His mouth covers mine, warm and sweet and strong. My breathing immediately quickens and I coil my arms around him, pulling him closer. As close as I can get. But still, he kisses me slowly, tantalizingly. Takes his time. His hands move through my hair and I slide my palms over his back, feeling the corded muscles tighten at my touch.

"Conor," I breathe against his mouth.

He pulls back for a moment, eyes swimming with a sea of emotions. "Is this okay? Are you okay?"

The concern in his tone is the loveliest sound I've ever heard. Seeing that he wants me, but that he's trying to take things slow to make me feel respected and cherished, is enough to make my heart explode. I have never, ever met a man like Conor Brady.

I smile. "More than okay."

I tilt my head back towards his, wanting more. And he obliges. It's the best kiss of my entire life, and I'm dizzy and shaking when we finally come up for air.

Conor runs a finger down my cheek. "It's getting late, I'd better get you home."

I shake my head. "I don't want to go home yet."

My drooping eyes must give me away, because he laughs gently and kisses my forehead. "You're about to fall asleep on your feet. Plus, it's not a date unless I drop you home and walk you to your door."

And so, like a true gentleman, Conor drives me home, walks me to my bedroom door, and gives me the softest, sweetest kiss goodnight I could have ever dreamed of.

"I had a great time tonight, Jess," he says, his voice husky.

I smile up at him. "Me too."

"Can I take you out again sometime?"

"I'd like that."

"Good." Conor squeezes my hands, then turns to leave. "Goodnight, Jess."

"Hey, Conor?" I call after him. He turns back around.

"Yeah?"

"Thank you for a perfect second date."

He grins. "Anytime, roomie."

23

CONOR

The days that follow our rooftop date are some of my favorite in recent memory.

First off, the Decatur house gets multiple offers, triggering a bidding war. Karla is ecstatic. And Chaz n' Chad are clambering to set up a meeting and invest in Brady Homes.

Secondly, the silent auction for Jess's artwork turns out to be a roaring success, and the lady who has the top offer on the house offers a sizeable extra chunk of cash to take the paintings along with the house. All of them. I haven't told Jess the amount yet, because I'm waiting for the deal to go through. But I can't wait to see her face when she finds out.

And last, but certainly not least, I've been walking Jess to her bedroom door every night since our second date. Kissing her goodnight and wishing her sweet dreams. Because I know that I have to—I want to—take this slow and easy with her. Show her, not just tell her, that she's special to me. That I truly care about her.

When she thought I was just using her, just wanted to take her to bed, I could hardly believe it. Did she truly think that I saw her as an opportunity for a passing fling?

She seemed so scared, so anxious, that it made me wonder again just what exactly went down with that boyfriend of hers. How is it that Jess seems to believe so little in herself?

Whatever it is that went down with Johnny, she'll tell me if she wants to, whenever she's ready. All I can do until then is try and make her feel cherished. Make her feel like enough.

Because she's more than enough.

So, I've taken her on a slew of dates. Every night, we've done something new: ten pin bowling (where she absolutely annihilated me), a drive-in movie (where we sat in the back of my truck on a pile of coats and held hands), the Georgia Aquarium (where she loved the whale sharks so much I bought her a stuffy).

Every date with Jess is the best date I've ever had. And, for the first time in years, I've gone from barely making it through a first date, to waiting excitedly, every day, for work to finish so I can take this girl on another adventure and create more memories with her.

I know Aiden is back next week, and we're going to have to face some harsh realities then. For instance, how can I possibly explain that I fell for his sister when he was away? But, I'm determined to show him that my intentions are good. Same as I'm determined to show Jess.

This evening, I'm taking her to my new house again for a change of pace. A work date, of sorts. Which, in a real, corporate workplace would violate just about every HR rule in the book.

Because dating my staging contractor, who also happens to be my best friend's sister and new roommate? That's like the trifecta of rule-breaking.

But Jess is worth breaking the rules for. I know it.

Jess's hand is warm and soft in mine as we walk up the

pathway to my house. As we step inside, Jess sucks in a breath. "Wow!"

I smile, watching her reaction—the way her eyes widen, her mouth opens in a perfect little "o", her tan skin crinkles around her smile. I'd happily spend days studying all of Jess's expressions, trying to commit each tiny detail to memory.

I knew that my house would elicit such a reaction. Because gone are the salmon carpets and pieces of ripped up wall. And in their place is a big, open-plan floor space that's a blank canvas.

She turns to me, and I can almost sense her excitement. "Do you know what you're going to do in here?"

I feel shy all of a sudden. Yet another uncharacteristic emotion that Jess drags out of me. "I, uh, was hoping that you'd go through my plans with me." My cheeks redden as I speak. "Give me your opinion."

"On designing the house?" she squeaks, and I nod.

"Two seconds." I retrieve a set of floor plans and a pot of pencils from a kitchen cabinet and roll the plans out across the floor. "Come take a look."

Jess sits, cross-legged, in front of the rolled out papers. It's a little cooler this evening, and she's wearing black leggings with an oversized, pale pink t-shirt that slouches off one, tan shoulder. She gathers her hair into a topknot as she leans forward to pore over the pages. Her glasses slip down her nose an inch or so, and I can't help but grin at how cute she is.

I sit next to her. On my knees. Because I have no idea how women manage to make sitting cross-legged look so easy.

With a pencil, I point out where I'm thinking of creating a brand new, L-shaped kitchen. Where the powder room will go. How accordion-style French doors will run along the back of the house, showing off the pretty, treed yard and pool. She follows along, frowning in concentration as I talk.

"What do you think?" I ask, still slightly nervous.

"Incredible! Absolutely incredible." She beams. "I can't believe how much you can change a space by moving some walls around."

I breathe a heavy sigh of relief, still unsure exactly why I'm so concerned about her opinion.

Because I care about her, so therefore, I care what she thinks. I watch her trace the drawings with a finger, enamored by their details.

"Anything you'd suggest?"

Jess shrugs. "Maybe find a space for a pantry in the kitchen? This is such a perfect family home. If you eventually have a family here, you'll want a pantry." She shifts slightly awkwardly, as if she's just touched on a taboo topic. Does the thought make her uncomfortable?

"Good idea." I nod. "Where do you suggest?"

We pore over the plans together for the better part of an hour, stopping briefly to place an order for Thai food delivery. We find a place for a walk-in pantry, and I take Jess's suggestions to stack the washer and dryer in the laundry room so I can add a sink, and to expand the hallway closet because, "you're always going to accumulate shoes."

When our food arrives (red curry for Jess and Pad Thai for me, the secret spice-wuss), we carry the cartons outside and sit by the pool. The sun is setting, and an explosion of red and pink streaks blaze through the darkening sky. It truly looks like an artist's canvas.

"So beautiful." Jess sighs, gazing at the sky as she pops a piece of chicken in her mouth.

"You're beautiful," I murmur. Yup, I'm being cheesy as

a wheel of gouda right now, but she *is* beautiful. I speak only the truth.

"None of that."

"You are," I insist. "I knew it the second I saw you."

Jess snorts. "Lying on the ground in a pile of dirt?"

"That very moment."

Jess's eyes dart around, and she bites the inside of her cheek. Then, she makes her own confession. "I thought you were pretty okay yourself... for a freaky Charles Manson type."

I burst into laughter. "Please, please, tell me that you're not secretly one of those twisted people who writes letters to serial killers in jail, declaring love for them?"

"It's called hybristophilia," Jess says seriously.

I recoil in mock horror. "There had better be a good reason why you know that."

She shrugs. "What can I say? I'm a true crime buff."

"Weirdo," I say affectionately.

"Less weird than washing all the dishes *before* putting them in the dishwasher."

"I told you, it clogs the drain otherwise."

"So unclog it after," Jess says flippantly.

I gag. "That is absolutely disgusting."

She puts her face really close to mine. "Disgusting?"

"Dis-*gust*-ing," I say solemnly. Then, I grin. "But, I still like you anyway."

Jess smiles and looks at me from under her lashes. "That's convenient... because I like you, too."

Her words are everything I want to hear. I slide my hand over to graze the sensitive, soft skin at the back of her neck. My lips find hers, hungry for her, and she responds immediately, clutching at my shoulders as we fall headfirst into the most incredible kiss.

I can't get enough of her. Her lips taste both sweet and

spicy. My mind swims, and when she makes a little noise in her throat, I tilt her head backwards so I can deepen the kiss.

Eventually, we break apart, breathing hard, but I make sure not to let her go.

"That was—"

"Wow," Jess finishes for me, her voice scratchy and high-pitched. "That was wow."

I gather her closer to me, pulling her into my chest for a hug. I bury my face in her hair, inhaling the citrusy scent of her shampoo.

"I could kiss you all night," I murmur into her hair.

"Then do," she says.

I lean back so I can look at her, a million questions racing through my mind. Until now, our kisses have been sweet, and soft, but no less intoxicating. Of course I want her. But, even more than that, I want her to know how much I care about her.

I'm here to play the long game with Jess. The one where we end up together. Hopefully forever. Which means taking things one step at a time, as and when she's ready. No need to rush into anything—because I'm not going anywhere. "Jess, I..."

Jess glances at my serious expression and smiles softly, her cheeks glowing petal pink.

"Just kissing," she clarifies. "I just want to kiss you and fall asleep in your arms."

Her eyes flicker when they meet mine, and my stomach jolts. "Well, I guess it's only fair that I give you what you want."

If she wants to fall asleep in my arms, I don't want to wait a moment longer to hold her close. To wrap my arms tenderly around her body so we can drift off into sleep together... At this moment, I've never wanted anything so much.

Jess clearly has the same idea, as she jumps to her feet. "Let's go home?"

"Let's go home," I reply with a smile.

As we drive, the air in the cab of the truck feels thick and heavy. The electricity—the tension—in the air is unlike anything I've ever experienced. It takes all of my willpower to focus on the road ahead, and not on the feeling of Jess's hand in mine. How her fingernails gently drag across the back of my hand, lighting all of my nerve endings on fire.

I thought this drive was only fifteen minutes. Why's it taking so long?

My heart pounds, and I realize that I haven't felt this excited about the prospect of kissing a girl since... well, probably since Rebecca Sanderson in the seventh grade.

I've never wanted anyone like I want Jess. And I want Jess for real. Not just physically—I want her heart, and I want to give her mine. Settle down and have a family with her. This all seems a little crazy, even in my mind as it produces these thoughts. But, when you know, you know.

All I know is that Jess is special, and I don't ever want to let her go.

I slide my eyes away from the road and over to her. She's sitting next to me with a pained expression on her face.

"What are you thinking?" I ask, curious.

She squeezes my hand a little tighter. "Is it a bit weird? That we're roommates, but, you know..."

"Going home to kiss all night?" I offer, and I'm rewarded with Jess's fierce red blush.

"Yeah, that," she says softly.

I chuckle. "I guess we'll have to tell Aiden before he's back."

Jess pauses, then nods. "Yeah... Can we wait to do that tomorrow? Call him in the morning?"

"For sure." I smile. "Tonight, it's just us."

"Just us," Jess echoes happily.

We finally—*finally*—pull up outside Aiden's house, and I'm suddenly struck by how incredible the timing was. That we ended up here, together, under the same roof. Fell for each other in the middle of such a crazy set of circumstances.

I'm about to kill the engine when Jess's phone rings, cutting through our blissful bubble.

I groan and bang my head against the headrest. "Please don't tell me that's Aiden, calling because he's got some weird sibling sixth sense and he somehow heard our entire conversation."

I glance at Jess, looking for the smile on her lips. Instead, she's gone pale as she stares at her phone screen. "Much worse," she whispers. "It's Johnny."

Johnny. I freeze, my fingers gripping the steering wheel.

He didn't call after the open house, like she thought he might. But, here he is, calling almost a week later. I'll bet he tried not to, but ended up cracking. Just had to keep tabs on her, didn't he?

The last thing we need is for Jess's ex to ruin our night. And doesn't he have a fiancée to call? Before I can think about what I'm doing, I grab her phone with lightning speed. Jess's mouth falls open as I slide the bar on the screen to answer the call.

"Yes?"

"Uh, what? Hello, Jess?" Johnny sounds even more annoying than his friend Dick. He also sounds drunk.

"Not Jess," I say calmly. "Can I help you with something?"

"Who is this?"

"I'm Conor. Who's this?" Okay, I'm enjoying myself now.

Meanwhile, Jess is gaping at me, a hand on each cheek. *Home Alone* style.

Johnny sputters, then laughs cruelly. "The same Conor who was with her at the open house last week? Mark said her crazy art was all over the walls."

"I sure am," I say coolly. "And the buyers loved the art, thanks for asking."

"Are you, like, together or something? Did Jess really leave me for a construction worker?"

"Jess left you because you're a fool. No other reason."

"Excuse me?!" Johnny rages into the phone, slurring slightly.

"You're excused," I respond levelly. "And, I'm a little busy right now. So I'll ask you one more time before I go, can I *help* you with something?"

"No, well, I—"

"Okay, we're cool then. I'd say it was nice chatting with you, Johnny, but it wasn't."

"Wait—"

"Oh, and Johnny?" I smile manically.

"What?" Johnny-Boy rasps.

"Please don't call my girlfriend again."

Before he can say anything more, I hang up the phone, adrenaline pumping through my veins. It felt so good to put that idiot in his place.

Then, I see Jess's aghast face, and my heroic bravado crumbles into dust. "Oh, Jess, I'm sorry. I didn't mean to overstep, I just—"

I don't get to finish my sentence because, before I know what's happening, Jess has thrown herself at me. Her mouth collides with mine, and I blink in shock before I react to the sensation of her kiss. Hungry and desperate.

And react, I do. All rational thought leaps out the window as I lean over and unbuckle her seatbelt. I pull her towards me, and she climbs across the center console and onto my lap, kissing me so fiercely that my head bangs against the headrest. I hold her against me, pressing her body to mine. Every one of my senses is in overdrive—the citrus smell of her skin, the intoxicating sound of her breaths coming hard and fast, the sweet taste of her lips...

"Thank you," she pulls back enough to whisper. "Thank you so much."

I touch my forehead to hers, catching my breath. "I should have thanked *him*. Because if he hadn't acted like such a jerk, we wouldn't be here right now."

Jess throws her head back and laughs. A real, deep belly laugh that reverberates around us, filling every inch of the air with hope and happiness.

I lean forward and place a kiss on the tender area at the base of her neck, reveling in the fact that I get to taste her skin. She shudders, tilts her mouth towards mine, and once again, we're tangled up in each other.

I fumble for the door handle, and somehow, we make it out of the truck and onto the pavement. I lean her back against the truck, tilting her head to deepen our kiss. She responds by balling her hands in my t-shirt and pulling me closer.

I've never loved kissing as much as I do right now. Ever.

"Come on," I say gruffly. "Let's get you inside."

I slide my hands under her thighs and gently pick her up, holding her body to mine. Her legs wrap around my waist and she clings to me like a limpet, giggling all the way to the front door.

Once we get there, I let her down so I can unlock the door. But, somehow, we end up pressed against the door, kissing frantically again, like we're a pair of teenagers.

I'm sure the weird girl next door is watching, but I don't care. I'm just deliriously happy to be here, lost in this moment with Jess.

I finally get my house key into the lock, and we both fall through the door in a heap, laughing maniacally and clinging to one another.

Then, I blink.

Why are all the lights on?

I look up, disoriented, and my eyes land on... Aiden.

Aiden, who's not meant to be home for another few days. Sitting in the living room with his arms folded. His face is etched with suspicion as he takes in Jess and me, red-faced, sweaty and breathless.

"Surprise," he says, his mouth twisting in a grimace.

24

JESS

Wake up, it's a beautiful morning! Wake up, it's a beautiful day! Birds are singing, bees are buzzing, chipmunks are... chipmunking. What do chipmunks even do?

Anyway, never mind that. The point is, last night happened.

Conor and I kissed until we were breathless. Over and over. And you know the way I thought our first kiss was the best kiss of my life? Yeah, WRONG. Like everything with Conor, even the kissing gets better. Every. Single. Time.

He wasn't wrong when he said he'd perfected his kissing game over the years. So much so, that I should probably send Rebecca Sanderson a thank you letter.

Seriously, it's *that* good.

And, it was all made even better by the fact that he called me his girlfriend. And sure, there's a good chance he said it simply to spite Johnny. But I'll take it.

And yes, my brother unexpectedly came home. Yes, I had to think fast and make up a weird story about how I was clinging to Conor because he was saving me from a particularly aggressive flying cockroach. And sure, it sucked that, following that, we all had to sit in the living room and listen to Aiden's really, really boring stories about LA (okay they weren't that bad, but they were pretty boring compared to what I'd just been doing with Conor).

None of that did much to dampen my mood, though. My feet were well and truly planted on cloud nine, and nothing could ruin that for me.

And I was kind of happy to see my brother, too, inopportune as his timing was. Until I discovered that he'd unceremoniously dumped all of my belongings onto the floor of his other spare bedroom so that he could claim his own room back. Ugh.

Last night, I settled into my new, much less comfy bed, assured that Aiden had nothing to be suspicious about. Then, a text came through.

Conor: Do you know that we're sharing a wall now?

As much as I wished that Conor was on my side of the wall—or that I was on his side—and he was holding me and kissing me like we'd planned, the thought made me smile. A smile that remained on my face until I drifted to sleep.

My heart skips as I throw off my covers and leap out of bed, almost slipping on the small shag rug. The spare bedroom comes without the luxury of an ensuite bathroom, so I grab my toiletry bag and dart out into the hallway, looking around furtively as I go. I don't want to risk running into Conor before I've freshened up.

I tiptoe down the hallway and... Success!

I throw open the door to the bathroom, glancing down the hallway one more time. And immediately run into something hard, solid and... wet.

I've been here before. I know exactly whose solid chest I've just barged into, because who could ever forget what a shirtless Conor Brady feels like?

I squeak and leap backwards, taking in the sight of Conor in all his freshly-showered glory. His hair is damp and tousled, his muscled chest glimmers with droplets of water. And—*oh my gosh, he's in a towel.*

"Eek!" I clap my hands over my eyes. "Sorry!"

I stumble backwards, and my back hits the wall. He laughs, a low, throaty sound, and then his hands cover mine, pulling them from my eyes.

"Good morning, gorgeous," he twinkles, looking at me like I'm something to eat. My stomach bubbles giddily at the sight of his smile. "Has anyone ever told you that you look beautiful in the morning?"

Before I can say anything, he kisses me on the mouth. Hard. His lips are cool and minty, and I reach out to grasp him, pull him closer. But, he's already on the move. My eyes lift in surprise, locking on him as he backs out of the bathroom with that maddening smirk on his face. I can only stand there, breathless and baffled.

"Missing you already." He winks, and pulls the door closed behind him.

My hand flies to my lips and my heart vibrates against my ribs, fluttering like a hummingbird. What just happened?

In a trance, I move to the mirror. Then, I nearly scream again as I take in my appearance. I have the craziest case of bedhead and ugly clumps of mascara dot the region under my eyes. That'll teach me not to sleep with makeup on.

Beautiful in the morning? I'm just amazed *he* wasn't the one screaming.

As I brush my teeth and swipe at my face with cotton pads soaked in makeup remover, I think about how Conor consistently defies my expectations. How he sees the best in me even when he sees me at my worst.

Did he mean it when he said that he was my boyfriend last night, or was that just for Johnny's benefit? He looked like he was going to say something about it when he hung up the phone, but my adrenaline-fueled pounce had immediately put a stop to any talking.

I'm curious to know what's going on in his head... and there's only one way to find out.

I rush back to my room and select a breezy, yellow sundress. Then, I tie my hair back into a ponytail.

By the time I make it to the kitchen, both Aiden and Conor are there—Conor making coffee and Aiden scrambling eggs. Because us Shaw siblings have enough sense to know that breakfast is the most important meal of the day.

The kitchen is spotless, as usual. Fernie sits in the middle of the kitchen island, healthy and flourishing in her brand new pot. I smile at my little plant, remembering the unfortunate, and very literal, run-in between Conor and me. Who would have thought things would go like this?

"Morning." My voice comes out all breathy and jittery, and both men turn to look at me.

"Morning, little sis." Aiden sets down his spatula and moves to give me a hug. "How was sleeping in your new bed?"

I lean out of his hug and stick my tongue out at him. "Terrible. My back's in agony."

Aiden smirks. "Your punishment for lying to me."

My heart stops and I just about choke on my own spit. Does he know? Did Conor say something?

"L-lying to you?" I stutter. My eyes swivel from Aiden to Conor, who looks a little pale all of a sudden.

"About sleeping in my room," Aiden clarifies, ruffling my hair. "Don't look so scared, J. I'm just going to make you take out the garbage and clean the bathroom a few times before I properly forgive you."

I exhale in relief and paste on a smile. "Anything to make it up to you, dear brother."

Boy, do I need my morning coffee. Now.

"I'll bet you just about lost it, living with this one for the past few weeks," Aiden says to Conor, blissfully unaware of the momentary panic he just caused. "She's messier than I am, I'm surprised you didn't move out."

"It was a struggle, that's for sure." Conor locks eyes with mine, and my stomach jolts at the look in his eyes. It's the type of look that makes me want to lock Aiden in his room and throw away the key so I can have this morning with Conor all to myself.

Wow, falling for someone has really brought out the selfish side in me. I take a huge sip of coffee.

"Speaking of moving out," Aiden presses on cheerfully, scooping eggs onto a plate. "How's the reno on your new place coming?"

"Getting there." Conor smiles easily.

"Can't wait to see it," Aiden says, then smiles jokingly. "Plus, it's about time you moved out, now that I've got my sister bunking here. You know what they say: two's company and three's a crowd."

Aiden laughs at his own, definitely not funny joke, but my too-big gulp of coffee goes down the wrong way and I choke for the second time this morning.

Because Conor will be moving out as soon as the renovations are done on his place.

But me? I'll still be here. Probably living with my brother til we're gray and old.

I look at Conor, who's now sitting at the counter and texting. He lifts Aiden's "World's Okayest Brother" mug to his lips, a coy smile on his lips, and I take a moment to stare at him. Drink him in. He's so perfectly handsome, and so successful in his work. He has his own house, his own business. He has everything going for him.

All I have to show for myself is four years' experience with circus waitressing and a single successful open house.

An ugly, but all too familiar, voice reminds me that the success likely had more to do with Conor's beautiful renovations than anything I'd done, anyway.

My phone vibrates in my pocket, shaking me from my thoughts. I tear my eyes away from Conor, grateful for the interruption.

Conor: Is your back really in agony? I know a guy who can hook you up with a really good massage.

Oh goodness, the butterflies are back. A whole army of them.

My face reddens, and I look to see that Aiden is safely engrossed in his egg-eating before I dare glance at Conor. When my eyes meet his, he smiles wickedly.

"Well?" he mouths.

I type furiously on my phone.

Jess: Stop it, Aiden's literally sitting right there.

Conor's eyes widen a touch when the message comes through. But then, he smirks and begins typing. I wait for his text in anticipation.

Aiden chooses that exact moment to insert himself into our bubble.

"Who you texting?" he asks Conor in that tone guys always use when they talk about girls.

Conor jerks up his head, and a ray of sunlight hits his face. And, let's just put it this way—he doesn't look *unlike* an angel. "Uhhh, no one. I'm, um, playing... Angry Birds?"

Aiden snorts. "That's weird, I didn't think anyone had played Angry Birds since, like, 2016."

"Conor's big into Angry Birds," I add helpfully. "Plays for hours every day."

Conor sets his phone on the counter and smirks at me. "It definitely keeps me on my toes."

"Well," Aiden shovels another forkful of eggs in his

mouth. "Maybe don't reveal your secret Angry Birds obsession to your date tomorrow night."

Conor turns suspicious eyes on my brother and crosses his arms across his broad chest. "What date?"

I turn to Aiden, too, my brow furrowed. I have no idea what Aiden's talking about... but I already know I don't like where he's going with this.

Aiden grins and puffs out his chest with bravado. "Remember those girls we went out with before I left for LA—Jennifer and Brooke? I arranged a second double date with them."

Conor, for once in his life, looks lost for words.

Aiden winks at him. "You're welcome."

If Conor looks speechless, I can't imagine how I must look right now. *Hell hath no fury like a woman scorned...*

It's probably not a good idea to punch your brother in the face when he's giving you free room and board at his house. Right?

I lean against the kitchen counter and clutch my coffee mug, barely aware of the radiating heat burning my palms. Aiden walks to the sink. Throws his dirty dishes in. Conor gets on his feet, too, and stacks the dishes in the dishwasher.

Aiden punches Conor in the arm playfully. "You don't look nearly as pumped as I expected. I thought you liked Jennifer." Then he stops, examines Conor's scowl and laughs. "Don't look so sour, didn't you say you wanted to see her again? I totally remember you saying that."

My stomach drops like an anchor. But, I fix my eyes on Conor, scanning for his reaction before I jump to conclusions again.

"I, uh—" Conor flails aimlessly. My stomach sinks further.

Aiden narrows his eyes. "Wait, did something *finally* happen between you and Karla?"

218

My jaw almost drops to the floor, but I recover just in time, my heart lurching. What does Aiden mean, *finally*? As in, that's who he expects Conor to end up with eventually?

Conor pales. "No, it's not that. It's—"

"Mindy, then?" Aiden guesses.

I'M SORRY, WHAT?

Conor shakes his head, and Aiden smiles. "Well, then. What's stopping you?"

Conor looks at me. This is where we're meant to tell Aiden what's going on, isn't it? But something deep inside my heart constricts painfully, a physical tightening like I'm being squeezed. Conor has his pick of a million women...

Just like Johnny did.

A familiar rush of bile fills my throat as doubt closes in. The walls slam back up around my heart. Big ones, with barbed wire at the top. And a flashing "No Entry" sign in red, neon lettering.

"Aiden, uh—" Conor starts. Then, he stops and shoots me a sideways glance.

And, all of a sudden, I know what I have to do.

"He'd love to go!" I blurt, my gaze locked on Conor. His beautiful, emerald eyes widen, and I nod, pressing on. Act first, think later, all that good stuff. I tear my eyes away to look at Aiden. "Look at you guys, going on a double date with a couple of hotties."

What the heck am I going on about? And since when do I talk like a frat boy? Do I actually want Conor to go on a date with another woman?

No, I don't. But, better to give him the option before he can pull a Johnny and tell me that I'm great and everything, but there's someone else. Someone who has it together in a way that I don't.

Dealing the first blow will surely make the impact of the metaphorical punch to the gut hurt less.

Aiden gives me the side-eye. "Uh, you okay there, J?"

I ignore him. Focus on Conor. Who's currently staring at me, scowling. And oh boy, does he look hot when he scowls.

No! Focus, Jess!

I stare back, stony faced. Wait for Conor to say something. Come clean. Claim he doesn't want to go. Anything at all.

But, after a bit of a staring stand-off, Conor's mouth twists. "Sure, Aiden. Let's do it."

And, there it is. The truth. I'm not his girlfriend, because Conor Brady doesn't *do* relationships. He does casual dating with lots of beautiful women. And I know we've gone on way more than just one date, but maybe that was simply because of our roommate situation. Which will inevitably come to an end soon. And then what?

I try not to visibly wince at the punch his words pack. At the thought of him and *Jennifer* together. I push myself up from where I'm leaning against the kitchen counter, unable to stay here a minute longer. "I'm going to go see Courtney."

Aiden does a perfect reenactment of *The Exorcist* head-swivel—he's even practically foaming at the mouth. "Courtney, as in, my *next door neighbor* Courtney?"

He says "next door neighbor" like it's a string of curse words. I almost forgot that they hate each other. I still don't know why. But, as I am angry with Aiden for setting up this stupid double date, I smile at my brother like I'm blissfully unaware of the feud.

"Yes." I put my mug next to the sink, purposefully sloshing coffee over the edge and onto the counter. I'm gratified to hear Conor practically gasp.

Extreme pettiness, thy name is Jessica Shaw.

"Why?" Aiden's slack-jawed.

"Because she's my new bestie. And, because she's setting us up on our own little double date for tomorrow night."

But she isn't.

She really, really isn't.

WHAT AM I DOING?

Aiden shakes his head, looking as dazed as if I'd just told him that I was going on a date with a little green Martian with three heads and octopus tentacles. Conor, meanwhile, looks like he's carved from stone. Beautiful, sculpted, and completely unwavering. What's he thinking?

"Great," Conor suddenly speaks, his voice a little too casual. He moves towards the sink and wipes up the coffee I spilled. "We should all go together, a quadruple date. It'll be cozy."

"NO!" Aiden and I yell in unison.

"That's not happening," I add.

"Why not?" He looks at me evenly, his voice flat. "Is there any reason you'd like to share, Jess?"

"No. No reason whatsoever." I grit my teeth. "In fact, I don't know why I was so hasty in saying no. A quadruple date is a fantastic idea."

Aiden, meanwhile, is still on the Courtney train.

"She likes you?" Aiden demands, scratching behind his ear. "She hates me."

I smile sweetly. "Isn't the feeling mutual?"

"Well, what better way to bury the hatchet than a big, group date," Conor says with way too much enthusiasm. I resist the urge to stick my tongue out at him.

Aiden's still scratching his ear. "Won't that be... weird?"

Yes.

"No," I say instead. "Not at all. I'll leave it up to you guys to make reservations—Table for eight tomorrow night. I'll tell Courtney now!"

Then, I high-tail it out of there before Conor can get another word in.

At Courtney's house, I seek refuge under a huge, pink patterned quilt and two enormous balls of fluff that seem to think they're lap dogs.

Courtney sits opposite me in an armchair, tapping her fingers against the armrest like she's the Godfather or something. "So, let me get this straight. Your brother came home. Almost caught you and Conor making out. Then, you lied to him, and told Conor to go on a date with someone else because...?"

"I don't know," I moan, burying my face into the golden, hairy back of Butch—or is it Cassidy?—and letting out a distinctly pirate-like, "arggggggggggggh."

Courtney takes another bite of what looks like a brownie and chews thoughtfully. Swallows. I wait for her words of wisdom.

"You're ridiculous," she volunteers. "I hope you know that."

I throw up my hands. "I just freaked out. Aiden said something about Conor getting together with Karla, and I couldn't help myself."

Courtney shakes her head and brushes stray crumbs from her lap. "Conor doesn't want that redhead. I told you, he never looks at her like he looks at you."

I sigh, my fingers tightening in the golden dog fur. Butch, as if sensing my anxiety, turns his head to lick my hand. "Yeah, well how do you know the same is true for Mindy? Or for Jennifer? How do I know that he's any more serious about me than all the rest of these women in his life?

That's what players do, Court. They date everyone and commit to no one."

Courtney tuts. "Well, did you give him the option to commit to you? Because you just told me that you practically forced him to go out with someone who wasn't you."

I frown. Open my mouth, then close it again.

"Did you even think to ask Conor if he wanted to go out with Jennifer again? Or did you just assume based on what Aiden said?"

I feel a little bashful all of a sudden. "No... I guess I didn't."

"Well, maybe it's time to start using that noggin of yours." Courtney gets out of her chair and taps the side of my head with her knuckles. None too gently. "Hellooooo, anybody home?"

I bat her hand away. "So, I may have overreacted a touch."

"A touch?" she yells. "I can't believe I'm saying this, but you're almost worse than your brother in the overreaction department. And he put a 'For Sale' sign on my car after I accidentally blocked him in."

Despite myself, I snort with laughter. "He what?"

Courtney's pretty blue eyes flash with indignation. "I got twenty-seven calls in half an hour!"

"And all you did was accidentally block him in?"

"Well, I mean, I did leave him that fake parking ticket. But, as a good-humored neighborly joke, that's all." Courtney waves a hand dismissively, like this detail doesn't matter. "Anyhow, my point being—you overreacted. Tell Conor that you don't really want him to go on the date, and I'm sure he'll tell you he doesn't either. Simple."

"Um, it's not quite that simple."

"Why not?"

"There's just one teeny little detail I haven't told you yet," I admit.

Courtney flops next to me and slings an arm around my shoulders. "I'm sure it's nothing we can't handle. What is it?"

"Well, I told Conor you were setting me up on a double date tomorrow night, too."

"WHAT?" she squawks.

"It gets worse." I brace myself for her inevitable explosion. "I told him and Aiden that we'd all go as one big group. Know any single guys who'd be up for an octo-date?"

Courtney lets out a colorful string of curse words that any sailor would be proud of.

I pull the quilt over my head.

25

CONOR

"Could you please pass the butter, *Jessica?*" I look across the table to where Jess is seated next to a perfectly nice man whose chair I'm dying to accidentally tip over.

"Sure, *Conor.*" Jess passes the butter to me, and I over-reach for the dish, making sure my fingertips graze against hers. She makes a sudden, sharp little gasp at the contact, and I don't miss the sparks that flicker on my own skin, too.

"Everything okay?" Jess's date—Rob—tilts his head to look at her.

"She's fine," Courtney interjects sharply.

"Are you?" I lean forward on my elbows, staring at Jess. "Fine, that is?"

"Yes." She sits poker-straight in her chair, poised as could be. But, her voice cracks like an egg over the "s" sound, betraying her whole unaffected act.

She blushes and looks away. In the dim light of the restaurant, her skin looks luminous, her eyes bigger and darker than ever. And, my goodness, does she look good tonight in that forest green, silky dress that slides like liquid over each and every curve. There's no way Rob would have a clue what to do with a woman like that in his life.

"Can I have some butter, too?" My "date" whines.

Not now, Jennifer.

I smile at Jennifer flimsily as I pass her the butter dish, and when our fingers touch, all I'm aware of are her extremely sharp nails.

Emitting a quiet sigh, I lean back in my chair and rub my eyes. I've had the longest day on earth. Chaz, Chad and Karla were all up in my business during our meeting about their proposed investment, and honestly, I thought I'd accidentally stepped onto the set of *Shark Tank*.

They spent hours poring over my financials, pointing out "unnecessary expenses" on my renos that I happen to think were *very* necessary—namely, all the things that I spent money on to preserve the character and history of the houses. Chaz was particularly aggressive about the bills on the Decatur house, even though it sold for over asking. It also got multiple offers that I *know* had to do with Jess's staging and the unique, simultaneous silent art auction.

I'm so proud of our efforts, proud that we managed to take a money pit and turn a profit. But, oh no, that's not enough for ol' Chaz n' Chad, who started rambling on about the "new direction" we need to take once they inject their cash.

In my opinion, though, their direction was going south—essentially cutting corners and producing identical, cookie-cutter houses that use mass-produced materials. In and out, quick and easy. Less effort, more dollars.

I've worked myself to the bone for so many years to grow and expand my business. It's why I teamed up with Karla in the first place. And Chaz n' Chad? I know they're offering me a unique opportunity to keep growing. But, in all honesty, something about their proposed vision feels deeply wrong.

I didn't go into flipping houses purely for the money. I

went into it to make people's lives better, to make their dreams come true. Like I did for my mom. It's worth taking time and effort with these projects.

But, no matter how much I pointed out the value in restoring homes—and how talented artists like Jess bring so much to the table—they wouldn't budge. They vetoed the idea of hiring Jess for our next house, which I didn't understand, at first, seeing as Jess worked for less money than any other stager I'd hired. Then, I saw the jealous look on Karla's face, and it didn't take me long to figure out who was behind that one.

I told them that their new direction was stupid. Didn't bother to mince my words, either. But, I was an island in that particular discussion.

So now, I've been left to "think about what I'd like to do"—which made me feel a little like a naughty child getting sent to time out. Which is not the best feeling when it's regarding your own freaking business you built from the ground up.

Chaz n' Chad may be successful, but I'm not going to let them belittle me or push me around.

So, as you can imagine, after a long day of arguing, the last thing I want is to be on a date with a woman I have zero interest in. Especially not while the woman I *am* interested in enjoys her date with another guy across the table.

I'm still not sure why Jess cut me off yesterday morning. I thought she wanted to tell Aiden about us, but instead she threw me into the deep end and insisted I go on a date with another woman. And then, she proceeded to rub salt in the wound by announcing that she was coming along... with her own date. Who's a total snoozefest, by the way.

The chemistry and tension between us is still palpable, so the only thing I can think is that Aiden freaked her out with all of his inane chat about other women. Made her pull back. Jess always doubts herself, and to be fair, the conversation didn't exactly paint me in the best light. Once upon a time, I might've gone on a second date with Jennifer. But, last month seems like a lifetime ago. And, what Aiden didn't know when he arranged this date is that I no longer want to date any other woman. Ever again.

Because Jess is it for me. The one. And I want her to know that that's how I feel.

Right after I spend the rest of this nightmare date proving to her that she wants to be with me just as much. I want her to believe in herself enough to stand up for what she wants and how she feels.

"Aiden, how're your shingles healing? Okay, I hope?" Courtney asks sweetly, jolting me from my thoughts.

Aiden gasps through a mouthful of wine, and practically sprays a fountain of Merlot into the air.

"Oopsie," Courtney sings. She hands him a napkin, then turns to Brooke, Aiden's date. "I hear that lukewarm colloidal oatmeal baths work wonders for cases where the rash is really bad. Or, you can make a cornstarch paste to rub into his back for him. Very effective."

Brooke looks like she's about to vomit her rainbow trout all over the table. Her eyes narrow in Aiden's direction. "You didn't tell me you have shingles."

"That's because I don't have shingles." Aiden glares at Courtney, who's happily chewing her ravioli. "I told you my roof needed new shingles, not that I *have* shingles."

Courtney shrugs, then blinks her big blue eyes, the picture of innocence. "Well, you can't expect me to remember everything you say."

"Easy mistake to make, honey." Courtney's date, whose name has slipped my mind, pats her arm patronizingly. "You ladies don't need to bother yourselves with construction, anyway. It's a man's job."

Before I have time to call out this blatantly sexist comment from what's-his-face, that whine comes again in my ear. "Conor? I need the butter knife?"

Why not use your regular knife, Jennifer?

"Oh. Sorry," I say instead, sliding the knife towards my "date" while keeping my eyes locked on Jess.

Sure, Jennifer is pretty, in that overly-made-up kind of way. But, she has nothing on Jess. Plus, she's been asking me rude questions all evening about how much money I make. And, she keeps putting her hand on my leg. What ever made me say that I'd want to go out with this girl for a second time?

"So, what do you do for work, Rob?" I ask through a smile as fake as his hairline.

"I'm an accountant." Rob wipes his mouth with his napkin. "How about you?"

Of course he's an accountant.

I keep my eyes carefully trained on Jess as she takes a sip of wine. "I flip houses."

"Oh, like they do on TV?" Rob asks through a mouthful of chicken nugget. Which he ordered off the Kids' Menu, claiming he was allergic to everything else.

"No." I know I'm being a territorial a-hole right now, but somehow, I just can't bring myself to care.

Jess's eyes dart around and she wiggles uncomfortably under my stare. Finally, she throws down her napkin and pushes herself to a stand. "I need to go to the bathroom."

I glance in Aiden's direction, and luckily, he's busy trying to persuade his date that there is no terrible, blistering rash lurking under his designer shirt.

"Me too." I get to my feet.

Jess narrows her eyes at me. "You can't come with me."

I give her a mischievous smile. "I need to go."

"No, you don't."

"Yes, he does," Courtney joins in. "The bathrooms are at the far end of the restaurant, you can walk together."

"Thank you, Courtney," I say with a nod in her direction. I have no idea why she's taking my side right now, but I feel a brand new sense of warmth towards our neighbor.

Jess glowers.

"Maybe I'll come, too," Brooke volunteers, pushing her chair back.

"No, you won't." Something in Courtney's shark-like smile makes Brooke reconsider her actions, and she tucks her chair back in immediately.

I smile. "Guess it's just you and me, Jessica."

Jess slams her mouth shut, turns on her heel, and starts walking quickly. Really quickly. Teetering in high heels that I try not to notice make her legs look a mile long. As I follow her, a loud sound like a whoopie cushion comes from the far end of the table, and I swear I hear Courtney mutter "really, again?"

Once we're safely around the corner, Jess turns on me.

"What are you doing right now?" she hisses.

"Having dinner. The food's good, isn't it?"

"I wouldn't know." She folds her arms across her chest. "I haven't had a moment to take a bite between all the chaos breaking out at the table."

"You're the one who suggested this, remember?"

"Because you wanted to!"

"Because I *what?!*"

Jess presses her lips together, her eyes fiery.

I glance around quickly. The restaurant we're at is one of those lame, fancy places with a stark, cold color scheme and overpriced spinach dip. I never choose restaurants like this, but apparently, it's Jennifer's favorite. However, the one advantage of places like this is that they always have nice, individual bathrooms.

Confident that nobody can see us, I grab Jess by the arm and pull her into one of the private restrooms. I lock the door behind me, then let her go.

"What do you think you're doing?" she demands, color flaring in her cheeks.

"Why did you think I wanted to go on a date with Jennifer?" I retort. The room is tiny, and I'm standing close enough to breathe the scent of the light perfume she's wearing. She smells like sunshine. "You didn't ask me, you just started doubting yourself. Doubting me. Doubting everything I've told you."

Jess's nostrils flare and she crosses her arms again. "Aiden said that you wanted to see her again."

"Jess, that was before I even met you. You can't hold that against me."

"Well, if you didn't want to see her again, you could have taken Mindy or Karla instead." Jess's voice is cold, but I don't miss her lower lip wobbling.

"What if I didn't want to take Mindy or Karla?"

Jess blinks. "So... you didn't want to go on a date tonight?"

"Oh, I wanted to go on a date." I inch closer to her and she takes a step back, but can't move any further. She's pressed against the sink. "But not with six other people in tow. And especially not with a woman who isn't you."

I raise an eyebrow, challenging her to show her cards, too. She opens her mouth. Closes it again. Then, she purses her pretty pink lips and lets out a long exhale, her expression full of remorse. "Really?"

The sweetness in her voice calms me, anchors me, and I feel more at ease than I have all day. I run a finger along her bare arm, delighting in the shiver she responds with.

"I want to be with you, Jess. Only you," I admit.

A tiny smile appears on her face.

"And, you want to be with me, too." I take a final step forward, moving to where she's leaning on the sink. "Am I wrong?"

Jess holds her breath, her eyes searching mine almost desperately. Then, she shakes her head. "You're not wrong."

My heart thumps at her words and I move my face close to hers. So close that there's only an inch between our lips. "Am I going to need to fight off Rob?"

Finally, Jess smiles. A sweet smile that makes me want to claim her lips all the more. "No."

Her warm breath brushes across my cheek and I can't stand it a second longer. I have a million things I want to talk to her about, but right now, my brain and my body are not communicating at all. Because she's just confirmed she wants to be with me, too. Because it's been almost two days since I kissed this girl properly, and that's two days too long.

Completely forgetting where I am, I lean towards her—

Knock, knock!

"Anybody in here?"

We jump apart before our lips can meet, and I almost trip over the toilet. Quite literally brought back down to earth with a crash.

"Occupied," I yell.

Jess looks a little starry eyed and she flushes scarlet as she eyes the door. All I can think is that Jess deserves to be kissed in a way nicer setting than a restaurant bathroom, and that I can't be on this sham of a date for a moment longer.

"Want to get out of here?" I ask, my voice almost a growl.

Jess looks at me, and that wild, passionate gleam sparks in her eyes. "We can't. What about Rob and Jennifer and Ai—"

"Follow my lead."

I have no idea what just happened.

One minute, Conor and I are seated on opposite sides of the table, with our own dates for the evening. The next, we're about to make out in a public bathroom.

I'm shook. (See, Courtney, I can do the down-with-the-kids lingo, too.)

As we exit the bathroom, Conor shrugs off his sexy navy suit jacket and drapes it around my shoulders. It drowns me, and I can't resist inhaling his scent of the fabric.

I take a moment to appreciate how good he looks dressed up like this. His five o'clock shadow perfectly accentuates the angles of his jawline, and his hair has juuust the right amount of product in it. His cologne smells so delicious I want to drown in it. He wears navy dress pants and a crisp, white button-down shirt, the cuffs rolled up and straining around his muscular forearms. The shirt is unbuttoned at the collar to reveal a tantalizing triangle of tanned skin.

Skin I want to put my mouth on. Now.

Before I can swoon and embarrass myself further in front of the restaurant patrons, he wraps one of those strong arms around me. His warm hand is tight on my shoulder as he directs me back in the direction of our table.

"What are you doing?" I hiss. When he suggested that we get out of here, I was having visions of climbing out the bathroom window and making a run for it—not facing the music first.

He doesn't reply.

"Conor!" I try to dig my heels in, but to no avail.

As we get close, six faces snap in our direction. Aiden looks perplexed, and Courtney, positively gleeful. Courtney's date, the unfortunate Farty Marty, and his pal, Rob the Bore, look vaguely intrigued. And Brooke and Jennifer both look like they're about to audition for *WWE Smackdown!*—ie, they're not happy. Not one bit.

I wince and hope that Conor has a plan. He'd *better* have a plan.

"Guys." Conor's voice is low and urgent. "Did anyone else order the steak fajitas?"

Six heads shake.

"Oh, phew. It was just the two of us, then." Conor shakes his head gravely, and drops his voice lower still, to a conspiratorial whisper. "Jess just threw up everywhere, I think it might be *food poisoning.*"

Jennifer gasps and shoves her salad away. Not that she was eating any of her food, anyhow.

"Should I, uh, take you home?" Rob asks me, half getting up and hovering in a strange crouch.

"No worries." Conor waves a hand. His voice carries so much authority, *I* almost believe the story he's spinning. "We're going home to the same place. I'll save you the gas, Robbie."

"Oh, uh. Thanks," Rob mutters, glancing around like he's not sure what to do next.

Aiden frowns. "You okay, Jess? You do look a little flushed."

Yeah, but it's not what you think...

I sniffle a bit, playing my part. I feel a little guilty about hoodwinking Aiden, but as this entire nightmare of an octo-date is kinda his fault, my guilt is outweighed by my desire to get out of here with Conor. Sorry, big bro. "I'll be fine. Just need to get home and sleep it off, I think."

"Come on, then. We'll head out." Aiden takes a swig of water and gets up. Touches Brooke on the shoulder. "Sorry for cutting the evening short, everyone."

"No!" I say. A little too loudly. Everyone gapes at me, and I take it down a notch. "I mean, uh—no, you don't have to come. Why spoil everyone's evening?"

"It was only Jess and me who had the fajitas," Conor adds.

"But, I drove here." Aiden drums his fingers on the table.

Oh, shoot. I'd forgotten that the three of us carpooled here tonight, on Aiden's insistence. His love for the environment is usually admirable, but right now, it's downright inconvenient.

Jennifer pouts. "I wanted Conor to drive me home."

"Aiden." Courtney holds out a hand and makes a "gimme" motion. "Your car keys."

"Why?" Aiden demands. They stare at each other for a long, loaded second.

"Because Conor can drive Jess home now, and I'll drop you home later. When we're done." Courtney sighs as if this is very, very obvious.

Aiden glares at her. "You don't get to decide that."

"I still don't mind driving Jess home if—"

"Shut up, Rob!" Everyone yells.

Rob shuts up. Poor Rob.

"Courtney." Conor takes advantage of the momentary silence. "Thanks for taking Aiden home. Now, I'm going to get Jess out of here before she throws up all over the table."

And with that unfortunate and thoroughly unsexy image, Conor spins me on my heel and marches me to the door. It's like that quintessential scene in every action movie, where the hero pours kerosene on everything, lights a match, and strides away, victorious, while the world explodes into carnage behind him.

I throw a morbidly curious glance over my shoulder to see what we've unleashed. Jennifer, still pouting, is already sidling up to Rob. Brooke crosses her arms, clearly annoyed. Courtney grins like a circus clown, and she shoots me a theatrical wink—which she quickly turns into a dramatic "there's something in my eye" act when Aiden glances her way.

And then, I turn my eyes towards Conor. He's walking quickly, purposefully. A man on a mission, who's just asserted his authority over an entire situation. And he's wearing the sexiest, most confident smile I've ever seen.

Never in my life have I wanted to be alone with someone so badly.

But, apparently, Conor has a totally different idea of what being alone will entail.

The second we're through the front door, I move to kiss him, but he holds me away, almost at arm's length. I try out a Jennifer-style pout to protest the sudden change of events, but Conor just runs his finger along my chin and smiles. "Shall we get changed first, so our little sick charade is believable if Aiden suddenly comes home?"

I nod. A few minutes later, I've just changed into old

sweatpants and a tank top when a knock sounds on my bedroom door.

My heart leaps into my throat, as I sit, cross legged, on the bed. "Come in."

Conor walks through the door, two glasses of ice water balanced in one of his big hands. He's wearing a light gray t-shirt and gym shorts, and his golden brown hair is damp and tousled. It will never cease to amaze me how quickly men can shower.

"Hi," he says.

"Hi." I look at the bedspread, suddenly shy. Suddenly very aware that Conor is in my room.

Conor sets the glasses on the nightstand, then sits on the edge of the bed. Like, the very edge. "Jess, I want to talk to you about something," he says quietly. "Something I should have talked to you about before trying to kiss you again."

His grave tone surprises me and my head immediately tilts in his direction. He looks serious. Too serious.

"Talk about what?" I ask, my palms tingling.

He runs a hand through his hair and the air fills with the clean scent of his shampoo. "You know when Aiden brought up the double date with Jennifer?"

I nod.

"Well, you barely even hesitated. You seemed so eager to send me on that date with someone else. And, I've been wondering why?"

I bite the inside of my cheek. It's a valid question. It really is.

I just don't know where to start. How do you tell the man you've fallen for that it's only a matter of time before he finds out he's too good for you?

But, Conor is looking at me with those clear green eyes, and I remember the way he got me out of that restaurant.

237

He cares about me, I know that. Maybe it's time I show him I care, too.

And that means doing the very thing that most terrifies me.

It's now or never. It's time to rip off the band-aid. Jump out of the plane. It's time for Conor to find out the girl I really am. I suck in a breath. "I didn't tell you the full story with Johnny. He... well, he cheated on me."

"What?" Conor's voice is practically a bark, and I almost jump out of my skin at the sound. He gets to his feet and paces like a caged tiger. A ferocious tiger ready to kill. "He *cheated* on you? Is that why you broke up?"

Shame clouds my vision and I feel a fat tear roll down my cheek. I bat it away. "Yeah. He had an affair. With Sarah, the girl he's engaged to."

There's a long, long pause. When I dare look up, I barely recognize the man in front of me. Conor's face is practically purple, his eyes ablaze. His fists are clenched like he's about to put a hole through the wall.

"Conor," I whisper, not sure what else to say.

He startles at the sound of my voice, then turns to me. And the second his eyes meet mine, every inch of rage drains from his expression. Those bright green eyes fill with softness, and he's by my side in an instant, gathering me in his arms.

"Jess, I'm so sorry," Conor mumbles into my hair. His voice is calm, but pressed against him, I hear his wild, erratic heartbeat. "I'm sorry he did that to you."

I move out of his embrace so I can look at him. Because I'm not done with this humiliating admission of truth yet. If telling Conor the truth about Sarah was jumping out of the plane, admitting this next part is the free fall.

"That's... that's not all," I whisper, my voice shaky. "It's why we broke up the first time, too."

Conor frowns, a small quirk in his brow. He opens his mouth, but I cut him off.

"A couple of years ago, he suddenly started working late. All the time. And, for a while, I believed him. Until I went to his office to surprise him. He wasn't there, and the look on his secretary's face told me everything I think I already knew, deep down."

I shudder at the gut-wrenching memory. How, even after the awful break-up, even after I'd tried to move on... Johnny had come back. And I'd taken him back. I was so quick to believe him when he said it was going to be different.

A powerful mix of pain and sympathy dance across Conor's face, weaving themselves into the crease in his brow, the downturn of his mouth. He sits very still for a moment, his eyes weary in the dim bedroom light. "Why didn't you tell me any of this?"

"I've never told anyone." I shake my head. "Not even Aiden, although I think he has an idea that things weren't great between Johnny and I. The whole thing was just... humiliating." I shrug weakly. "And besides, who wants to be with a girl with baggage like that?"

Conor runs his hand down my arm. "We all have baggage, Jess. And you need to know that you did nothing wrong. This is on him. He treated you horribly, and you didn't deserve any of it. Not for a second."

I bite down on my lip, desperate to believe him.

Then, Conor's eyes widen a touch. "Hang on. That's why you told me to go on the date." His voice is sharp, cracking slightly. "Because you believed I'd do that to you, too?"

A bubble of shame swells in my throat and another tear slips from my eye as I nod. "Look, Conor, I'm the girl who gets left for women like Jennifer and Karla. Women who have it all together, have their lives figured out. Women who don't take back their cheating ex-boyfriends."

My voice is stronger than intended, but Conor doesn't back down. He faces me, his eyes riveted on me. Supporting me.

I deflate under his kind gaze, shaking my head. "I'm a mess, Conor. Why would you want to be with a mess?"

To my surprise, Conor's lips tip upward slightly. He presses the backs of his fingers to my cheek, his feather-soft touch brushing away my tears. "Jess," he whispers, his hands moving to cup my face. "I wish you didn't go through any of this. I wish Johnny had treated you as you deserved, and I wish I could erase every piece of that pain. I'm so sorry I can't do that for you. But, what I can do is tell you the truth."

His eyes are locked on mine and I realize I'm not breathing. All I'm aware of is the place where his hand connects with my face, and the words coming from his beautiful lips.

"You're not a mess," he says in a voice both gentle and firm. "You've been put in messy situations, and it would be enough to derail anybody. But instead, what you've gone through has made you stronger, braver, more empathetic."

The world spins, and I rest my forehead against Conor's in a desperate attempt to steady myself, process what he's saying.

He smiles softly before continuing. "So many people would be hard and bitter after being treated the way you have. But you? You keep fighting, you keep believing the best in people. You're a loyal friend and an incredible sister, and you're sweeter, more talented and funnier than anyone I've ever met. When I look at you, I don't see a mess. I see a masterpiece. I see every single piece of your beautiful heart as a brush stroke on canvas, and the result is a work of art."

His words wash over my skin like melted chocolate and suddenly, I'm no longer in free fall.

Even after everything I've told him, every time I've tried to push him away, he's here. My parachute. I've tried to slice the strings twice now, put myself back into the plummeting failures I believed defined me. But, he held on, buoying me. Hellbent on catching me before I fall.

But, not before I've fallen head over heels for him.

He's still gazing at me, his eyes glimmering as they focus, unwavering, on me. As if what I say next is the most important thing in the world to him.

And I know, in one sudden swoop of certainty, that this is real.

He's got me.

27

CONOR

A career guy. That's how I always described myself—a guy who put blood, sweat and tears into running his own business so that he could... what, exactly? Buy a nice vehicle, a nice house, fancy clothes for meals at fancy restaurants?

Aside from the desire to look after my mom, I realize now that all of my ambitions in life have been entirely selfish. All of my motivations revolved around getting things.

And I don't want things.

I want Jess.

As we sit in her bedroom together, my hand pressed against her cheek as she shares something so deep, so personal, so meaningful, I know of one thing to be true—I've fallen in love with Jess, and, if my heart is steering me right, I think she loves me, too.

But, if I want to be a good boyfriend to her, map out a future with her, then the first thing I need to do is stop being married to my job. Get a quickie divorce and get the hell out of dodge. Or something. I never really understood that saying.

First thing tomorrow, I'm telling Chaz n' Chad that the deal is off. I'm telling Karla that I'm scaling back—one project at a time from now on. And, before that, it's time I tell Jess the very thing that's been weighing on me. That it's *her*. That I want to be with her for real. That I love her more than anything.

I run my hand along her cheekbone, her skin smooth and impossibly soft under my calloused fingers. My heart beats quickly with my upcoming confession. "Jess, I—"

"I KNEW IT!"

A triumphant yell shatters the moment as Jess's bedroom door flies wide open.

"I was right." A very flustered, red-faced Aiden wheezes as he extends a pointer finger at us, shaking it back and forth like he's a Halloween witch. He's grinning like a maniac in victory—Aiden has always had a competitive streak. Then, he seems to remember exactly WHAT he was right about, and his smug smile slips right off his face.

"You weren't answering your phones!" Courtney bursts into the room hot on Aiden's heels, her expression panicked. And... wait, is that Brooke behind her?

Yup.

Oh, and there's Jennifer. Glaring daggers. Fantastic.

All I need now is for Jess and Courtney's weird dates to... oh, never mind. They're here, too. Rob and what's-his-name pop their heads around the doorframe to get in on the action. Why not make it a real party?

Jess scowls at her brother, hands on her hips. "Can someone please tell me what's going on?"

"I think *I* should be asking *you* that," Jennifer snaps, lips drawn together like she's been sucking on lemon slices. "What happened to food poisoning?"

Rob adjusts his glasses. "We're very sorry to intrude like this—"

"SHH!" Aiden yells. The irony of which is not lost on me.

243

He takes a step towards me and I steel myself for what's about to happen. This is the least opportune way for him to find out, but at least it will be out in the open now.

"You weren't answering your phones," Aiden repeats, like that explains everything. "So we came to get you."

Courtney looks between Jess and me, her eyes deeply apologetic. "We tried calling you. I promise, I tried everything to stop him from coming here, but—"

Aiden's face gets even redder as he wheels around to Courtney, his eyes brimming with fire. "You KNEW about them?!"

Courtney's cheeks turn bright pink. "Well, I—"

He doesn't wait for an answer. He turns back to me instead—his head swiveling back and forth so fast it's like he has front row seats at Wimbledon.

And I'm about to get knocked out.

"You and Jess?" Aiden's voice drops about an octave and it's like the entire room ices over.

I keep my eyes on Aiden and hold up my hands carefully. I nod. "Yes. But, Aiden, there's something you need to know..."

"This is stupid. I'm out of here!" Jennifer whines, clearly having no time for this drama. She twirls on one stiletto and clatters off down the hallway. I grimace at the thought of the marks her shoes might make on the wood, and then berate myself. Like *that* matters right now.

Less than a second later, Brooke teeters off as well, and Aiden is momentarily distracted. He pops his head into the hallway behind Brooke. "Call me?" he croaks, and then shakes his head, running his fingers through his hair. "Ah, who am I kidding? She ain't going to call."

Aiden sets his sights on me again and his rage fires up once more. "This is your fault!"

Before I can speak, Courtney exhales loudly and rolls

her eyes. To my intense surprise, and amusement, she shoves Aiden—a guy who towers over her—out of the way and steps past him. "NOT NOW!"

But, before I can open my mouth, Jess has read my mind yet again. "It's okay, Court," she says softly. "It's time we tell him."

"We should probably be going," Rob mumbles, the first right thing he's said all night.

"Then go!" Courtney, Aiden, Jess and I yell in unison.

At least we agree on something.

I take another deep breath. "Aiden, I'm—"

"Conor," Courtney barks, waving her arms like she's directing a plane on the runway. "Your sister is in labor."

WHAT?

"That's why we're here," she continues. "Aiden got a call when no one could get through to you."

I look at Aiden, who confirms. "Mia's water broke this evening. A neighbor took her to the hospital, but Pete's in Savannah for work today. He's been calling you. He's on his way back now, but until he arrives, you're the stand in, Conor."

"And, currently, you're absolutely sucking at your job," Courtney pipes in cheerfully.

My mouth goes bone dry and I scramble in my pocket for my phone. Sure enough, it's in silent mode—and showing fifty-two missed calls from Pete, Aiden and Courtney (wait, why is Courtney showing up as a contact in my phone?)

The blood drains from my face. I'm not sure I'm ready to watch a child being birthed. I'm not sure if anyone could ever be ready for that. Jess puts a reassuring hand on my back, and her touch soothes me some.

Until Courtney opens her mouth again.

"Get a move on!" She grabs me by the shirtsleeve and

yanks me to my feet. I don't miss that she's freakishly strong for someone so finely built. "That baby ain't gonna wait for you to check your phone all evening."

Fair point, well made. Now standing, I continue to stare at Courtney, awaiting further direction for some reason. She rolls her eyes, then barks out another order. "Aiden, drive Conor to the hospital. He looks like he's in too much shock to drive."

Aiden stands obediently, but his body language is tense, coiled like a tiger. He glares at me. "Don't think this baby thing gets you off the hook. We'll be finishing this conversation later."

"Wait, what about Oliver?" In the midst of all the chaos, I manage to get a single, coherent thought together.

"The neighbor's watching him right now," Courtney says briskly, then turns to her friend. "Jess, get dressed into something you can actually wear outside without scaring people. We'll go over there and babysit."

All three of us blink at her and she claps her hands like an overeager gym teacher. If she had a whistle, I'm sure she'd be blowing it right now.

"Well, don't just stand there. Get to it!"

28

JESS

It's a very, very long night.

Like, the kind of night that merits a week-long Caribbean all-inclusive vacation at the end of it. Complete with a lounger by the pool, and copious pina coladas. Not Courtney's recipe, obviously.

Which is a tad selfish, as I'm not the one in indescribable pain from bringing a human life into the world.

But, Oliver is a cranky, irritable charge who doesn't want a babysitter—he just wants his mom. "Auntie Jess," as he so affectionately used to refer to me, has been replaced with "WAHHHHHHHHHHH!" and "I WANT MY MOMMY."

I feel bad for the little guy, I really do. But, I also feel bad for my eardrums. Courtney's "soothing" rendition of "Baa Baa Black Sheep" is not helping. Pete calls me once in a while to check in and see if we have any updates—it's usually only a four hour drive from Savannah, but he's hit numerous construction delays. Of course.

And, I've just been hit in the face by a fistful of peach yogurt. Wonderful.

After a few hours of this, the very sticky, yogurt-and-tear-stained toddler falls asleep with his head in my lap, and Courtney and I dare not make a sound. Instead, we stare, zombie-fied, at *Bubble Guppies* blaring on the TV.

I gently pull one of my arms loose from under Ollie so I can check my phone. Still nothing from Conor. Or Aiden.

"What do you think is happening?" I whisper to Courtney. The fact that we haven't heard anything is making me super anxious, and my stomach has pretzeled into a million knots.

"Don't worry. I'm sure that if Conor and Aiden had a fight, Conor would win," Courtney replies, smiling at the thought.

"Not helpful," I hiss.

My brother is an extremely reasonable person in general. And even though he found out about Conor and me in, arguably, the worst of circumstances, I'm sure they've managed to have a calm, rational conversation about the whole thing.

I hope.

When it comes to their silence, the real worry is that something might've gone wrong with Mia's labor. The thought makes the pretzel knots in my stomach tie tighter, and I squeeze my eyes shut, praying that Mia and baby are both doing okay...

The next thing I know, Pete is shaking me awake. "Jess?"

"Hurrrrrrrrrgh," Courtney moans. She's cuddled up to me on the couch, open mouthed and drooling on my shoulder. Not for the first time, I feel a bloom of gratitude for my new friend. It was sweet of her to stick around tonight when she absolutely didn't have to.

I blink a few times and Pete comes into focus. He smiles kindly, before prying a still-sleeping Oliver off my lap and gathering him in his arms.

"Pete? Whattimeiset?" I slur like a drunken sailor.

"6am."

I bolt upright, like someone lit a rocket under me. I'm now wide awake. "What happened? Is Mia okay?"

Pete nods and grins. "She got taken in for an emergency C-section at about 2am. Adelyn Joy was born half an hour later."

"Oh!" I exclaim, relieved and delighted. "That's such a beautiful name."

"Shhhh," Courtney whispers, before she turns her head and makes a little snoring sound.

Pete's positively beaming, bouncing as he cradles Ollie to his chest. He strokes his son's hair lovingly. "Seven pounds, four ounces. Twenty-and-a-quarter inches. Both mom and baby are doing well."

I have no idea if any of those statistics are good or not. But, given that Pete looks so pleased, I take it as my cue to smile and congratulate him. "Did you make it back in time?"

"I did. I'm just so thankful that Conor was there with her in the meantime. Aiden, bless him, was asleep in the waiting room when I got there." Pete looks a little teary-eyed. "Nothing like good friends and family."

I remember Pete's toast at the BBQ a couple weeks back —"*to friends who feel like family.*" At the time, it choked me up because I didn't recognize that feeling. Aiden has always been my closest friend, and a wonderful big brother, but outside of him, I didn't particularly feel close to anyone. Especially after Johnny.

But, fast forward a few weeks, and I get it. Not only do I care deeply about Pete, Mia, Oliver, and now, Adelyn, but I also have Courtney at my side. And, best of all, I have Conor... who went quickly from sexy roommate, to new best friend, to the guy I'm head-over-heels for. The guy who's got my back, and likes me because of my flaws, not in spite of them.

My heart warms and I retrieve my phone from between the sofa cushions. But, there's still nothing from Conor. I can only hope that Aiden hasn't put him in his own hospital bed in a fit of misguided overprotectiveness.

"Is Conor still at the hospital?" I ask.

"Both Conor and Aiden were there when I left. Aiden was going to find coffee, then wake Conor so they could be with Mia and meet the baby," Pete says. I have to avoid swooning—picturing Conor holding a newborn baby is enough to whip me into a fluster. "I came home to get Ollie so he can meet his little sister."

"I'll bet he can't wait to meet her." I smile tearfully, overcome with joy for my friends.

"Thank you for being here last night, Jess." Pete gazes at his still-snoozing son lovingly, and then uses his thumb to wipe a white smudge off of Oliver's cheek.

"Yogurt," I offer, rather uselessly.

Pete nods like this explanation suffices. "I'll give this little guy a bath and feed him breakfast before we go, so feel free to head over there whenever to meet the baby."

"For sure." I groggily begin the arduous task of removing myself from the couch, which is beckoning me to snuggle back down for a few more Z's. "I'll pop home and shower, then go straight over."

It's inconvenient, because I'd love to get to the hospital as soon as possible, but the shower is necessary as I have half a carton of peach yogurt stuck in my hair and haven't brushed my teeth in twenty-four hours. Gross.

I'll admit that I'm eager to meet baby Adelyn, but I'd also like to check up on the whole Conor and Aiden situation. I should take it as a good sign that Aiden is getting Conor coffee, but it doesn't exactly fill me with confidence that I haven't heard a word from either of them all night.

What on earth went down at the hospital?

"Come on, Sleeping Beauty." I wiggle Courtney's shoulder in an attempt to get her to stir.

She grumbles something incoherent, but sits up, wiping the drool from her mouth. She stands, stretches, and tosses me her car keys. But, because I'm not paying attention, they bounce off my chest and fall to the floor with a loud *clank*.

"Can you drive?" She yawns. "I'm too tired."

"Least I can do." I pick up the keys, then give my friend a little hug. Just because.

I park Courtney's Jeep on our street just as the sun begins to peek above the trees, tinting the leaves a shimmering gold. It's that perfect, quiet time of day, when the entire world seems to pause.

"I'm going to sleep for a week." Courtney stretches in the seat beside me. "That was exhausting... Remind me to never have kids!"

I laugh at her joke, but inside, I'm gooier than a pan of undercooked brownies.

Because, although I'm equally exhausted, and the tantrums and screaming were beyond difficult, Oliver falling asleep in my arms made my heart swell. Everything about that moment—how Ollie smelled like baby powder, how his little starfish hand clutched around my finger, how his long eyelashes fluttered on his round cheeks—made me think about how much I want that very thing in my own future.

I want to create my own family, create somewhere I truly belong. Even the mere thought of Conor holding little, newborn Addie makes me dizzy with the idea of him holding *our* baby someday.

Because, ever since I got back to Atlanta, my life has begun to feel full and vibrant again. The future is brimming with possibilities, and I'm slowly but surely gaining confidence. I want to take risks and put my own happiness first.

Painting makes me happy. Conor makes me happy, too.

And, what might just make me happiest of all is the fact that Conor believes in me so fiercely that I'm starting to believe in myself.

I slide out of the Jeep and take a breath of fresh morning air. The perpetual, muggy heat of the summer is finally giving way to blissfully temperate sunrises and balmy twilights.

I've never really liked fall all that much. Not just because I don't really get the appeal of cute ankle boots or Starbucks' PSLs (I'm a grande white chocolate mocha customer, rain or shine), but because I never liked the idea of everything having to fall apart—to die off—in order to regrow the following spring.

But now, for the first time ever, I feel like the impending fall and I have a bit of an understanding. In life, seasons are inevitable, and sometimes things have to fall apart completely to yield real growth. And no matter how tough that feels in the moment, the eventual growth is worth the pain of loss. Because beyond loss lies something new. A new beginning in life.

And speaking of beginnings in life, I have to get showered ASAP and get to the hospital to see Mia, Adelyn, Aiden and Conor. The man I've fallen in love with. And if I'm not mistaken, was about to tell me he loves me, too... before the entire octo-date clan gatecrashed our moment.

Hope and happiness warm my chest, and I give Courtney another hug goodbye ("What's with the sudden love-fest, Shaw?") Then, I sprint towards Aiden's front door, the refreshing shower water already calling to me. Because you know that if Aiden's not home, I'm going to be using his fancy ensuite steam shower instead of the boring, ordinary one for guests.

As I make my way up the driveway, I spot a large, bubble-wrapped package on the front doorstep. I frown and approach cautiously.

What on earth could that be? The mailman doesn't usually come until the afternoon.

As I get closer, I notice that there's a note attached to it. It's unfolded and taped on top for all to see. So, I'm not really snooping if I read it, right?

I crouch down to decipher the scrawly handwriting.

Returning these to their rightful owner. Some silent auction haha.

—Karla

An entirely different feeling begins to bubble in my chest, the sinking feeling of suspicion. I lift the corner of the wrapping paper and confirm that this package is what I think it is—my paintings. From the open house. The ones that were up for auction.

Which means, if they're being returned to their "rightful owner" now, that nobody bought them. Making their rightful owner *me*.

Conor told me there were multiple bids. That people were going crazy for them, they loved them. That he didn't want to tell me the final number the paintings had sold for because it was a big, exciting surprise.

I reread Karla's note.

Haha. Haha. Haha. Haha.

Her scrawled laugher mocks me and tears prick the corners of my eyes, making her words blur on the page. "Some silent auction" is right.

Conor actually made me believe that people *liked* my paintings. That I could do this thing for real, I just needed to believe in myself.

My fragile balloon of hope for the future slowly starts to deflate, leaking air from a puncture. Instead of going into the house, I turn around. Walk towards my car. Anxiety grows in me with every step as I ask myself the same question over and over.

Why would he lie to me?

29

CONOR

"You're awake," Aiden says gruffly as he stands directly in front of me. He's still wearing his dress shirt and slacks from last night's ridiculous group date... though it could have just as easily happened last year. Five o'clock shadow peppers his jaw, and his eyes are puffy. And yet, the fire of a thousand suns rages within them.

He's clutching two cups of coffee, but by the look on his face, I'm not sure if he brought the second one to give me, or to pour on my head.

"Yeah," I croak nervously. "It was a long night."

I sit up from where I'm slouching on the orange, plastic hospital chair, and rub my eyes. I'm still wrapped in a fog of sleep. The waiting room smells like an unfortunate combination of bleach and stale coffee, undercut with the faint metallic smell of blood. All together, it makes me feel a bit like puking into the nearest trash can.

I wouldn't say I'm a squeamish man. I donate blood regularly, and I often find myself leaning forward, intrigued, when there's an operation scene happening on the show *House*.

But, nothing could have prepared me for the miracle of childbirth. It's always tough to see someone you love suffer... And seeing my sister in so much pain is not something I want to relive in a hurry.

Pete was hours late, so I sat by Mia's bedside through the whole beginning of the labor. I did exactly what the nurse suggested, and dutifully fed her pieces of ice—until she bit my finger, that is.

Apparently that was her way of communicating that she didn't want any more ice.

Things got all the scarier when it came time for her to push. I held onto her hand for dear life, squeezed my eyes shut, and sent up a prayer. The fingernail marks in my hand may be there permanently.

But, in all seriousness, Mia was an absolute champ. She was calm in the face of her husband's absence, with the knowledge that he was racing up the interstate to get to her in time. And, she was calmer still when the doctor said that the new plan was an immediate, emergency C-section.

Me, on the other hand? Yup, I had to sit down because I felt faint.

Faint. At the mere mention of a C-section.

I was mortified. But also dizzy and in need of an orange juice. So, let's just say I went from being helpful to being a hindrance in one fell swoop.

Luckily, my prayers were answered in the form of Pete showing up in the nick of time to go into surgery with Mia. Otherwise, there was a chance they may have had two patients laying on the operating tables.

I spent the rest of the night in the waiting room, rocking back and forth, traumatized... Just kidding.

Mostly.

But one thing's for sure—I have a whole new appreciation for just how badass, strong and amazing women are. Seriously. What they go through to have children makes us men look like a bunch of puny, prepubescent teenagers at the gym, wearing brightly-colored tank tops as we try, and fail, to bench press even half our bodyweight (which may, or may not, be a sad but true story about fourteen-year-old Conor and his friends).

The only upside to Pete being so late to the hospital was that Aiden was asleep in the waiting room by the time I got out. I was way too exhausted to talk, especially about Jess and me. After taking out my phone to text Jess and then realizing that there was no service in the hospital, I slid into an uncomfortable, but very welcome, dreamless sleep.

Now, it's morning. And Aiden and I are the only ones here—save for Cynthia, the plump, smiley receptionist who's currently watching us like we're the latest episode of *Big Brother*.

I wonder where Jess is. Is she coming?

Aiden considers the cups in his hands, like he's still deciding what to do with the spare. Silence stretches between us like a tensed elastic band. One that's about to snap.

"Coffee?" he says.

Relief floods my veins and I tentatively, gratefully, take the cup. "Thank you."

He gives me a small nod. "Pete came through a couple of minutes ago. He's running home to get Ollie, and asked us to be with Mia and meet your new niece while he's gone."

"Our new niece," I correct automatically. Because, in our tight-knit friend group, Aiden will become "Uncle Aiden" to the baby just as much as I'm "Uncle Conor."

Friends who feel like family, right? Which is why I need

to explain myself to Aiden as soon as possible. For the sake of our friendship, which is one I truly value. I never meant to break any trust with him, and it's time to face the music.

"Aiden, I—" I begin, but he holds up a hand.

"Let's do this afterwards." He looks as tired as I feel. "Mia comes first right now."

"Okay," I agree. Because not only do I know that he's right, I also know that I need to let this conversation unfold on his terms. As much as I want to ask him if he's heard from Jess, I know this isn't the time, nor the place.

And so, we walk down fluorescent-lit corridors filled with humming machines to Room 5107, where we meet Adelyn Joy Stevenson for the first time. She's beautiful. Perfect. Amazing in every way. And, by the way Aiden and I both react to the tiny human before us, this little lady is going to be one extra-spoiled little girl.

Like seriously, I'm in love.

"Congratulations, you did awesome." I kiss my sister on the forehead before returning my gaze to little Addie, lying in her cot by the bed. She's got the same nose as Mia and me, which makes me smile. "How are you feeling?"

"Exhausted. Sore," Mia says tiredly. She's deathly pale, her voice is quiet, and she winces every time she moves, but the pure love and infatuation burning in her eyes is enough to tell me that the pain was all worth it for her, now that Addie's here.

Not for the first time in the last twelve hours, I let myself imagine being in this situation with Jess someday. How it would feel to be at her side for the birth of our daughter. Or son.

Hopefully I'd feel a little less faint than I did this time.

After greeting Mia and cooing over Addie for a bit, Aiden sinks into a chair near the bed. I hover awkwardly close by, instead of sitting in the other chair. I have a feeling

Aiden doesn't particularly want me sitting next to him right now.

But, perceptive as ever, Mia notices my hesitation. She looks suspiciously from me to Aiden. "Is something going on with you two?"

Maybe it's a touch of deliriousness from lack of proper sleep, but my mouth kicks into gear before my brain does and I answer Mia's question honestly. "I'm in love with Jess."

"Duh," Mia says, at the same time as Aiden practically yells, "YOU WHAT?"

Aiden's face turns white as he casts a panicked, sideways glance at the peacefully sleeping Adelyn. Satisfied that she's not stirring, he lowers his voice to a whisper-hiss and repeats, "*you what?*"

Mia flaps her hand dismissively, making her wince again. "Oh, please, he's been in love with Jess since the moment she walked through your front door. The guy had no hope from day one."

I pull a face at my sister. "Well, that's not quite how it went..."

"You're *in love* with her?" Aiden sounds stunned. Beyond stunned. Like a man who's just found out water isn't wet. "I didn't even think you knew what love was."

I cross my arms defensively. "Uh, right back atcha there, buddy."

He shrugs, unoffended. "Exactly. I thought you and I felt the same about it all—love, relationships, dating... Which is why I warned Jess you dated tons of women, and might make a pass at her."

Rude.

I look at my friend sharply, definitely offended. "Ex-*cuse* me?"

"Okay, okay," Aiden relents grudgingly. "Not tons, but

plenty. Enough that last thing I expected was for you to go and fall in love with my sister—I mean, *come on*, it's such a cliche."

"Look, I didn't mean for you to find out this way. And, I know it looks bad, but believe me—"

"Jess seems really happy since I got back." Aiden fixes me with a sudden death glare, his menacing tone clashing with his much more pleasant words. "Did you do that?"

I blink, unsure of exactly how this conversation is actually going. "I do my best to make her happy every single day. To show her that she's wonderful, and that my life is so much better with her in it."

"Yes," Mia adds, eyes glittering. "He means yes. He did that. They make each other stupid happy, it's adorable to watch. You'll see."

Aiden looks from me, to Mia, then back to me. "Johnny made her miserable."

"I know," I tell Aiden. "Jess told me all about it, and honestly, I'm in awe of her. Jess is one of the strongest, kindest, most compassionate people I've ever met. And, I know it's really soon for her to get into another relationship, but, I'd never put myself in the picture if her wants and needs didn't come first. In my eyes, and in hers. Because I want to build a life—a future—with her."

"My best friend, and my sister," Aiden repeats, more thoughtfully this time.

"You're beginning to sound like Ross from *Friends*," Mia says. Which makes us both laugh.

Aiden screws his nose up, and he looks remarkably like Jess for a very frightening shadow of a second. "I need a minute to get used to this."

Mia and I are quiet as Aiden rubs his forehead, closing his eyes. My stomach is twisted into a nervous knot as I wait for his next words—because even though neither Jess, nor I, need his permission to be with the person we love, Aiden means a lot to both of us. And as such, his blessing means a lot, too.

Finally, he sighs. "Does she know you love her?"

I shake my head. "I was going to tell her last night, but—"

"You got interrupted," Aiden finishes.

"Exactly."

Aiden adjusts the collar of his shirt before he leans forward, his gaze trained on me like he's some kind of prize hunting dog, and I'm the unfortunate fox.

"So, tell me, Conor. If she doesn't know you love her yet." Aiden's voice is dangerously quiet. "Why the hell are you still sitting here?"

I shoot him a sharp look, my face a question mark.

Aiden nods, and it's all I need.

He doesn't need to tell me twice. I frantically pull on my sweater and run to kiss my sister's cheek.

Mia laughs, then groans in pain and uses a few choice four-letter words. "Get out of here before you split my stitches!"

"Sorry, sorry!" I shoot Mia an apologetic look, then clap my best friend on the shoulder as I run past him. I get to the door before doubling back on myself. "Uh, I'm going to need some car keys."

Aiden throws me the keys with a hint of a smile. "I'm proud of you, bro.... But if you screw this up with Jess, if you hurt her, you're a dead man. Understand?"

I'm pretty sure I could take Aiden in a fight, but he doesn't need to know I think that. So, I nod in agreement. "Loud and clear."

Aiden smiles for real, this time. "Well, what are you waiting for? Go get her."

And so, with everything finally put right, I jog down the corridors towards the hospital exit.

Because if this was actually an episode of *Friends*, it would be The One Where Conor and Jess Get Their Happy Ending.

I sit in the parking lot of Piedmont Atlanta Hospital for a few minutes, watching the sun climb higher in the sky. Around me, people come and go in waves—happy families clutching balloons, a woman on her own with a frightened, pinched expression, and, as I finally climb out of my vehicle, smoothing my yogurt-matted hair, a man carrying a little girl with a broken arm.

"Hello!" She waves her hot-pink casted arm, shooting me a gap-toothed smile, curly black pigtails bobbing.

"Hi, there." I grin back. "Cool cast."

"I'm getting it off today," the little girl says, her expression now solemn. "Daddy says I have to be very brave."

Her dad raises his eyebrows at me conspiratorially. "I told Daisy that she has nothing to worry about. Getting the cast off won't hurt nearly as much as when she got it put on."

"But they have to cut it off!" Daisy's voice rises in panic. "What if they cut my arm?"

"They won't," her dad reassures her, tucking a stray curl behind his daughter's ear. "Trust me."

I fall into step beside the father and daughter, and smile gently at Daisy, who's chewing her lip. "How did you break your arm?"

"Rollerblading." Daisy turns shiny dark eyes on me. "I went down a big hill."

"Wow!" I say. "You rollerbladed down a hill? I've never been brave enough to rollerblade down a hill."

Daisy gives me a small smile. "Really? It's pretty easy."

"For you, maybe. But, I would be way too scared." We reach the front doors of the hospital, and a chilly gust of antiseptic-tinged air conditioning greets us as we step into the lobby.

Daisy shakes her head at me. "I wasn't scared."

"Well, if you weren't scared of rollerblading down a big hill, there's certainly nothing to be scared of when you get your cast off."

"I'm very brave," Daisy declares, her little face screwing up in determination.

"The bravest!" I reply, as we step into a vacant elevator.

Daisy insists on pushing the button for the right floor, and as she busies herself, her father mouths "thank you" over her head. I smile, and when Daisy's done, I scan the information plates and hit the button for the floor with the Maternity Ward.

"Can we get ice cream after, Daddy?" Daisy asks, her panicky tears forgotten. I grin.

"We sure can, honey."

Ping!

The elevator doors open at their floor, and I wish Daisy luck while I wave goodbye. Now standing in the elevator cab alone, I take a deep breath, and let it out slowly, shakily.

Because I know I need to take my own advice. I know I need to be brave, and trust. I've already fallen down, and I proved to myself that I could get back up again. The worst pain is over. I've been broken, but the bones are now reset. I can take off my cast and move forward.

The elevator doors spring open and, filled with a surge of adrenaline and purpose, I propel myself forwards. And run straight into a very familiar muscular chest for the third time in recent weeks.

"Oof!" I groan, as I put out my hands to steady myself.

"Jess!" Conor's eyes light up, and he puts his hands on my shoulders. His big hands feel warm and welcoming. "You're here! I was just coming to look for you, I have to tell you something..."

It's time for me to face my fears head on, instead of running away. Be brave. Like Daisy.

"Why did you lie to me?" I blurt, cutting him off. "You didn't have to lie to me, you know. I could have handled the truth."

Confusion rivets itself into frown lines across Conor's forehead. "What are you talking about?"

"The paintings! The silent auction! Why did you tell me there were multiple bids?" I continue. The old Jess would have swept this under the rug, pretended that everything was fine. I would've let myself be lied to. But, not now. I know I deserve the truth. And, if Conor and I have any hope of a future together, we need to have the tough conversations, and do the hard thing when it's necessary.

"There *were* multiple bids," Conor says. A pretty nurse walks past and shoots Conor a flirtatious smile, but his eyes remain carefully trained on me, searching my face.

"So why were all my paintings on our front doorstep this morning? With a note from Karla saying she's returning them to their 'rightful owner?'"

Conor's face turns red. Very red. Like, redder than I've

ever seen him. I didn't know the man was even capable of blushing—he's usually cooler than a polar bear lounging on a glacier—but right now, he's beetroot.

"Uh... because I'm the owner."

"What?"

Conor smiles bashfully. "There were a ton of bids, and the lady who bought the house was the top bidder. But, I just couldn't let them go. So, I submitted a last minute bid to the silent auction people."

"You sneaky little hobknocker!" I am, quite literally, stunned.

He looks at me from under his lashes. "I'm sorry I didn't tell you. I... I was going to hang them in my new place when it's ready."

"Why on earth would you do that?"

"Because I love your art, Jess." Conor's fingers tighten on my shoulders and he looks into my eyes. "I love *you*, Jess. And, since the moment you threw that stupid fern at me, I knew that you were the one for me. There's nobody I'd rather build a life, a future, a home with. Home is where the heart is... and my heart belongs to you, Jessica Shaw." He smiles a small, hopeful smile that makes my heart ache with love for him. "If you'll have it, that is."

I let out a slow, shaky breath, the force of Conor's revelation settling on me, slipping over my shoulders like a cozy sweatshirt that fits just right.

"I love you too, Conor Brady," I say, looping my arms around his neck and pulling him close. Because Conor and me, together? *We* fit just right. And despite the million reasons we shouldn't have fallen for each other, each of those pieces have slotted into place perfectly.

Conor leans in to kiss me, and I'm immediately lost in him. But, after a couple of seconds, he pulls back. Sniffs.

"Jess?"

"Hmm?" I say dreamily, still wrapped up in the sensation of our kiss.

"Why do you smell like yogurt?"

31

JESS

Ten Months Later...

"What do you think?" I ask, gesturing in a *taa-daa!* motion. It's a warm, sunny, spring day in Atlanta, and the air is heavy with the sweet honey scent of azalea blossoms.

Courtney stands beside me, looking chic as ever in a white linen jumpsuit that clashes with her big, black backpack. But, her expression is entirely unimpressed as she lowers her sunglasses and squints at the adorable (if I do say so myself) navy van with white, scripted writing that's just pulled up in front of us.

Or, maybe she's just unimpressed to see who's riding shotgun.

Aiden jumps out of the passenger seat and jogs over to give me a hug. "Hey, J." He grins sunnily, then narrows his eyes as his gaze shifts. "Courtney."

"Charming as ever, I see, Aiden." Courtney crosses her arms over her chest and returns the dirty look in dividends.

"That's Prince Charming to you."

"More like the frog," Courtney snaps back.

"Hey, she kissed the frog, too. Remember?"

"Stop it guys," I say halfheartedly, knowing my words are useless. This is nothing new with Aiden and Court—in fact, the most surprising thing about that little exchange was Aiden's remarkably good knowledge of Disney princess movies.

"Do you like the van or what?" Conor slams the driver's side door and strides towards us in a way that makes me want to reconsider our little party and drag my husband straight to the bedroom.

Our bedroom. In our house. In our bed, which we've slept in together, curled around each other like bookends, every single night for the past five months. Ever since we said, "I do."

My big brother joked that he would give us his blessing the second Conor made an honest woman out of me. So Conor rose to the faux-challenge and he wifed me as quickly as we could make a wedding happen.

And every day between then and now, Conor has made me feel more loved and more cherished. Even when I leave coffee rings on the countertop.

After we officially got together, Conor moved in with Mia and Pete until our wedding. Instantly bonded to little Addie, Conor was happy enough to live in their bright, very loud madhouse with a couple of tiny new temporary roomies. And Mia said he was an extremely helpful house-guest, even getting up to change a few diapers in the middle of the night. She referred to him as their "Manny", which I think he secretly liked.

I continued to stay with Aiden, enjoying quality time with my best and only big brother, and Conor and I spent every spare moment working on the new house—and we designed every square inch of the place together. It turns out that we work well as a team, our talents seamlessly over-lapping and smoothing out each other's edges.

When the house was finally complete—my paintings on every wall—we had a beautiful ceremony in our backyard. And then, I pushed Conor in the pool. For revenge, you know. Just because I'm married doesn't mean I've gone all soft and lovey dovey at every opportunity.

"Hey, love." I smile up at Conor as he wraps his strong arms around me, and nuzzles my hair. Both Courtney and Aiden redirect their glares in our direction.

Yeah, so I might have been lying about the lovey dovey thing.

But, love does incredible things to a person. And, if my best friend and my brother would just drop their whole tortured-enemies fandango, maybe they'd end up with something incredible, too. But hey, that's another story for another day.

"Sorry we're late!" Mia calls as the Stevenson family's own new van—a seven seater, three row, soccer-mom-fantasy of a vehicle—pulls up outside our house.

"Not late," I amend. "Perfectly on time."

Tonight, we're hosting a little garden party for our friends. Luke and Mindy, who are now a couple, will be in attendance. Mindy and I will never be besties, but she calmed right down after she and Luke got together. She also never tried to steal my boyfriend. Not that she would have been successful.

Karla, on the other hand, will not be in attendance. She and Conor have gone their separate ways, professionally. Last I heard, she'd gotten into specializing in downtown penthouses for city-slicker types. Which seems to be more her speed.

The party doesn't start for another hour, but we've gathered Courtney, Aiden, Mia, Pete and the kids early for the big van reveal.

Pete smiles and waves as he climbs out of the soccer-mom-mobile and begins unbuckling Oliver. The second he's free, the toddler runs in our direction, arms wide.

"Auntie Jess!" He wraps his little pudgy arms around my shin, and I ruffle his hair.

Courtney, meanwhile, swoops over to assist Mia with baby Adelyn, who apparently single-handedly changed my best friend's mind about the whole "no children" thing. She scoops Addie up in her arms, cooing to her and stroking her big, chubby cheeks.

"Don't drop the baby," Aiden mutters, more to himself than to Courtney. Because even *he* knows it would be a bad idea for her to overhear that one.

Mia runs over and envelops Conor and me in a big, group hug. "I love your new van, guys. Love, love, love it."

Her eyes are big and sparkly, and while Mia always brims with positivity, she's suspiciously enthusiastic about the van. Like she knows something.

I side-eye Conor, but he just shrugs and mouths, "I didn't tell her."

"The Brady Bunch," Pete slowly reads the writing on the side of our new business vehicle.

Mia applauds and I grin at the way the name sounds. Grin at the thought of everything it means for us.

You see, Conor and I had so much fun renovating our house and designing a dream home to spend forever in together, that he realized working like this was infinitely more rewarding—and enjoyable—than flipping cheaply-bought fixer-uppers and selling them to nameless, faceless buyers via realtors and open houses.

When Conor considered the past few years, the only projects that stuck out to him were the house he flipped for his mom, and the work he did at Aiden's house. His high-light was seeing the faces of people he cared about after the job was done, and being able to say "welcome home".

And so, after our wedding and our whirlwind honeymoon in Costa Rica (less sightseeing than I'd expected, but we did see a lot of the inside of our hotel room), we've been working on our brand-new, *joint* endeavor.

We rebranded Brady Homes to be our new, family business—The Brady Bunch. We focus on modernizing heritage homes, while retaining their original charm and character. And then, we come up with picture perfect design, furniture and artwork to tie our transformations together.

And, to my absolute delight, my art is so popular that I actually sell some on the side. To people who don't need renovations, just a breath of fresh air in their home decor. I even got a call from an anonymous buyer in New York City last week, but I don't have time or brain-space to dwell on who that could possibly be. I'm too busy being happy and fulfilled and pursuing my dreams.

And, of course, The Brady Bunch has one other meaning...

"I'm just not sure about the name." Courtney frowns again. "On the *The Brady Bunch* TV show, they had, like, a million kids. And Bunch suggests a few. You know, like a bunch of bananas? And there's only two of you..." Her eyes suddenly narrow. "Unless..."

Heads swivel to look at me, and I can't keep the smile off my face.

I glance at Conor. Nod.

Mia squeals.

Courtney lets out a massive "WHOOOOO!"

And Pete and Aiden just blink in confusion.

My gorgeous, handsome, incredible husband puts a hand on my big brother's arm. "You're going to be an uncle, again."

I don't know who starts it, but suddenly, we're hugging each other. And, as I lean into the warmth of the closest people I have in my life, I feel my husband's arm around me, strong and steady. And (I blame hormones for this one), just as suddenly, I'm crying.

"I love you, Jessica Brady," Conor whispers in my ear. I tilt my head to look at him, and the sight of his glowing green eyes makes my stomach flip with a now-familiar mingling of love, desire and sheer, unbridled happiness.

"Love you, too." I smile at him through my tears of joy.

Because, finally, I'm home. Where I belong.

Thank you so much for reading!

If you enjoyed this book, please leave me a review. As a new author, reviews mean everything to me. I appreciate each and every one of them.

A NOTE FROM KATIE

To everyone who read this book - THANK YOU!

You're amazing, wonderful, fantastic and I am beyond grateful that you took a chance on reading The Roommate Situation.

I was so excited to write a book. And then, I was absolutely terrified. Seriously, trying to be funny on purpose? Way more stress-sweat than I was anticipating.

So, to my incredible beta reader, editor, and all of you fabulous Bookstagrammers who picked up an ARC, thank you for believing in this project. And, to my sister-in-law, thank you for biting your hubby on the hand during labor. That was very funny.

I'm so grateful to each and every one of you, and I really hope you loved Conor and Jess's story. I can't wait to share Courtney and Aiden's with you soon.

Big love,

Katie B.

ALSO BY KATIE BAILEY

Donovan Family

So That Happened

I Think He Knows

Only in Atlanta

The Roommate Situation

The Neighbor War